THE SOUSHARI SAGA

BOOK ONE

THE **SOU**TH **SHA**LL **RIS**E **AGA**IN

R.L. Dubé

Editing by Cara Highsmith, Highsmith Creative Services, www.highsmithcreative.com

Cover and Interior Design by Mitchell Shea

ISBN-13: 979-8-9857338-1-5

eBook ISBN: 979-8-9857338-2-2

LCCN: 2022907014

Printed in the United States of America

First Edition 14 13 12 11 10 / 10 9 8 7 6 5 4 3 2 1

DEDICATION

To Barbara who told me to write just one book at a time.

THE **SOU**TH **SHA**LL **RIS**E **AGA**IN

CHAPTER ONE

"A job interview is a two-way communication to probe for cultural and team fit. No matter on which side of the table you sit, you should be asking questions that are important to you without fear."

—Salil Jha

Bubba Smith was uncomfortable and more than a little nervous. This wasn't his first job interview, but it definitely was his most interesting. His potential boss, Kianna Smythe, towered over him. She had to be over six feet tall and next to his five and half feet, which he insisted was average, he couldn't help but feel intimidated. Her being a woman and of obvious mixed race were not factors that bothered him. His daddy had always taught him it wasn't what was on the outside that mattered.

But the location for the interview? Why on earth would she want to meet him at this abandoned dead-end alley in this gang-riddled neighborhood? The smell of rotting garbage and overflowing trash bins coupled with the graffiti covered walls and broken windows made a clear and compelling statement. 'Get out of here and get out of here NOW!' Yes, Atlanta was considered a Special Economic Zone in the Southern Commonwealth and yes, it was "'legally'" a racially integrated community; however, it was also true that birds of a feather flock together, and white faces like his were rare in these parts of town.

Kianna Smythe greeted him with a warm and comforting smile. "Hello, Bubba. Glad you could make it. You seem a little uncomfortable. Are you going to be okay?"

"Well Miss Smy... um, is it Smith like mine, or rhyme with eye?"

Kianna smiled. "Just like your last name Bubba."

Bubba sported a crooked smile. "Got it. Well, Miss Smythe, to be honest, I am a little taken aback by where we are doin' this interview. Seems like we're just fixin' for a lickin', if you know what I mean? And that does make me a tad nervous."

"Fair enough. First things first. From now on, I would appreciate it if you addressed me as Kianna. Next, the reason you mentioned is precisely why we are here. You might say we are 'poking the bear'."

Bubba's jaw dropped. "Are you kiddin' me? I wish I had known that afore hand. I'd of brought my pistol."

Kianna shook her head. "I am not a big advocate of guns, Bubba. I see them as something that provokes a potentially fatal reaction in a situation that could be resolved in a more amicable manner."

"Well, that's all well and good, but explain that to the guy who's aimin' one at you that's cocked and ready to fire."

"Let's cross that bridge when we come to it."

At that very moment, the bridge came to them.

Seven young black men came down the alley engaged in a lively conversation and seeing Bubba and Kianna, they stopped dead in their tracks. The fact that these two interlopers were smack dab in the middle of their turf was disconcerting enough, but the oddity of these two together took them completely off guard. The leader —a lanky dark-skinned man— called out. "Hey! Whatch y'all doin' in our hang? If y'all gonna be here, y'all got to pay to play. That can be cash or blood. Y'all choose!"

2

Kianna rose up and stared calmly at the seven young hoodlums. "I beg your pardon, but this is a public space and my white friend and I have every right to be here. Is that not correct, Bubba?"

Bubba's voice showed the distress he was feeling. He nervously said, "Yes, Miss Kianna, but I ain't lookin' for no fight."

The leader laughed. "Well, *Mistah* Bubba, you ain't lookin' cause you found one."

With this comment he reached behind him and pulled a pistol from his waistband. Upon doing so, another gang member also brandished a Glock while the other five members flashed nunchucks and knives that glistened in a ray of sunlight penetrating down into that avenue of potential pain. "What's it gonna be *Miss Kianna?* Cash or trash?"

Kianna stood there defiantly. "I believe there is a third option you have failed to consider. What if I choose to defend myself as well as my young friend here? A fourth. You can quietly let us go our own way and avoid the inevitable pain and suffering that will be visited upon you."

The leader smiled and then started to laugh to the point of tears. "Y'all kiddin'. That there's the best joke I've heard in a long, long, time. You tellin' me you and that little honky gone kick our asses? Unless I miss my guess, y'all ain't packin' no heat."

"You are correct. We have no guns. But you misunderstood what is going to happen next. My young friend is just going to watch. I am the teacher here, and you are going to get a lesson in manners and humility. Oh, by the way, you do have the opportunity to surrender at any point. That offer is always on the table. One other thing:- what is your name, young man? I like to know whom I am addressing."

"The name is Ramone, and this is going to be fun!" With that, he raised his pistol and pointed it directly at Kianna.

Being an experienced Go player she knew that the corners and edges of the fight area were the easiest and most efficient to control, so, she immediately moved to the back of the alley. The benefit of taking on multiple attackers is that they usually don't know how to fight as a team. Larger groups are easier to combat because the individuals tended to get in each other's way. Though they didn't want to hurt their own, everyone here was literally a man for himself. Kianna stopped thinking of them as people and thought of them as kinetic objects moving in the space around her. This made it easier for her to plan her first move. Her priorities had to be the two men with guns. When multiple handguns are in play, regardless of your skills, agility, instincts and reflexes, it is difficult to dodge two opponents shooting from two different locations at the same time. Kianna focused on the closest armed man and quickly plotted a strategy. She felt it best to keep one man between her and the closest gunman, even though that opened her up for attack from behind. Drawn like a fly to dead meat, the man with a ten-inch blade rushed at her. Using his energy, she side-stepped and used not only his momentum but his body mass to propel herself toward the nun-chuck guy between her and the gunman she was pursuing.

The first knife-wielder became a literal steppingstone to her target. As she passed by the man with the nun-chucks, he lashed out with his weapon but almost immediately found himself flying across the alley into the wall in front of him. She simply diffused his momentum toward her and changed the direction of his movement toward the alley wall. This was one of the most basic principles of Aikido, the martial art she was employing in this conflict. She rode her first attacker's body like a surfboard toward the gunman. Now that she was within striking distance, she pulled a homemade bokken from a concealed side sheath. Using the short wooden rod to extend and amplify her energy, she struck the hand holding his gun. With a sharp

4

cry of pain, he dropped the pistol. She quickly scooped it up and broke it down in less than two seconds, scattering the parts around the alley.

This left the problem of Ramone who was trying to position himself in order to get a bead on her. She locked his gaze and read him like a book. She made her body the smallest target that it could be and moved toward him, waiting for him to fire. The eyes, being the roadmap to intention and action were where she trained her focus. She had taught herself to know when action would follow an eye movement. She learned over time that one-tenth of a second after the eye-shift began, the finger would pull the trigger. Years of practice had taught her body how to respond and she moved out of the trajectory of the bullet. Directly behind her, and in the path of the bullet, was the gunman she had just disabled. She did not need to look back to see that he was hit by Ramone's first and only shot. She could read it in Ramone's eyes. Since the human mind is not capable of focusing on two things at the same time, she knew that Ramone would be vulnerable for two seconds. This was an infinite amount of time for Kianna. Within one and a half seconds, Ramone was no longer armed, and by the time two seconds had passed, his gun was useless and spread around the alley like so much discarded insignificant jetsam. She put a subtle pinch hold on Ramone, and he passed out. This hold was one she had learned during her recent martial arts study in China.

This left the other two who held knives and a single nunchuck wielder. She did not need to attack them. In fact, she preferred it that way. Having no choice, they rushed her not realizing they were simply playing into her hands. They quickly became her unwilling dance partners and within half a minute found themselves strewn around the alley. The whole battle lasted a little less than a minute.

Walking over to Bubba who was standing slack-jawed at the side of the alley, she said, "I think we should go over to my office to finish this interview. We can talk on the way."

Bubba shook his head. "Pardon my French, Miss Kianna, but what the hell just happened? If I had heard this from someone else and hadn't seen it with my own eyes, I woulda told them they were stretchin' a gnat over a rain barrel. Color me impressed!"

As they walked down the street toward the Smythe Detective Agency office, Bubba could hardly contain himself. "Is that why you scheduled the beginning of the interview there? Did you know that was going to happen? What did you do to them?"

Kianna maintained a placid and peaceful demeanor. Much to Bubba's amazement, she was neither winded nor filled with adrenaline. She was simply in the moment.

"Bubba, one thing at a time. To help you understand, we started the interview there because it's important for an interviewee to know what sort of job they may be getting into, and occasionally I find myself in situations where I need to defend myself. You need to be aware of that and not just read about it in a job description. To merely tell you that your life could be in danger, would be like a finger pointing at the moon. The experience you go through is the moon. Now, your second question ... ?"

Bubba caught his breath and was starting to gain control of himself. "Did you know that was gonna happen?"

Kianna smiled. "No, Bubba, I did not know for sure; however, it was not exactly a surprise. That is precisely my point about knowing what you are getting into."

Bubba asked, "Okay. So, what kinda karate was that? I never seen nothin' like it!"

Kianna said, "Well, it is not karate. It is called Aikido. It is a Japanese martial arts technique that is primarily for self-defense, and if you come to work for me, I will expect you to learn it and master it. Would that be a problem for you?"

"Lord no! I would love to learn that. But could I still keep my gun?"

Kianna frowned slightly. "As I said, I am not a fan of the gun. I will not rule it out at this point, but I will have to think about it. Look, my interview techniques are rather unconventional, but I prefer a one-on-one dialogue and not the pro-forma questions most ask because it allows me to see the real person rather than the best-face-forward persona traditional interview settings dictate. I have answered some of your questions, though I am sure you will have more. For now, I have only one question for you. Why did you respond to my advertisement?"

Bubba smiled and chuckled. "Well, that's easy. It's what you said right up front. You were looking for a young, white, Christian male. That just plumb struck me as mighty strange. In these parts those things are usually a given. Maybe not the young part always, but the white Christian male part is pretty much assumed 'cause, those are the people gettin' the jobs. It's kinda like sayin' you expect someone to breathe air. What is the deal with that?"

"Wonderful observation on your part Bubba." Just then they arrived at the doors to the Smythe Detective Agency. Taking a key out of a hidden pocket in her loose-fitting trousers, she placed it in the lock on the door. As she opened the door, she said, "I am looking for a key, Bubba.", holding up the one in her hand to illustrate her point. "Keys are used for opening doors that are often closed and locked tight against entry. The employee that I will hire will help me open more doors than I can on my own."

"I'm not sure I follow you, Miss Kianna."

"Even though Atlanta is officially an integrated community, I'm sure you know that does not mean people of my gender and skin color are widely accepted or expected to hold the position I do. However, if I have a front person who is white, Christian, and male, more people are more likely to hire us."

"Oh. I get it. Does that mean you're not a Christian since you were asking for one?"

Kianna got quiet for a second and then carefully responded to Bubba. "An individual's belief system is very personal. Until we know each other much better, I would rather not go into my complex theology. I hope it suffices to say I am a Christian."

Bubba laughed. "Honestly, whatever religion you practice don't mean a whole hill a beans to me. I was just tryin' to clarify. My daddy raised me up to respect other people and what they believe is their own business. Unless of course they're tryin' to push it down your throat. If you ain't doin' that, I'd say we're good."

"That is an absolutely wonderful sentiment," Kianna said as she nodded her head and let out the most pleasant laugh that Bubba had ever heard." They settled into some chairs in the client meeting area, and she continued, "That gives me great insight into the person you are. Now, is Bubba a moniker or your legal name?"

"No ma'am. Bubba's my given name right on my birth certificate. My full official name is Charles Bubba Smith. Bubba was the name of my mother's brother. Uncle Bubba is a hoot. Kinda proud to be named after him. Some of my friends nicknamed me C.B., but most people just call me Bubba. I do run across some people who call me Chuck or Charlie, but they just don't know no better. Do you mind me askin' bout your last name Miss Kianna? I've never seen Smith spelled that way."

"I do not mind at all. I carry my mother's surname. The heritage of my mother's family goes back to the time before the War Between the States during the mid-1800's. In those days, slaves often took their master's last name. She was a Smith, just like yours. In fact, your family probably owned members of my family at one time." Bubba's eyebrows lifted. "We have come a long way since then."

Dismissing the rising tension, she continued. "Somewhere along the line, however, an ancestor changed the spelling to S-M-Y-T-H-E, which is how it was originally spelled in England. As I said, our family still pronounces it like your last name. In England they pronounce it with a long I. Personally, I am glad my mother uses the common pronunciation, as otherwise it sounds too pretentious. I do not know who my father is or even if he is still alive, but that is not something I am prepared to discuss at this early stage in our relationship. Enough of that for now. Tell me about your family."

Bubba got quiet and straightened himself in his chair, his body taking on a posture of pride. Family was important to him. "My daddy is a good man. He works for the Southern Commonwealth in their data services division. He raised me right and proper. He believes in doin' the right thing and he brung me up the same way. My momma passed when I was only about two years old, so I don't much remember her. But Daddy speaks real fondly of her. He misses her. Sometimes I catch him lookin' at her picture and he gets all misty eyed. I just look the other way."

"Your father sounds like a good man."

"Oh, he is Miss Kianna."

Ki got a serious look on her face and met Bubba's eyes with a sternness

9

that gave him a start. "Time to get serious here, Bubba. According to your application you are twenty-two years old. I believe that is a good age. You have not developed too many bad habits at this stage of your life, and you are fresh from what sounds like an excellent home environment. You seem to be very honest and do not have any difficulty expressing what you think. I believe that is an important attribute in an assistant. And, by the way, I think it would be fine if you just called me Ki. I usually reserve that for family and friends, but we are going to be working together closely, and I have a feeling you and I will become a family of sorts.

Bubba lit up like the sun breaking through parting clouds. "Thank you, Miss Ki. I feel honored indeed ... and I guess that means I got the job?"

"Well, normally there would be a longer vetting process, but my gut instinct tells me you are the right choice, so yes. I am offering you the position. The pay is reasonable, hours are flexible, and benefits are negotiable. Oh, and just Ki will suffice. You can drop the Miss. I believe I understand why you use the title 'Miss', but for me it is a demeaning term. It is often directed toward women like me in a condescending manner."

"I'll try Miss ... oops. I did it again. I'm sorry. For me, it is a way of showin' respect. To stop using it is like usin' your left hand when you are right-handed. It just don't feel natural."

"Well, we will work on that. My question to you now is, considering the potentially dangerous nature of my work, the fact that I am black, and I am an older woman, do you think you could work for me?

"Well, Miss Ki ... Damn! Ki, if you are willin' to hire me, I couldn't care less about the older woman and black thing. It's how people treat each other that's important. I would take it as an honor and privilege to be your personal assistant. Of course, until I learn that there Eyekeedo, I'm hopin' you'll watch my back like you did today."

"Yes, Bubba. You can count on that. Oh, and Bubba, one other thing. I am going to make one more concession. I understand that "Miss" is engrained in you and is a habit that will take time to break. I will try to live with being called Miss Ki for the time being."

"Thank you, Miss Ki. I truly do appreciate that."

CHAPTER TWO

"America preaches integration but practices segregation."

—Malcolm X

Kianna Smythe was born in the year 2087 and raised in the Atlanta Special Economic Zone (SEZ) in the free and independent State of Georgia within the nation known as the Southern Commonwealth. Along with ten other states and portions of four more, Georgia seceded from the United States of America four years after the formation of the Commonwealth. The legally sanctioned secession was in response to the prevailing and growing divisiveness in the country and people squaring off along ideological and cultural lines: people of color versus whites, progressives versus conservatives, capitalism versus socialism, patriarchy versus egalitarianism, and science versus faith.

The Southern Commonwealth formed in 2023 CE and was loosely modeled after the European Union. It was not so much a governing body as it was a coalition of like-minded communities that implemented policies which would bond the separate states into a unified whole. The Southern Commonwealth guidelines aimed to ensure the free movement of people, goods, services, and capital within the internal market. They sought to enact legislation in justice and home affairs; and they were intended to maintain common practices on trade, agriculture, fisheries, and regional development. A common system of monetary exchange was established and referred to as the Dixie Dollar. English was designated as the official national language, and Christianity the national religion. A singular department of transportation oversaw the Commonwealth states, and for national defense, they had a collective of state militias. Unlike the central government of the United States of America, the Southern Commonwealth by seceding from that union, became a coalition of free and independent states where each state government could establish their own individual standards for education, laws, and taxes.

Throughout Georgia and the rest of the Commonwealth, most counties were racially segregated to some degree. For the most part, each county contained either people of color or whites, —but rarely both—, who managed local businesses, school, and municipalities. Because each county had the power to enact their own segregation laws, there was a mixture of standards within the states. People gravitated to the regions that espoused their personal perspectives. There were even a few smaller counties that established total racial integration similar to what Atlanta had.

Atlanta, due to its large population of progressives that fostered a general atmosphere of widespread racial integration, had received special dispensation from the Southern Commonwealth so that mixing of races in work and social life was permitted. In this Special Economic Zone (SEZ), schools and eating establishments were racially integrated. Because of the relative openness of this society, this is where Kianna Smythe decided to base her private investigative operations.

The Smythe Detective Agency LLC was a lifelong dream of Kianna's. As a child, she was absolutely enthralled by puzzles and word problems. Assessing her environment, deducing clues, and finding answers were just compulsory for her, whether she was taking on a universal question or just solving a matter of practicality. When Ki was eight years old, her mother had a problem with the clothes dryer. Knowing her burgeoning skill set, Ki's mother gave her the challenge to see if she could figure it out. Within twenty minutes, the dryer was repaired. Not only did it save her mother good money that would have gone to a repairman, but this accomplishment also gave her a huge sense of satisfaction and well-being. Ki was comforted by the fact that she had some modicum of control over a world that seemed beyond her influence. Without any prompting from her mother, she set about to understand how *all* the appliances in their house worked. Later, she came to the conclusion that she could put her problem-solving gift to good use and earn a solid living by becoming a private eye. It became a goal for her and drove her toward fulfilling her destiny.

Another area of proficiency that she cultivated in her youth was awareness of her surroundings. She learned that it is hard to solve problems unless you know the facts. She tuned in to details that escaped most others and used them to suss out situations adroitly and solve problems. She created a personal challenge for herself: to catalog exactly what her mother had done all day based on evidence she gathered through scanning the room. She would inventory the smallest details around the house and compile a report of what tasks her mother had performed at home, whether she had gone on errands, and what she bought or did while she was out. Her information came from subtle clues such as those found in traces of debris or scents on her mother's clothes or body. She also created a memory map each morning of the entire house—furniture placement, arrangement of décor, locations of stains, or messes, etc. That way she could compare it to any changes in the layout while she was at school. For her tenth birthday her mother got her a vintage book by Sir Arthur Conan Doyle. It was the collected short stories of Sherlock Holmes. Needless to say, she was captivated and knew she had found her calling.

Another aspect of her desire to be a private eye was her mother's rape. Her black mother was accosted by a white man thirty-four years ago. Kianna was the product of that assault. Police were not able to come up with any leads following the event. The case went cold and any hope that her mother had of holding the man accountable for his actions went onto the back burner. The trauma of such an event never really leaves; it covers its victims in an emotional residue.

Kianna's heart's desire was, to find this man not only for her mother's closure, but also her own. She needed to confront him and look him in the eye. She knew she could never change the past, but she felt this burning need for some form of resolution. She believed that as a private detective, she could at least have the chance to offer other women who suffered the same atrocities some form of justice.

Kianna's new personal assistant, Bubba Smith, could not have been more different. He was born and raised in Pickens County, Georgia, the quaint, backwater village of Dog Hobble Hollow. The closest sizable, populated community was the town of Jasper, where he went to school. It was a segregated county, and his exposure to people of color only happened after he got into the upper grade levels at his school. It wasn't until some of his friends got cars that he even ventured outside the county and discovered just how sheltered his life had been. He was a tow-headed, freckle-faced lad who had the good fortune of being raised by a father who not only taught him how to behave, but modeled it as well. Sadly, his mother passed away from ovarian cancer when he was only two, so, his father was his mentor and guide in navigating life. Bubba could not have asked for a better teacher and parent. In an effort to be a hands-on father, Franklin, studied electronics and computers, which allowed him to work from home most of the time and be available to help Bubba find his way in the world. With mom gone, he and his dad only had each other for companionship at home. Conversations were often long and compelling. Being innately courteous and kind, Bubba never had problems making friends, and really knew no enemies.

Bubba had worked a couple of odd jobs locally, but he realized that if he wanted to make something out of his life, he would need to look further afield than Pickens County. After Bubba graduated from high school, Franklin Smith applied for and landed a job with the Southern Commonwealth's Data Services Division. When his dad left for Blount County there was nothing to hold Bubba there so he decided to cast his net wide and thought Atlanta might be a good choice. There was more money to be made, and a lot more to do in the big city. He had a couple of friends from Jasper who had secured jobs in Atlanta, so he was able to share an apartment with them, and wasted no time seeking employment. His father had taught him a great deal about computers, however, he was interested in doing something more exciting than data entry.

Bubba was immediately drawn to an advertisement for a personal assistant with a newly-formed investigative firm called Smythe Detective Agency. The job description itself was compelling, but what really hooked him were the criteria for the qualified candidate: young, white, Christian male. That was him to a T! When he called the number, a woman answered the phone and arranged for an interview the next day. If he had been familiar with the neighborhood where she told him to meet her, he probably wouldn't have showed up. Ultimately, he was glad he did.

Kianna Smythe and Bubba Smith were the human embodiment of yin and yang – the ancient Taoist icon of opposites. Aside from their physical differences, they were about as polarized in their cultural roots as one could imagine. Yet, despite that, or possibly because of it, they seemed to fulfill something in each other that created an immediate bond between them. On more than one occasion during the first couple of weeks of working together, they discovered that they each had the ability to finish the other person's sentences.

When Bubba reported for work, Ki familiarized him with the office and her expectations for him as her assistant. Her management style was objective-oriented. She was not overly particular about how he did his filing and organizing as long as he kept her up to speed and that the information was readily available when needed. Because of who they were, their approaches to client communications were markedly different. Ki tended to be concise and no nonsense. She found social niceties to be an unnecessary expectation that obfuscated understanding and interfered with the job she was being hired to do. She focused on the facts and had no patience for anything that shrouded them. Ki believed she was being efficient. Bubba, on the other hand tended to be chatty. He sought to establish relationships with their clients, and he relished the social engagement. Bubba saw this as providing basic Southern comfort food for the ears.

One area that created some contention early on was religion. Bubba thought it might be nice to socialize some with Ki and so asked her, "Say, Miss Ki. Where do you go to church?"

Ki looked quietly at Bubba for about half a minute, which evoked for him the sound of crickets. Finally, she spoke curtly, "Why do you ask?"

Bubba, responding to the uncomfortable silence said, "Oh, I was just tryin' to get to know you a little better and have a conversation."

Ki sighed and said, "I shared during the interview that I was a Christian. Once we know each other better, we might revisit this conversation, but all you need to know for now is I am not part of any congregation. This may not make much sense, but I have found I am too Christian for most people. My faith journey has been long and arduous and is deeply personal. That is about all I am comfortable sharing for now."

Bubba sat there stunned. "I am so sorry, Miss Ki. I didn't mean to pry. I'll just drop it until you bring it up again. Does that work for you?"

Ki smiled. "Yes, Bubba, it does work for me."

Suddenly the power went out, shutting down everything electrical, except the lamp on her desk. Then it too faded out like it was on a rheostat.

Bubba said, "Did you see what that lamp did? Or was I just imagining it?"

Ki frowned. "Yes, Bubba. I did see that, and, no, you were not imagining it."

"You know, Miss Ki, I don't know lots 'bout electricity, but that doesn't seem normal."

Ki shook her head. "No, it is not normal. It tells me the lamp must be connected to a capacitor in some way. I am seriously disturbed by this. I scoured this place from top to bottom before moving my office here and found no signs of anything like this then."

"Is it safe?"

Ki nodded. "Yes. That is not the problem. It is just extremely odd, that is all. I am going to have to look into it further."

Pulling a flashlight and screwdriver out of the desk drawer, she quickly dismantled the lamp. Unfortunately, the only thing she could find that was out of the ordinary was there was indeed a capacitor in the lamp. But she still had no idea why it was there or how it got there.

The electricity was still out so she said to Bubba. "It is still a mystery, but, since we are forced into a break and it is close to lunch time, what do you say we go get a bite to eat?"

Bubba smiled. "That sounds great to me. I'm so hungry, I could eat my elbows! You know this part of town better than I do. Is there a place you had in mind?"

"There is a place a couple of blocks from here. Good home cooking."

On the way to the restaurant, Kianna was quiet. Not that this was abnormal, but Bubba had noticed usually there was a small smile on her face. Now there was a small frown.

Bubba said, "Penny for your thoughts?"

"Oh, I am sorry. I am still thinking about that lamp and the capacitor. It is a puzzle that has me stumped. I do not like being stumped." She made a mental note to check other electronic devices in the office when they returned.

Once they sat down and had ordered, Kianna looked around the restaurant. It was a pretty typical lunchtime crowd. She saw a white couple, a black family of four, a single black man with what appeared to be his son. There was a white teenager just entering the restaurant. A racially integrated group was pretty normal here, but Ki picked up on something that was different. For some reason, people were looking over at her and Bubba, and then whispering to each other. Also, she detected a precipitous drop in the noise level throughout the place. "Bubba, have you noticed anything unusual here?"

"No, not really. What do you mean?"

"Well, people seem to be paying close attention to us. I wonder why."

"Oh. That's simple, Miss Ki. We're a mixed-race couple. You don't see much of that anywhere in the South."

Kianna was struck silent. Why didn't she catch that? She liked Bubba even more now. Usually, she was the one person in any crowd who could effectively read a room and Bubba had bested her. That made her smile.

Bubba's cell phone rang.

"Hi Daddy! I'm doin' just fine. Sittin' here with my new boss and havin' lunch. What's up in the Commonwealth?"

Bubba sat there listening and then said, "I'll ask her. I think that's a great idea!" Holding the phone to the side, he said, "My daddy says there's gonna be a big shindig goin' on down in Blount County and he was wonderin' if the two of us might be interested in attendin'. He thought it would be a good chance to hobnob, rub elbows, and chase up some possible detective work. It's next Saturday evening. Interested?"

Realizing what a great opportunity it would be for finding some bigger clients, Kianna said, "Yes. Absolutely. I look forward to meeting your daddy. Tell him we will definitely attend."

Bubba put the phone back up to his ear. "We're good to go, Daddy. Lookin' forward to it. How should we dress? . . . Okay, business casual it is! See you then. Love you too, Daddy!"

CHAPTER THREE

"Networking is not about just connecting people. It's about connecting people with people, people with ideas, and people with opportunities."

—Michele Jennae

Kianna and Bubba pulled through the wrought iron gates of the enormous estate, both feeling very conspicuous in her older model sedan. The well-tended, crushed clam shell driveway wound an unimaginable distance through exquisitely landscaped grounds. Kianna took in the beautifully orchestrated sense of old-world charm. The drive was lined on both sides by Live Oaks draped in fuzzy Spanish Moss and terminated in front of a grand, columnated Southern mansion with an elaborate entrance adorned in sumptuous plantings. She had mixed feelings about this ostentatious display of wealth and power. While she appreciated the exquisite beauty and elegance of this space, she was simultaneously repulsed by the ego and desire for affirmation from the dominant society on full display here. Both Kianna and Bubba felt like intruders on this rarefied world. The Bentleys, Rolls, and Maybachs parked along the drive were gleaming in the sunlight. By contrast, Ki's ready-for-a-wash automobile was like a thistle sitting among roses. Bubba's daddy had said the attire for the evening was business casual, so Ki felt appropriately dressed in a modest, but stylish pantsuit. Bubba's pink polo shirt, dark green chinos, and slightly beat up Nubuck oxfords were a little more reflective of the country club aesthetic, but his slightly disheveled mop top betrayed the illusion of refinement. And it was clear the dress code was interpreted differently by the couples they saw loitering on the broad front porch. The men were all wearing light-colored blazers, ascots, and open-collar shirts with khaki pants and shiny loafers. The women were wearing stylish floral print dresses and low-heeled shoes. Both the men and women were perfectly coiffed, tailored, and manicured.

When Ki and Bubba pulled up to the front of the mansion, two valets opened the doors of the car and let them out. There was no question the two of them would be the topic of much conversation this evening. It was no surprise that there was an immediate lull in the conversation as soon as they approached the front stairs to the veranda. They realized they were fish out of water, but were now committed, and with heads held high they made their entrance.

Bubba spotted his father across the living room and waved to him but failed to get his attention. Franklin Smith was standing by a grand marble fireplace with a small group of men who were being deferentially attentive to a jovial well-dressed man gesticulating with a cane. Ki was less worried about underdressing for the occasion once she saw how the man who clearly was the host of this soiree went in the other direction in a caricature-like fashion. The western bow tie, black-rimmed glasses, and white suit combined with the shock of white hair, curled mustache, and pointed goatee reminded her of pictures she had seen of Mark Twain. She had a sense that it was not a coincidence.

Just then, Franklin caught sight of them and eagerly motioned for them to join him. The clustered guests parted in front of them like the Red Sea did for Moses as they made their way across the crowded room. Once again, they felt all the eyes in the room on them, and especially the focused attention of the man with the cane. Franklin stepped forward and announced loudly to the room, "Ladies and gentlemen. I would like to introduce my son Bubba and his boss Miss Kianna Smythe from the SEZ of Atlanta, Georgia. They run a detective agency up there and I thought I'd invite them here to mingle with you good people and maybe drum up a little business at the same time. Feel free to ask them any questions and if you have any private eye work that needs to be done. Please do not hesitate to introduce yourselves."

To say that the introduction went over like a lead balloon would be an understatement. People suddenly felt the need to be wrapped up in some urgent conversation with anyone close by. Franklin Smith walked up to Bubba and pulled him in for a big hug and heartily shook Kianna's hand. "I am so glad to finally meet you, Miss Kianna. Bubba has told me a lot of wonderful things about you."

Kianna smiled. "It is a pleasure to make your acquaintance as well, sir. Bubba is equally complimentary of you. He is a good employee. You have raised a fine young man."

"Why thank you Miss Kianna. I appreciate your kind words." Franklin then gestured to the distinguished gentleman who was the magnet of everyone's attention. As the man glad-handed his way across the room toward them, it became evident he wanted to be personally introduced.

"Excuse me, but I would be remiss if I didn't introduce you to the man who is my boss and president for life of the Southern Commonwealth. Bubba, Miss Kianna, may I present Colonel Beauregard Thomas Whitehead, or as he prefers to be called, Colonel Tom."

There was a noticeable shift in the crowd's attention. As he took Kianna's hand and kissed it, you could have heard a pin drop in the room.

"My dear Miss Kianna," his Southern drawl dripping off his tongue, "it is truly a pleasure to meet you. We don't often get guests from the Atlanta

SEZ. It is so good to see a living example of a business forming with whites and blacks working together. We need to encourage more of that sort of thing in our handful of non-segregated counties. It does my heart good to see such collaboration between the races."

Kianna was taken aback. Hers was the only black face at the party outside of the servants and kitchen staff. This gathering was clearly for people who were about as far from wanting racial integration as she could imagine. Kianna received Colonel Tom's obsequious greeting with the understanding that, as a politician, he was playing a role. Even though the office of president in the Commonwealth was a lifetime appointment, his ego exceeded his position and needed the ongoing assurance that he was the most favored, and that included the opinion of this interloping black woman. Kianna read this on him like a billboard and indulged him in her response.

"How courteous of you. I will remember your sincerity."

Colonel Tom did a slight bow. "I will not take up any more of your time Miss Kianna. I am sure there are others here who would love to bend your ear." Summarily dismissing her, he turned away from her and toward her subordinate. "Bubba, do hang back a moment. I would like to have a moment with you one-on-one."

Bubba turned crimson and beamed with delighted surprise. He wasn't sure whether to bow, curtsey, or hug the Colonel. He fumbled a moment before deciding to thrust his hand forward.

"I can't begin to say how honored I am to be in your presence, sir. My daddy didn't tell me you would be attending personally."

Colonel Tom laughed. "Bubba, I'm not anyone special. I put my pants on every morning in the same manner as everyone else—one leg at a time. I must say you favor your father in your good looks. He speaks quite highly of you. I dare say good things are ahead of you, son. Now, I do regret I must attend to the other guests. I wish you and Miss Kianna the best of luck with your venture."

"Thank you, sir. Thank you!"

And with that, the gregarious Colonel Tom went off to greet another cluster of people waiting in the wings.

Kianna whispered to Franklin and Bubba, "That man is like a force of nature. He is the epitome of a smooth-tongued politician"

Franklin nodded hesitantly. "Yes, Miss Kianna. He is indeed. Colonel Tom strives to embody the lofty ideals and conventions of the Southern aristocracy."

Kianna thought better of challenging Franklin and decided to save her comments for another day. Right now, she and Bubba needed to make themselves available for any opportunities that would arise from the glowing reception provided by Colonel Tom. His endorsement would likely yield a greater willingness among the guests to approach them. She could sense the discomfort in many of them, but she was not sure if this was due to their pretention or embarrassment over a real need for her services.

Most of the guests were politicians in service to the State of Georgia, but there were a few visitors from bordering states paying their respects. As was most often the case in these social gatherings, the men and women congregated in small sets with old friends or political allies. The ladies most commonly chattered about gardening, cooking, or domestic service issues and the men were pontificating about hunting, fishing, sports, or some piece of legislation they were working on.

The guests who did introduce themselves to Kianna and Bubba were mostly couples breaking away from their social clusters to seek further information about their services. In a conversation with one group of four,

Ki said, "A lot of what we do is fairly mundane. We investigate crimes to help the police, uncover deceit, infidelity, stop identity theft, and perform background checks on job candidates for employers. Exciting cases like solving a murder are a rarity, but not unheard of."

Toward the end of the evening, they were approached by an attractive middle-aged woman who appeared to be unaccompanied. Speaking with a refined Southern lilt, she said, "Good evening. My name is Mrs. Penelope Lee, the wife of Senator Marquis Lee from the great State of Louisiana. I apologize for his absence. He truly wanted to be here, but he had other affairs to attend to this evening, otherwise he would be here. His job keeps him busier than I would like."

Kianna nodded and extended her hand to Penelope. "Glad to meet you. May I call you Penelope?"

"Why of course, Miss Kianna. I am fascinated by the work that you do. I'd love it if you told me a little more. I may have a need for your services."

This was the first solid lead of the evening for getting some work. Kianna brightened up and smiled at Penelope. Taking Penelope by the arm, she escorted her to an outlying gazebo in a more private part of the estate, and Bubba followed on their heels.

Once they were settled, Ki said, "I get the sense that what you want to discuss is not for public consumption and some privacy is warranted. I think, rather than giving you a list of our services, it would be more effective if you explained your situation, and then I can tell you how we might help."

Penelope gasped. "Good heavens! How on earth did you know that?"

"My dear Mrs. Lee, it was obvious, at least to me."

Catching her breath, Penelope nodded. With some trepidation she said, "Well, I'm not quite sure where to start. I guess the first thing you need to know is that I believe my husband is having an affair. He is very powerful, so I cannot confront him until I have proof."

"I understand. And how long have you suspected this has been going on?"

"About two months."

"I am going to take a guess that this is with someone under your employ and not a social peer. Is that correct?

Both Penelope and Bubba stared silently at her in awe over her accuracy.

Kianna went on. "Part of my job is to study subtle cues in body language to learn more than people are willing to tell me. When you mentioned 'he had other affairs to attend to,' there was a slight, involuntary spasm in your left cheek. Then when you mentioned that his job kept him busier than you would like, your pupils dilated, so I knew this was a common occurrence, which made me suspect his troubling behavior had to be happening close to home. The most common reason for marital discord is infidelity, so it was not a stretch to figure he was involved with a domestic servant, who, of course, would be a person of color."

Penelope hung her head, struggling with the overwhelm of having her worst fears verbalized.

Kianna gave her a moment, and then continued. "I see you are wearing a two-carat flawless diamond stacked with a smaller solitaire and your wedding band. This suggests your husband gave it to you recently and unexpectedly. Perhaps he said it was simply because he loved you. Of course, your gut was telling you the ring was *drachenfutter*."

"I'm sorry, what is that? I think I know what you mean, but that's not a term I've heard before."

"Yes, it is an uncommon word. It is German for 'dragon food.' In other words, it is a gift that is given out of guilt from a spouse who is trying to atone for inappropriate behavior. I imagine your suspicions were aroused by this point, and you started paying more attention to your husband's behavior."

"Yes! I noticed Latitia seemed to be more attentive to my husband's needs, and there were times I found them together talking secretively. You were off on one thing though. The woman of interest is not a domestic servant, although she is colored. She is his personal assistant. Everything else was dead on. It's like you had a camera following me around in my own house. I suppose that begs the question: Where do we go from here? Are you available for hire?"

Kianna stood and smoothed her pants, becoming even more formal in her tone. "Once Bubba and I have returned to our office, he will send you a contract to sign, along with details on our fees and retainer requirements. Bubba, make sure to get her contact information."

Bubba pulled out his phone and took down Penelope's phone number, email, and address in Louisiana.

"Now, Penelope, we also need to know the senator's schedule for the next few days. It will be crucial for you to continue in your daily activities as usual and do your best to not change your demeanor when you interact with him. I know that may be difficult given what you suspect, but if you give him any indication you are on to him, he will stop what he is doing and we will not be able to get the evidence you need. Bubba, set aside a few days next week for the two of us to visit the Great State of Louisiana. I do not expect us to need more than four."

As Bubba and Penelope finalized their exchange of information, Kianna scanned the garden and patio area. She noticed a distinguished, late middle-aged gentleman standing alone sipping a cocktail. He was approximately fifty feet away and was staring at her. There was something familiar about him, but she could not, for the life of her, figure out where she might have seen him before. With her steel trap memory, that was unusual for her. She concluded he must resemble someone from her distant past. As their eyes locked, he tilted his glass in a sort of salutation. She nodded her head in response and he winked at her. Kianna found this to be unnerving and quickly turned back to Penelope who thanked her for her willingness to help her out. When Ki looked for the man again, he had disappeared.

CHAPTER FOUR

"Betrayal is a riddle we want to solve"

—Sascha Arango

Latitia Hicks grew up poor in Concordia Parish, Louisiana, and lived only a hop, jump, and stone skip across the Mississippi River from the free and independent State of Mississippi. Her momma raised her and younger brother Ned in a neat-as-a-pin shack along the shores of a stagnant oxbow lake. The lake supplied the family with plenty of catfish and gar, and a small plot of vegetables kept them from starvation's door. Their clothes were homespun and plain, and on special occasions they bought premade clothes purchased mostly from the bargain bin at Goodwill. Latitia's saving grace was that they lived in a black segregated parish. Because of this she had the advantage of being educated in one of the finest elementary schools in North America. The school had very few resources, but the parish spared no expense in providing the best teachers that money could buy. These teachers cared deeply about their students, and the students in turn cared deeply about their learning. Learning was their most likely path to freedom because it was also the path to power.

Latitia knew that if she were to rise above the systemic poverty inherent in this society, she needed to have a plan. Above all things, her momma had raised her to be organized. She would say, "Latitia, if you ever expect to become someone in this world, you need to live in a clean and well-arranged space. If your surroundings are a mess, then you can expect your life to be a mess too. Be attentive to details and keep things straight. You are young and there are opportunities out there to be had. Pay attention and take advantage when you can."

Latitia learned early on there was a demand in the local businesses for the particular skill set her mother had cultivated in her, which meant she could bring more money to her family's home. With money came a certain form of control and at least the illusion of freedom and security. Over time, she became recognized as an asset to any industry and the black-owned businesses in her parish competed for her talents and skills. Eventually her family benefited from the profits she helped those companies acquire. Before long, she made enough money to rent a home in Jonesville and help her mother and her brother as well. When she realized how much more money she could make working for white people, she decided she could swallow a bit of her pride in exchange for that possibility. After securing a position as a house manager for a wealthy white man in Iberville Parish, she thought her dreams had come true. Then, one day, a head-hunter approached her and felt she was the perfect candidate for a job opening as a personal assistant to the newly elected Senator Marquis Lee. There was stiff competition for the job, but eventually her skill and experience won out the day. She realized over the next few months that by sacrificing a good bit more of her pride there were other benefits. Those fringe benefits included extravagant gifts and lifestyle perks not listed in the job description. But like so much else in life, there always seemed to be a quid pro quo. There was always a price to pay.

Senator and Mrs. Marquis Lee lived near White Castle, Louisiana, at the Nottaway Plantation. Sitting on the banks of the languid but powerful Mississippi River, Nottaway had been a tourist attraction for several decades, but the up-and-coming Senator had petitioned the state senate to make the mansion, grounds, and outbuildings the permanent residence of the sitting Senator representing the free and independent State of Louisiana in the Southern Commonwealth. It was made clear at the polling booth that the electorate felt that it was only appropriate that any man who filled that prestigious and meaningful role should be ensconced in an exquisite manor such as this. It was a home worthy of a powerful man. So, as soon as Mr. Marquis Lee became Senator-elect Marquis Lee, he moved his entire family and personal servants into the lush and spacious quarters.

Since he would be entertaining much more frequently, he added some personal staff to his existing retinue, including a butler and a personal assistant. Of course, his entire service staff was comprised of people of color largely because he relished their obsequious manner. He did not see their fawning behavior as being insincere, but rather it was merely his due because of the high position he held in the Southern society. Latitia Hicks, his personal assistant, turned out to be his biggest asset. She was an attractive and meticulously organized woman, and she brought a high level of professionalism to his office. Since hiring her, his personal and business communications became more refined and impactful, being also timely and concise. In addition to her business skills, Latitia also spoke three languages and had a nearly photographic memory.

Latitia started each day by presenting the Senator with his daily schedule, itemizing and prioritizing issues for his limited and valuable time. This particular morning, she greeted him saying, "Good morning, Senator Lee. It looks like you have a light schedule for today. I have scanned your emails and there appears to be only one item that requires your immediate attention. A Mr. Franklin Smith, who heads up the Data Services Division for the Southern Commonwealth is sending a letter of introduction for his son, Bubba Smith who is traveling through Louisiana on business this week. He was hoping you could spare a minute for Bubba to pay you a visit and see your grand home and estate. He would consider it a personal favor if you would give him and his assistant a personal tour. He gave you his son's personal cell phone number, so I took the liberty of calling ahead to determine his arrival date and get some available times for a tour. He said, sometime in the next day or two would be ideal. The email is in your inbox."

"Thank you, Miss Latitia. I do think we should work to accommodate our Mr. Smith. What does my schedule look like for the next few days?"

"Tomorrow afternoon looks good, as does the following morning."

"Great. Let's make it tomorrow afternoon. Confirm that with him and put it on my schedule. Block them in for a couple of hours. I think that should be sufficient. It is up to your discretion on the timing. Thank you, Miss Latitia."

The senator finally lifted his eyes from what was in front of him and looked at Latitia, letting his gaze linger. He reached out and delicately touched her hand. Latitia also looked directly into the Senator's eyes. She put her hand lightly on his shoulder, and then coyly averted her eyes. This was a signal both had become accustomed to. Although she knew what was to follow and she knew the pleasure of it, a large part of her felt tarnished. Only through reducing it to a matter of pragmatism could she reconcile their actions and make the indiscretion palatable to some small degree.

*****

The next afternoon at precisely 1:30 p.m., Mr. Charles Bubba Smith of Smith Enterprises LLC stood at the front door of the Nottaway Mansion accompanied by his tall, black lady assistant, a Miss Kianna Smythe. The family butler answered the door and invited the couple in, escorting them to wait in the library while he announced their arrival. A few minutes later,

Senator Marquis Lee made his entrance. Senator Lee was someone who checked all the right boxes. He was tall, ruggedly handsome, courteous, and charismatic. Lee's tailor-made suit and perfectly coiffed hair set the tone for their meeting; and, he exuded self-confidence and superiority from every pore, he had an uncanny way of making you feel welcomed as well. He flashed a warm, sincere smile at Bubba and Kianna, firmly shaking Bubba's hand, and then gently lifting Kianna's hand to place a whisper-soft kiss on her fingertips. Once they had dispensed with the niceties and rituals of formal greetings, they went on a one-hour tour of the expansive house and grounds. Bubba conversed with Senator Lee about his family and the Southern Commonwealth, laughing at all the right quips and anecdotes from the Senator. Bubba knew how to play the male-bonding game. Kianna, on the other hand was like the air itself, ever present but not noticed. She only spoke if specifically asked a question. Eventually they ended up in Senator Lee's formal office and were introduced to his personal assistant, Latitia.

Senator Lee motioned to his assistant. "Miss Latitia, this is Mr. Bubba Smith and his personal assistant, Miss Kianna Smythe, from the Atlanta SEZ."

Latitia offered a small curtsy and said, "A pleasure to make your acquaintance, I am sure. Mr. Smith, it is good to put a face with a voice."

Senator Lee, smiling, leaned over to Bubba. "Could I interest you in a glass of some fine imported Tennessee whiskey?"

"Certainly, sir. I prefer it neat."

"Excellent. Miss Latitia, would you be so kind as to fetch us a couple of glasses of that beautiful amber liquid?"

Latitia poured and served the whiskey, then placed an etched tumbler in front of each man.

"Thank you, Miss Latitia. Miss Kianna, you are welcome to adjourn with her to the parlor. Bubba and I are going to chat about things that won't be of interest to you."

He winked knowingly at Bubba, and Kianna knew this was not a suggestion but a courteous way of asking her to leave.

Latitia smiled curtly at the senator and then nodded to Kianna to follow her out of the room. Kianna rose without a word and followed Latitia into the adjoining parlor, closing the doors behind them.

After savoring the view of the ladies leaving, the senator turned his attention back to Bubba. "May I call you Bubba?" Bubba nodded his assent. "So, tell me Bubba, exactly what kind of business are you engaged in?"

Bubba stroked his chin. "I think it would best be described as Data Management. I handle information of all types."

"Interesting. Does your work ever enter into the realm of politics?"

"Why yes, it does, and it can be remarkably interesting indeed. We manage data for a number of individuals, government agencies, and non-profits involved in espionage and clandestine operations. Those fingers often dip into the political field. Extortion seems to be quite lucrative these days."

"Extortion. Why, that sounds positively indecorous. I would love to learn more about how you handle such cases . . . purely for informational purposes, of course."

"I regret I have a busy schedule for the rest of the day, but maybe we can arrange another time to chat about it when I next find myself in your neighborhood," Bubba said, hoping to not appear too eager for information.

"Yes, I would enjoy that very much. Have your Miss Kianna arrange something with my Miss Latitia, then we can discuss it in a more formal meeting."

"Certainly. I'd be happy to go into greater detail . . . just for your information, of course. That way, if you . . . or anyone you know had such a need for that service, you'd know who to call."

Bubba took out a piece of paper and jotted down a note. Rising and extending his hand to the senator, Bubba said, "Senator Lee, I cannot begin to tell you how much I appreciate the gracious sacrifice of your time and your courteous reception of me and my assistant. I do not, however, wish to overstay our welcome and, as I said, I have some personal business that requires my attention."

Senator Lee rose and took Bubba's proffered hand. "Mr. Smith, it has been my distinct pleasure to meet you. And thank you for filling me in on your most interesting profession. There may come a time in the near future I will prevail upon you to tell me more. But until then, I will bid you adieu."

The senator went to the parlor doors and without knocking opened them wide. "Excuse me, ladies, but Mr. Smith has another commitment and must be leaving us."

Bubba greeted Kianna and handed her the note he had jotted as she exited the parlor.

"Miss Kianna, attend to this matter at your earliest convenience."

Taking Latitia's hand, he made a slight bow. "Miss Latitia, thank you for helping to make this visit not only informative, but also a most pleasurable one."

Once Bubba and Kianna had left the room, Senator Lee turned to Latitia.

"Miss Latitia, you had mentioned yesterday my schedule was open tomorrow morning. Later this afternoon, call Mr. Smith and see if he can shoehorn me in for a short business meeting at 9:00 a.m. in my office. You can apologize for the short notice, but it is a matter of some importance that I speak with him soon."

"Yes, sir. By the way, I really enjoyed the company of Miss Kianna. Our short conversation was quite pleasurable. I look forward to seeing her tomorrow provided Mr. Smith's schedule can accommodate your needs."

Marquis looked into the distance as he said under his breath, "I certainly hope so, Latitia. I certainly hope so.

*****

Kianna read the note as they walked to the car.

He bit on the extortion bait like a yellow jacket to a sugary drink on a hot day.

"If I do not miss my guess, I suspect you will hear from our esteemed senator before the afternoon is out."

No sooner than had she uttered those words, her phone rang. Latitia's name was on the caller ID and Kianna said, "Good afternoon, Latitia. How may I help you?"

"Kianna, I know, this is short notice, and I apologize, but is it possible to have Mr. Smith pay a professional visit to Senator Lee tomorrow morning at 9:00 a.m.?"

"Latitia, it is so good to hear from you again, and so soon. Let me consult Mr. Smith's schedule for tomorrow. Bear with me a moment."

Kianna waited nearly forty-five seconds and unmuted her phone.

"Did you say 9:00 a.m.? The soonest I can manage would 10:15, and it could only be for forty-five minutes. Is that acceptable?"

"Kianna, that would be perfect. His morning is wide open. Thank you so much for accommodating the senator. We will see you tomorrow."

Bubba was smiling. "Well, this will be interesting."

CHAPTER FIVE

Shakespeare and his work will always be relevant. He wrote those pieces hundreds of years ago and we haven't really changed as humans, have we? We have to deal with love, honor and adultery now — people were the same then, too - that's what's so wonderful and powerful.

—Michelle Dockery

Bubba sat across from the senator and after engaging in the usual pleasantries, he said, "Well, Senator Lee, what exactly interests you about extortion and blackmail?

"I like a man who gets directly to the point."

He hesitated before going forward. "Bubba, I assume we are speaking with the full confidentiality that comes with a gentleman's agreement."

"Senator, I will do you one better. If you lay a dollar on the table right now, I will consider that a retainer and your privacy will be protected as with all of my clients."

The senator grinned and pulled a leather wallet from his desk and extracted a single bill and slid it across the desk to Bubba. Bubba was surprised when he looked down to see the denomination was considerably more than he expected.

"I believe in paying well for quality work. Now, with that out of the way, the reason I am interested in learning more about extortion is because

I have been approached by an individual who is, shall we say, attempting to gain favors from me. He has made it clear that if I refuse his requests, he will reveal to my family and political associates certain indiscretions I prefer to keep private."

Bubba looked directly into Senator Lee's eyes. "In order to help you effectively, I need to know the exact nature of this indiscretion."

Senator Marquis Lee went quiet for nearly a minute, and he stared past Bubba. He then spoke very quietly. "I have broken the seventh commandment in the Decalogue. I have been unfaithful to my wife. While many of my political allies will be inclined to let this sort of thing pass, my wife and my political adversaries are not likely to be so forgiving. In your professional opinion, what is the likelihood of this person to make good on his threat?"

*****

Latitia embraced Kianna. "I am so pleased that the senator wanted to see Mr. Smith again. I truly enjoyed our conversation yesterday. To speak with another person of color who is doing the same type of work that I am doing is delightful."

Kianna smiled and returned the hug. "If you would not mind, I would like to ask you some questions. I have a feeling the men folk will be occupied for a while."

Latitia smiled and said, "Go right ahead. I have nothing to hide. Provided, of course, you don't get too personal."

"Well, that is the thing. Some of the questions I had in mind are quite personal."

Latitia furrowed her brow. "Well, that is interesting. I suppose we will have to see about my response once you ask the question."

"Fair enough. Before I ask my questions, I wanted to comment. I must say, Latitia, you are one of the most organized people I have ever met. I am not easily impressed, but you have impressed me. When we were in your office earlier, not only was it tidy, but every item was carefully and meticulously labeled and not even a stray paperclip cluttered your desk."

Although Latitia was uncomfortable accepting compliments, a small smile crept onto her face. "Thank you for the compliment, Miss Kianna. I take pride in being well prepared for any eventuality, and to do that I need to be well organized. Knowing where everything is and when something is supposed to happen is essential to ensure I can execute my roles and responsibilities with precision. Most people don't really notice, and I am frankly amazed that you did. If you don't mind me asking, what impressed you?"

"Well, everything, actually. Your attention to the most minute details in your personal style, the structure in your office space, and even the painstaking uniformity of your handwriting reveals you have honed your organizational skills beyond what even a position like this demands. If I were to venture a guess, I would say you have been this way since your childhood."

"My, you do pay attention, don't you? You are right, by the way. Early on, my momma instilled in me the importance of being fastidious, not only in my appearance, but also in whatever work I did. It has been essential to my success in every job I have performed, not to mention my schooling. Did your momma help you hone your astonishing skills of observation?"

Kianna smiled. "As a matter of fact, she did influence me significantly. We used to play a game where I would look for clues around the house to figure out what had changed while I was at school. Assessing and understanding the world around me eventually became a significant part of who I was and who I am to this day. But what I use as a blessing can become a burden at times because I see things I might have been better off not seeing. I imagine the senator relies on you heavily."

Laughing, she said, "Absolutely. I swear that man couldn't find his hat if it was on his head!"

"How long have you been in the employ of Senator Lee?"

"Oh, it's been about six months now."

"Would you say that is enough time to know what he is like? You know, as a man?"

Latitia pondered the question and finally said, "I am not totally sure that one can ever know another person. I have lived with *me* my whole life, and yet I am not entirely sure I know myself, so I don't know if I would ever feel confident in judging a man like Senator Lee. Why do you ask?"

"Latitia, I fear you have been spending too much time with the good senator, or maybe you are a natural born politician. Your response has the rather shiny surface, yet ultimately meaningless fluff of political spin and you did not answer my question. This is the point where my questions become more 'personal'. Why did you use the term 'judging' him?"

*****

The senator now silently stared directly into Bubba's eyes. Bubba stared back at him and said. "My first question is regarding the accuracy of his claims, and second whether he has any proof of said indiscretion,"

"Unfortunately, the truth of the matter is, I did have a dalliance with Miss Latitia Hicks on more than one occasion. As for the second question, this person claims to have video evidence."

"There is a good chance that if you don't follow through on his demands, he will indeed share the information with your wife and your colleagues. However, if you were to confess the crime, he would have no leverage against you and would likely go away. As long as you keep your nose clean, you would never have to hear from him again."

"You say that I would need to confess to cheating on my wife in order to make it go away?"

"I am afraid so. I am curious though. Latitia Hicks does not strike me as someone who would engage in or be a party to such behavior. How did you sway her from what appear to be high morals and integrity? For that matter, I am frankly surprised you would even approach her."

"As for myself, one could say I have a strong libido. Someone else may call it sexual addiction. For me, there is something compelling about tasting 'forbidden fruit'."

The senator leaned back in his chair and studied Bubba for a moment, and Bubba feared he may have overstepped, but the senator surprised him by continuing. "I am not the sort of man to kiss and tell; but, given our arrangement, I will share some of the details of my relationship with Latitia."

Bubba smiled and said, "I can assure you, my lips are sealed."

Bubba said this knowing full well there was a hidden tape recorder getting everything down for the record, and he would not ever need to utter a word about it, as the senator would be doing all the talking.

"Good enough. When I first met Miss Latitia, she was prim and proper and hyper-focused on her work. I must admit I was immediately drawn to her, and I'm not proud of this, but soon my compulsion to have her was more than I could resist. I knew she would not be won easily; her integrity and sense of propriety were clearly and firmly ensconced, but I couldn't fight what I was feeling. I knew it would require the right approach and a great deal of finesse. I finally determined that sympathy might be the key, but not just pity. I feigned a bad mood or severe emotional distraction.

If she commented on it, I would say it was 'personal'. I might let it slip that Penelope didn't understand me and my needs, that I felt alone in my marriage, but then I would tell her not to worry about it. Little by little, she began to see me as the victim of a loveless union and incessant brow-beating from a shrewish wife, and she longed to help me see my value and experience the love I deserved. I would apologize, of course. I would say how hard it was being a man with these unfulfilled desires. The first time we were intimate, she just held me, held my head close to her breast and kissed me. From there I knew I would be fast-tracked to her bed."

*****

"Umm . . . Kianna, I'm not sure how to respond to that. As his personal assistant, I am privy to much of the senator's professional and personal concerns."

Kianna gently touched Latitia's arm. "Latitia, please know that I do understand your loyalty. It is admirable. I am equally guarded with my personal life, but Bubba is an open book, always willing to share nearly everything that crosses his mind. I imagine you have encountered the same with Senator Lee. I am not asking you to share anything he told you in confidence. I'm just wondering what you may have observed."

"What is it like working for Bubba? He seems so young to hold such a position of authority. And there is a boyish charm I can't help but find appealing."

"Well, to be honest, I would not say that I work *for* Bubba as much as I work *with* him. And you are correct. His honesty and lack of cynicism are two of his personality traits that truly appeal to me. He teaches me important lessons all the time."

Latitia sat quietly for a minute and seemed to be on the edge of saying something, but she kept hesitating. Kianna could sense the wavering tension and finally said, "Latitia, what is on your mind? It seems clear there is something you want to say. Let me assure you, I can keep a confidence."

Latitia seemed to relax some and said, "Kianna, it feels good to be able to talk with a sister of color and someone who speaks to me as an equal. I really appreciate that. In this house, the only person I normally speak with is the senator. Mrs. Lee tries to avoid me for some reason and the servants in the manor don't see me as one of 'them'. Because I feel a connection to you, there is something of a personal nature I would like to share."

Kianna smiled. "Of course. What is it you want to share?"

Latitia's face fell into a frown as she said, "I am ashamed to admit I have crossed a line in my relationship with the senator. It has taken on a more intimate nature than it should have. It all started as sympathy for Marquis and his troubled relationship with Mrs. Lee."

Kianna feigned shock. "Really? How is the relationship troubled?"

"Well, I believe that every human being has a need for a caring and compassionate companion. From what Senator Lee has shared with me, his wife is not an understanding or loving person. And, as he explained, she does not have the same level of desire for physical intimacy that he does, and that has created even more of a wedge between them. I expressed my sympathy, and at first that was as far as it went. Marquis is a charming and persuasive man, and I have to admit I am physically attracted to him. I was weak and succumbed to that attraction. I truly regret that, but now I get the sense that I am somehow obligated and I fear I could lose my job if I don't acquiesce."

"Latitia, I am so sorry to hear that. Do you remember when I said earlier that my observation skills at times are more of burden than a benefit?" Latitia nodded. "Well, I have seen enough in the short time I was in the room with both of you to gather that there was more to the relationship than employer and employee. You've been open with me, so I feel I need to be totally above board with you. Bubba and I are not here for a tour of the mansion.

Latitia started to tremble, and tears started to well up in her eyes.

"Oh my God! I trusted you!" she gasped.

*****

The senator turned to Bubba and asked, "What about you. Have you ever thought about using your assistant for more than clerical duties?"

Bubba started laughing hard, almost to the point of tears. Finally, he regained control and was able to speak. "Oh, if I were to ever do anything like that, Miss Kianna would put my ass into the hospital, and it would be a good month before I saw the light of day."

Senator Lee did not quite know what to make of this. Recovering, Bubba sat forward and leaned into the senator and spoke in a serious and subdued voice to him. "Now, there is something I need to share with you before the ladies rejoin us."

The senator looked at Bubba suspiciously. "Whatever do you mean?"

"Well, you see, Miss Kianna and I aren't exactly what we claimed to be. While it is true, we deal with data, it is more about the investigation of data. Miss Kianna runs a private investigation firm called Smythe Detective Agency located in the Atlanta SEZ, and I am not her superior. She is mine. We were invited here by your wife, Penelope, to look into her suspicions about your extra-curricular activities."

The senator's face was getting redder, and he looked as though he was about to explode.

"You have already quite graciously, albeit unwillingly, confirmed what she feared was true and given us ample evidence for her purposes. As we speak, Miss Kianna is speaking with Miss Latitia, and I am quite sure her version will add a great deal of color to the story we have to tell your wife."

The senator rose again. "You have nothing but hearsay. That will not get you anywhere!"

Bubba calmly looked at the senator. "Remember the pickle you are in regarding the extortion. You now have the opportunity to make a clean breast of it. Yes, your ego will be battered and bruised a bit, but you will come out of it whole. On top of all that you just may save your marriage and career."

The senator had made a career of avoiding discomfort, so this suggestion held little appeal for him, but he could still see the sound reasoning in it for the long term. This quelled his rage enough to allow Bubba the opportunity to finish.

Bubba smiled. "There is one other important bit of information I need to tell you." Bubba pulled back the lapel on his jacket to reveal the hidden microphone. Senator Marquis Lee blanched and sat heavily into his chair.

"You also need to know that Miss Kianna is an extremely talented and observant detective who has already compiled enough physical evidence in this room to hold up in in a divorce court, if it came to that. Is there anything else you would care to say for the record?"

After Bubba had revealed the truth, Senator Lee sat back in his chair and was at a complete loss for words.

*****

"My name really is Kianna Smythe, however, Bubba is *my* assistant, and *I* am his boss. I run a detective agency out of the Atlanta SEZ, and we were hired by the senator's wife, Penelope, to investigate his possible sexual infidelity."

Latitia sat stunned and mortified. When she spoke, her voice was soft and laced with vulnerability. "I really don't know what to say to that."

"Latitia, there are very few people on this planet who can hide any truth that insists on being known. That said, I am also very practiced at what I do. I can tell by your dark mahogany skin color and your regional accent that you come from South-Central Louisiana. That is an area that is rife with very low economic resources, so I naturally presume you grew up in abject poverty upriver from here, close to Mississippi. Most people subsist on caught fish and produce from small gardens as well as any wild victuals there might be found. Because you lived close to the land, your mother instilled in you, early in your life, to be conscientious about maintaining a certain order and discipline in your life. That has resulted in a very organized and borderline obsessive-compulsive lifestyle. This makes you extremely good at your job. I know you have a brother and a mother who is still alive. This is evident because of the family picture you have prominently displayed in your office. Your father is out of the picture for unknown reasons. He either abandoned you all or he died not long after your brother was born. Your family lived close to the land, and you raised, caught or captured most of your own food. I know you cherished your education and did well in school because you are a very intelligent young lady and you recognized early on the importance of knowledge as a way of rising out of the systemic poverty that is so inherent in that society.

On a more current note, in the outgoing mail, you had a stamped envelope addressed to your mother and from what little I know of you and your good character, you are a good daughter and send money home to her every month. Then, based on the open calendar on your desk, I can see you arrive in your office at seven in the morning. Based on the food remnants and the residual odors, it seems you had scrambled eggs, toast and bacon

56

for breakfast with only one cup of coffee although you would like to have two. That last bit, I deduced from your desire to have order and discipline in your life and that plays out in self-discipline.

Regarding your sexual tryst, it appears you had sexual relations on that settee across the room, I would say two days ago, probably around three in the afternoon. The cushions are disturbed which you normally would have straightened except you are embarrassed by your activities and you have avoided touching them. I reasoned the timing of your encounter basing it on your schedule and the open spot that was blocked off in your daily calendar."

The look of shock was evident on Latitia's face. Latitia broke down into an uncontrollable sobbing mess. She was shaking and hugging herself as she let her raw emotions and tears come forth. As those feelings bubbled up, the full implication of her actions with the senator began to dawn on her. Kianna tried comforting her.

"Latitia, I know you feel guilty, and I know how easy it is to find justification for something that feels good, even if you know in your heart it is wrong. However, my job is to gather information for my client. It is not my job to pass judgement on any of this. It may be uncomfortable for you, but I do have a few more questions, and I think you will feel better if you relieve yourself of this burden."

Between her spasms of sobbing, Latitia was able to finally bring herself under some control. Finally, she said, "What do you want to know?"

"I know the physical relationship started roughly two and a half months ago, but I need to know if you had any role in initiating the affair. Did you seduce him in any way?" Latitia shook her head no. "Did he force himself on you?"

Latitia bowed her head and shook it vigorously back and forth saying, "No! It was fully consensual. At first, I didn't even touch him, but it grew beyond that pretty quickly. He really seemed to feel something more than just physical desire for me. And I just felt so sorry for him because he is such a good man and was so lonely."

Kianna frowned. "Well, Latitia, 'good' men do not typically engage in this type of behavior, and while we cannot know what goes on inside the relationship between two other people, I did not get the sense from Penelope that she felt this was a loveless marriage. I cannot say he was disingenuous. That remains to be seen. That said, he may have an opportunity to redeem himself. It really lies in his wife's hands."

Latitia resumed her crying but with considerably less energy.

Kianna said, "You may not want to do this, but we need to talk to Bubba and the senator and see what they have to say."

Kianna opened the door to the senator's office to find Bubba and the senator sitting in silence. Bubba had a slight smile on his face, however the senator was not looking happy. Obviously, Bubba had filled Senator Lee in on what he and Kianna were doing there. Latitia refused to make eye contact with the senator, and she sat off in the corner of the room with her head hanging down. Kianna addressed the room.

"Latitia, Senator Lee, let me start by saying that our conversations were recorded in order to provide Penelope with both sides of the story in each person's own words." Latitia's eyebrows rose when she heard about the recordings.

"Is there anything else that either of you would like to add before we turn off the recording devices?"

Both Latitia and Senator Lee shook their heads no.

"You may want to consider what we all need to do in order to bring this messy situation to a close. Shortly, Bubba and I will be meeting with

Penelope to report our findings, and then coming back here to decide on an appropriate course of action. Are we clear?"

Both Latitia and Senator Lee nodded their heads.

CHAPTER SIX

"Resentment is like drinking poison and then hoping it will kill your enemies."

—Nelson Mandela

Penelope Lee listened to the tapes of Latitia and Senator Lee, but Kianna could tell that their words were merely confirmation of what she had expected. Penelope spoke quietly. "Well, Miss Kianna. Where do we go from here?"

Kianna looked Penelope in the eye and said, "That is entirely up to you. Ask yourself how you feel about this man. That is number one. Number two, consider what the revelation of this could do not only to his career but also your lifestyle and that of the other victim here, Miss Latitia Hicks. And finally, number three. What do you want the future for yourself, Senator Lee, and Latitia to look like? This is not a decision to be made lightly. You currently hold all the cards, but I recommend the six of us sit down and have an open and honest discussion about their choices and what it means for everyone's future."

Penelope rose, and with a determined voice said, "Let's get this over with."

She led them through the house to the senator's office. As she entered, her husband rose and started to speak, but Penelope cut him off.

"Marquis, keep your mouth shut until I have had my say!"

Senator Marquis Lee knew he was in no position to be defensive with his wife, so he silently sat down and waited for her to unload on him. Everyone in the room wanted to put this all behind them. Penelope cut to the chase.

"Marquis Lee, to say you have hurt me deeply would be an understatement. When you betray the trust of someone who loves you, you cut deeply into their heart, and it leaves a scar that constantly carries a reminder of those wounds. There is nothing you can ever do to erase the pain." She paused and the senator cleared his throat. "Marquis, I am not finished. Sit still. Your turn will come. Now, to be clear, I want you both to understand that I know you are at fault here, not Miss Latitia. I believe she has been treated almost as poorly as myself. I do not doubt the veracity of anything I heard from her in the recordings. Regardless of how this eventually plays out, I wish no further negative consequences to befall her. Is that clear?" The senator nodded vigorously and Latitia had a look of genuine relief on her face. "Second, as much as it pains me to say this, I do still love you, but, mark my words, there will be consequences for this stupid, self-centered behavior, but how this is resolved will be between the two of us."

The senator rose and looked to Penelope for approval to speak. Penelope gave a slight nod and Marquis said, "I know what an arrogant and self-centered ass I have been. Although apologies are totally inadequate, I feel compelled to at least express them."

Turning to his wife, he hung his head and said, "My dear and precious wife, the sorrow is deep, and I apologize from the bottom of my heart, knowing the pain I have caused you. I promise to you right now that I will never do anything of this nature to you again. I will undergo counseling for my sex addiction, and I will happily go through marriage counseling if that is something that will help us regain our previously happy marriage."

Latitia looked shocked.

"Yes, Latitia. Our marriage actually was a happy one, regardless of the picture I painted when I was deceiving you. I am deeply sorry for how I manipulated you. I realize I have lost the best personal assistant in the entire Southern Commonwealth, but I guarantee that I will find a comparable and better paying position for you with another high-ranked individual in our good commonwealth. Provided, of course, you want my help."

Marquis then turned to Kianna. "Miss Kianna. I am grateful for the tact and discretion you employed in your investigation. If I can ever offer a recommendation to any future clients, do not hesitate to call upon me. I do feel vastly relieved that this whole affair has been exposed. As I shared with Bubba, I am being blackmailed by a person who claimed to have video evidence of my tryst, which he said he was going to reveal to my wife. Now, I am no longer susceptible to his extortion."

Kianna interjected, "I was not surprised to hear someone was blackmailing you to attain political favors. What were they requesting?"

"Introductions to certain political groups. My name would have offered an essential level of credibility with them. He had a particular interest in Georgia and the Southern Commonwealth. I got the sense he was part of a lobbying group looking to have influence over some pending legislative action. If you would like, I can give you everything I know about him. I never did meet the man, however, so a physical description would be impossible. He did say his name was Herr Offen Braun."

"Thank you, senator. I am positive that the name he shared with you is an alias. However, whatever you would be willing to share with me would be much appreciated. I am all about gathering information."

CHAPTER SEVEN

"It was always so hot, and everyone was so polite, and everything was all surface but underneath it was like a bomb waiting to go off. I always felt that way about the South, that beneath the smiles and southern hospitality and politeness were a lot of guns and liquor and secrets."

—James McBride

On the drive to southern Georgia to meet Bubba's father, Ki and Bubba discussed the proper way to bring the Southern Commonwealth's attention to what they had discovered regarding the blackmailer and what he was trying to accomplish. Ki was hesitant to broach the subject since it was revealed in the course of a separate investigation that was of a very personal nature. Bubba, however, thought it was important to alert his father and Colonel Tom to what was going on and the potential consequences for the Commonwealth's security.

"Miss Ki, we don't need to tell Daddy how we found out, but I got a real bad feelin' about what might be happenin'. We got to say somethin'. Don't you agree?"

Ki nodded. "Yes, Bubba. I do think what we heard warrants some disclosure, but we cannot reveal this came from Senator Lee. That would violate all sorts of ethics codes, and it would not look good to a potential client if we were to share information entrusted to us by another. When we meet with your father, let me take the lead."

"No problem, Miss Ki."

Ki had never had the desire to visit the headquarters of the Southern Commonwealth before and she was ambivalent about the arranged meeting there. Ki had grown up in the Southern Commonwealth, which put much more emphasis on the states having the center of control and political power. When the Commonwealth finally came into its own nearly eighty years ago, one of the first things done was to reduce the size of the federal government. The states were united in having a common vision, but the states were independent entities that were more like separate countries. Because of this, when Ki visited other parts of the United States a couple of times in her youth, it was on a tourist visa. Once, she had an opportunity once to visit Washington, DC. She found it to be entertaining, and she loved the Mall area with all the museums, but it was disturbing how much emphasis there was on centralized power. The Capital Building, the Supreme Court, the White House, and all the pomp and circumstance surrounding those edifices was quite disconcerting to her.

The Commonwealth was united under a singular culture. That culture was one that harkened back to the days of the antebellum South. These factors were essential for understanding what the Southern Commonwealth was looking to achieve in the layout and design for their national headquarters in the town of Nahunta in Brantley County, Georgia. Nahunta was a small, quiet town that practically dripped old-world Southern charm and sensibilities. The Southern Commonwealth's office complex was modeled after a Southern plantation. The façade of the primary office was lined with massive columns, and the sprawling grounds featured Spanish Moss-covered Live Oak Trees. There were also numerous outbuildings mimicking the style of the main building to house various departments, but it was not a compound. There were no massive security fences or armed snipers on the rooftops. Nearly every employee packed a gun, so there was little concern for the safety of the premises. Parking was underground so it would not disturb the scenic presentation and patina of Southern gentility and charm.

While the aesthetic was superficially pleasant, there was not only the ever present awareness of what plantations once were, but there was blatant display of that history. Civil War heroes from the mid-to-late-19th century were memorialized in statues and plaques outside and numerous paintings hung inside the buildings depicting select scenes from what was unwaveringly referred to in the Southern Commonwealth as the War of Northern Aggression. Understandably, it was a source of pride that was inconceivable to Kianna. Yes, it was part of the South's history; but according to the version of history she received at her mixed-race school in Atlanta, that Great Civil War was called the War for Emancipation. It is often said that history is the myth written by the winners, and now that the South was independent, they had won the right to dictate how the history was characterized in their region.

Much like she resented the power displays in Washington, DC, celebrating anything that honored war was disturbing to her. Brothers killing brothers, cousins killing cousins. It was reprehensible on so many levels. She really hated any reminders of the divisiveness of that era. Another disturbing aspect for her was the way people of her heritage had been treated as less than human and the wanton disregard for life, regardless of it being white or black.

Ultimately though, in dealing with that history of suppression she had to fall back on the three commitments she had made at a Buddhist retreat center over a decade earlier. The first commitment was to do no harm to oneself or others. The second commitment was to show compassion to oneself and all others. The third commitment was to accept life as it unfolds, which proved to be the most difficult of all and one she found to be an ongoing struggle. Although it was not possible to fully keep any of these commitments, by holding them in her heart, she found they held influence over her life to a significant degree, and a certain level of tolerance and acceptance of those things she had no control over became achievable.

Ki and Bubba took the elevator up from the parking garage to the main floor and reception area of the mansion. The receptionist, one Peggy Sue, was on the edge of being cloyingly sweet; yet, somehow, in her it seemed authentic and not contrived. She was extremely courteous and efficient. Peggy took their coats and led them to a vast, well-appointed library where they waited for Franklin.

Ki ran a cursory glance over the periodicals neatly positioned on the end tables and casually perused the titles of the books lining the bookshelves and was quickly reminded of where they were and the existing paradigm, should she have doubted for even a moment that it might be other than it seemed. Ki knew that in her line of work understanding your client's character was essential for better meeting their needs. When asking questions, those questions must be couched in language that resonates with the client. It is far more productive to build bridges rather than walls. The reading material on display gave Ki all she needed to know for communicating with this unique client. She suspected that Bubba would serve as an effective foil by handling the formalities of client management, which would allow her to focus on the more pertinent matters of the case. Bubba was proving to be a valuable asset, confirming she took the right approach in screening an assistant.

A smile crept onto Bubba's face as he stood up to greet the man approaching them. She immediately recognized him from the gala a couple weeks before. He turned and addressed her.

"Hello again, Miss Ki. I understand you were able to be of some assistance to Mrs. Penelope Lee regarding a personal issue. I understand from the good senator that everything has been resolved and the muddied waters are starting to clear. Senator Lee says he would recommend your agency with no hesitancy."

"Well, that is wonderful to hear, Mr. Smith. Please pass my regards on to the Senator and his wife when next you see them. Bubba and I are here, on an unrelated matter, and we are hopeful you will find what we have to say important and helpful to the Southern Commonwealth's general welfare and security."

Franklin frowned. "That sounds serious. Should I get Colonel Tom to come down and hear it as well?"

"We will leave that to your discretion, but suffice it to say, we believe it is very serious."

"Please, go ahead."

"It has come to our attention through a reliable and confidential source, that the Southern Commonwealth may be the target of an elaborate extortion and information hacking operation. It is not clear what the specific goals are for the group behind this attack, but it would be wise to be on the alert for any suspicious activities."

A look of concern fell over Franklin's face. "Thank you, Miss Kianna, for coming to us with your concern. There is something I should share with you, but please understand what we are going to talk about is strictly confidential. We don't need to be spreading rumors or concern through the community. Our PR department would not take kindly to that sort of thing. It is indeed quite providential timing that you are reporting to us because our national database has, in fact, been compromised and we fear relatively sensitive information has been leaked to some of our political foes. The other component, which is confounding, is that whoever is behind this also shared information with us about our political counterparts."

Ki frowned. "Can you tell us the nature of this information?"

Franklin shook his head and said, "Unfortunately, I cannot. If you would excuse me, this is definitely something the Colonel should know. I will be right back. I apologize for leaving you like this. Do make yourself comfortable."

After Franklin left, Bubba turned to Ki. "It looks like this might turn into a job."

"Time will tell, Bubba. Time will tell."

A short time later, Franklin Smith rejoined them. "Colonel Tom says he would like to meet with all three of us. Are you okay with that?"

Ki nodded. "I welcome a meeting with him, but, is there anything I should know before we meet with Colonel Tom? Not following politics, my only familiarity with him is the colorful and ostentatious pageantry I observed at the gala."

Franklin grinned. "To use the term 'colorful' would be understating the case. He is largely about image, but don't let that fool you. He may come off as a good ol' country boy and maybe a bit of a rube, but nothing could be further from the truth. Behind his Southern charm and passive aggressive demeanor, he is one sharp cookie. So stay on your toes." Glancing at his watch, Franklin said, "Let's go ahead on up and meet with the big man. Follow me."

They followed Franklin up the wide winding staircase that looked like something out of the movie *Gone with the Wind*. Ki could not help but be impressed by the attention to historical detail throughout the entire complex. In some respects, it felt like an attraction at one of the Disney entertainment centers. Based on Franklin's description of Colonel Tom, she had a feeling that the cartoonish parallel was going to be taken to the next level. She was not disappointed.

"Colonel Tom. I'm sure you remember Miss Kianna Smythe from the gala one week ago. And, as you already know, this strapping young man is my son, Bubba."

Colonel Tom took Ki's outstretched hand and with a slight bow, he kissed her fingers. Looking up into her eyes, his face came alive. "My dear, Miss Kianna. It is so good to see you again."

Ki felt her stomach turn, so she recited the three commitments in her head, and it helped her weather the likely saccharine platitudes that were sure to follow.

He then turned and grasped Bubba's hand. "It is so good to see you again, son."

Bubba couldn't take his eyes off Colonel Tom. "Sir, it is a pleasure to see you again. Thank you, so much, for taking the time to talk with Miss Ki and myself about the problem you are facing. I am hoping that we can be of some assistance."

Colonel Tom smacked his forehead, "Now, where are my manners. Please have a seat and I will have Miss Peggy Sue fetch us some refreshments."

With this, he reached over to his desk and tapped on an intercom and said, "Miss Peggy Sue, would you kindly send in some hot tea and those lovely little cakes that you make?"

Peggy Sue bubbled over the intercom, "Of course, Colonel Tom. I'll have them brought in post haste."

Less than a minute had passed when there was a light knock at the door and there was a soft male voice. "Sir. You requested some hot tea and cakes?"

Colonel Tom looked up. "Yes, Tamba. Please bring them in."

A tall and distinguished young black man wearing a tailor-made suit pushed an ornate silver cart toward them with a complete tea service and a tiered pedestal arrayed with a variety of small cakes.

"Tamba, would you be so kind as to serve our guests?"

Tamba made a slight bow. "Of course, Colonel Tom, sir. It would be my pleasure."

While Tamba delicately placed cakes on serving plates, Colonel Tom said, "Tamba, this young colored lady has her own business up in Atlanta. She is a private eye and works for both white and colored. That is very enterprising, don't you think?"

With no show of enthusiasm, only focus on his task of distributing cups of tea, Tamba stated, "Yes, sir. Very enterprising indeed."

"Would you like to have your own business someday, Tamba?"

"Oh, no, sir. I would have no idea how to do that. I'm happy to be working here, sir." As he handed a cup and saucer to the Colonel. He stepped back to the cart and asked, " Would there be anything else sir?"

"Thank you, Tamba. That will be all for now. I always appreciate your fastidious service Tamba."

"Thank you for the compliment sir. Just ring when you want this cleared away, sir."

While enjoying the tea and cakes, the group engaged in informal banter, as was expected, according to social graces. A few minutes into their dialogue, Ki excused herself to powder her nose. She simply had to get away from the tea ceremony in order to avoid saying something in frustration that would ruin the chances of working for this especially important client. Kianna found all the pomp and circumstance of social niceties to be frustrating. She preferred to cut to the chase. This politician really rubbed her the wrong way. But, remembering commitment number three, she headed back to Colonel Tom's office about five minutes later and put on her best game face.

Once Ki had returned from the lady's room, Colonel Tom turned to his guests. "Well, why don't we get down to business? Franklin, won't you please fill our guests in on what has been happening here as of late that has us tearing our hair out? I believe you mentioned to me earlier that you might have some ideas regarding the source of this intrusion."

Franklin stood up and paced the room as he spoke. "Of course, Colonel Tom. We experienced a data breach that led to sensitive information being retrieved by a hacker. In looking at his or her 'footprints' in our network, the hacker seemed to be merely wandering around, looking at mostly innocuous information. I got the sense they were just exploring, but it was evident someone had been there. The information they lifted from our system included the names, addresses, and contact information of some of our private supporters. They also copied the weekly personal agenda for Colonel Tom. While that is information generally available to anyone, the fact that our system was breached is troubling in and of itself.

"An interesting thing is that it didn't look like they were trying to hide their activity. It is like having a hobo from the street walk into your kitchen while you're eating a bowl of cereal. Then they start helping themselves to your food, using your plates, and eating utensils, ignoring your presence the whole time. Now, imagine the interloper then turns to you and says, 'Sorry to hear about your mother's illness. Hope she is feeling better.' Then he gets up and leaves."

Ki got a puzzled look on her face. "Excuse me? I'm not sure I follow you."

Franklin added, "I received a personal email commenting on my choice of underwear for the day. How could he know such personal things about me that could not have been gleaned from our database? I mean, it doesn't get much more invasive than that."

Colonel Tom was scratching his chin. "Gentlemen, I hesitate to bring this up, but I too received a personal email with similar 'how the hell did someone know this' content. I don't know what is going on, but I can tell you this, I am not feeling very comfortable in what is supposed to be my sanctum, and I want to get to the bottom of this as soon as we can."

Franklin spoke up again. "There is one final aspect to the mystery that is quite perplexing. I believe the same person who sent Colonel Tom and I our 'personal' email, did provide something else. There were two forwarded copies of documents from NAM and Ebonée. Those two political groups are both headquartered in Atlanta so it should be convenient for you to explore this issue further. The one from NAM was a coded message that has defied any of our attempts to decrypt it. The other missive from Ebonée was an agenda with dates, times, and locations of some violent protests they are planning. The email simply said, 'Enjoy'. It was signed, 'A friend'."

Ki sat there, non-plussed. "Fascinating. I do believe we can be of assistance. But, first I need to know whether you are planning on hiring us or if you think your in-house staff can handle this."

Colonel Tom and Franklin conferred quietly on the couch for a couple of minutes, and then Colonel Tom said, "Yes, we would like to retain your services. Do you have a specific contract for the Southern Commonwealth, or do you use a boiler plate contract?"

Ki reached into her side bag and pulled out a contract. "I anticipated we might come to this decision, so I took the liberty of drafting this specifically for the Southern Commonwealth based on research I have done on your organization. Once you review and sign it, we can get started. I will need copies of all you have from this mysterious hacker. If you could, please make those hard copies, and do not communicate with me via email or any other form of electronic media. Also, Colonel Tom, I will need a hand-written note telling me about your personal exposure. It will be kept in the strictest confidence."

She handed the contract to Colonel Tom; after quickly skimming the document, he signed it with Franklin witnessing it. Colonel Tom then went to his desk and scrawled a few sentences on a piece of paper that he folded in half twice and handed directly to Kianna. Franklin told her he would pull together hard copies of all the emails and a document covering what areas in their computer system were examined by the hacker. He said he would have a courier deliver them to her office later that day. She thanked them for their time and she and Bubba headed for the car and the long drive back to Atlanta.

CHAPTER EIGHT

"We do not create our destiny; we participate in its unfolding. Synchronicity works as a catalyst toward the working out of that destiny."

—David Richo

On the drive back to Atlanta, Ki and Bubba discussed what they had learned. Bubba was driving and glanced over at Ki.

"You were awful quiet during most of the meeting. Why weren't you doin' more . . . um . . . detecting? You know, asking questions to get more information out of them."

Ki sat back in her seat and smiled.

"Good question, Bubba. I'm glad you are tuning in to my methods. The key to being a good detective is keen observation and receiving information in whatever form it comes. I was taking in not only the information being spoken, but the information communicated in the subtext as well. Tone of voice, facial expressions, and body movements are as important as the words themselves, and often they are more important. The people employed at the National Office who do not hold leadership roles are equally valuable to my investigation because they are a part of the fabric of the place, and they have just as much influence on what is happening here. Being too focused on Colonel Tom and his information could cause us to lose sight of that.

In this case, it was all critical. Finally, there is a strong possibility Colonel Tom's office, and possibly the building itself is bugged. I did not want to risk sharing what I am thinking with anyone who may be listening. I could be reading this wrong, but I believe we will find I am not."

Bubba sighed. "I got a whole lot to learn, don't I?"

Ki smiled. "We all do, Bubba. We all do."

When they got back to the office, Ki showed Bubba how to put up an investigation board. There were three large corkboards along the south wall of the office. Ki pinned a large label at the top that read: OBSERVATIONS. Under that, she attached smaller signs with four categories—the Problems, the Proof, the Players, the Perpetrator. Under the problems she assigned *future extortion, information leaks,* and *privacy* as subcategories. Under the players she listed *Senator Marquis Lee, Colonel Tom, Franklin Smith, Peggy Sue,* and *Tamba.* Pointing at the *Players* category, Ki said, "I have a feeling this will increase over time. The first thing we must understand is what our goal is here. Who is the perpetrator and what is their motivation in sowing this low level of threat within the Southern Commonwealth? Identifying this person will let us resolve the problems. As long as the perp is unknown, we are helpless to a large degree."

Bubba scratched his head. "Low level of threat? I'm not sure I follow you there."

Walking over to the board, she pointed to *the Proof* and said, "Look at the data. What did he or she do? First of all, they really didn't lift any significant data. Granted, they hacked into the system, but all they did was examine what was there. The only two things they copied were a personal agenda and some names and addresses. The Southern Commonwealth publishes that on their website every week. In other words, this is no great secret. Everything the perpetrator took was public information. The personal details revealed about Colonel Tom's private life are presumably not all that salacious. In other words, a very low level of discord. The data mined is not a cause for concern; the reason for alarm is in the action itself. I believe the perpetrator of this crime is laying the foundation for what will be a rapidly accelerating attack on this institution. Right now, they are sending the message, loud and clear, that they can come in any time they want and take whatever they want, and they have access to very personal information. They are also positioning themselves as a 'friend' by sharing what they stole from NAM and Ebonée. However, I expect extortion threats will eventually surface. This is evident from what they did to Senator Lee. One possibility is they could lock up all the data in the Southern Commonwealth's system and hold it for ransom."

Bubba's face lit up. "Oh, I see! We shouldn't just look at what happened, but rather look at where it could go. Nip it in the bud, so to speak."

Ki nodded her head. "Very good, Bubba. Now, next we need to look at the people in more detail." She moved back to *the Players* board, and explained, "Let's start with the minor players in this unfolding drama. Most of the time, the people in the background are ignored because of where they are on the organizational chart. Those in entry-level roles do not receive much credit from executives, or even middle management. That is usually a fatal error. It can be surprising how much information is conveyed by these people because, more often than not, they are treated like so much wallpaper. At some point in the next week, we will want to interview both Peggy Sue and Tamba. Bubba, please make a note to schedule that interview and put it on my calendar. Now, Bubba, did you observe anything noteworthy about Peggy Sue?"

"Well, she sure was pretty. And she was very helpful. Oh, and she made us feel right at home. Did I miss anything?"

Ki smiled gently. "You are absolutely correct in your observation, Bubba. However, all those things are what she wanted us to see. Here are the things I picked up through subtle cues: First, she is concerned about her son, LeRoy. I would venture to guess it is because of his most recent grades in high school. Second, she is hiding something about her relationship with Colonel Tom. Last, she is not being paid nearly what she thinks she should be for the services she provides."

Bubba went all gape jawed again. Ki was a surprising woman in so many ways.

"I know you are good at what you do, but dang, how in the name of all that's holy did you ever get all of that from meetin' her just once?"

"As a private eye, information is your stock and trade, so you need to be highly attuned at all times. Information is around us and available constantly, but to do what we do, it's paramount that we are scooping it all up and logging it for future use. If I know more than most, it is simply because I pay attention. For instance, when we were walking toward the reception desk, I noticed Peggy Sue was glancing down at something on her desk and her face showed telltale signs of stress. When I went to the bathroom, I made a point of walking past her desk so I could glance at what was there. I saw a picture of a boy who looked to be around seventeen or eighteen years old. In the picture, he was wearing a name badge and it said LeRoy Montague and I noticed an opened envelope from a local high school. This is the time of year schools send out report cards to parents."

Bubba nodded, a bit awestruck. "I see. I see. Mighty impressive, Miss Ki."

Ki continued, "As for her issues with Colonel Tom, I'll tell you what I detected, but use your own observation skills the next time you see the two of them together. Watch her face—the way her eyes move, how her cheeks flush. Those and other overt signals tell me there is much more going on between the two of them than they let on. At this point, I don't know what it is. I have my suspicions, but it is only a matter of time before I know all the details. Concerning her dissatisfaction with her pay, that is merely a foregone conclusion. She is a woman, and she is working for the Southern Commonwealth. In the eyes of this patriarchal aristocracy, she is subordinate in any number of ways. She also represents an image they want to portray when painting a picture of this society. She is attractive and caters to the ideals of Southern charm. Therefore, while she is important, she is also not valued. Because to truly value her would require they elevate her to their status. That is not likely."

Bubba shook his head. "That is incredible! Now I can't wait to hear what I missed about Tamba and Colonel Tom. Not really sure I want you talking about my daddy though."

"I'll only say this about your daddy, Bubba. He loves you very much. I caught him glancing at you several times, and his eyes reflected the deep and abiding love and pride he feels for you. I will also say he is fully aware of the potential for escalation and what that means, and he is extremely concerned. Showing up when we did was fortuitous for the Southern Commonwealth. And thankfully, our 'in' through your father fast-tracked our access and allowed us to bypass the normal screenings we might have encountered.

"Now, regarding Tamba. I do have some concerns there. I am always suspicious of those whose behaviors contradict what would be expected in a circumstance. Especially, when one does it so convincingly as Tamba. Being so obsequious to Colonel Tom seems quite authentic on the surface, so there must be some part of him that sees himself as nothing more than a manservant, or else he is a good enough actor to fool even me. I am inclined to believe he is a very good actor. I will know more after we interview him, but for now, I suspect there is more going on with him than meets the eye.

"Now, let us talk about good ol' Colonel Tom. Your daddy gave us some insight into the character of Colonel Tom and his larger-than-life persona. He was dead on. Based on his description, I could have written a script for Colonel Tom, and what he said would have followed it verbatim. For instance, when he asked Tamba about going into business for himself, he was poking a hornet's nest. He wanted to send me the message that he was white, male, and in charge. He was also smart enough to know I was not fooled by his passive-aggressive quips. That much was evident when I asked him to give me a handwritten note detailing what the culprit revealed to him. It read, 'That is none of your god damned business!'. I can guarantee if they were not extremely worried about this situation, we would not be employed by the Southern Commonwealth despite your personal connection. I am definitely a burr under Colonel Tom's saddle."

Bubba shook his head. "I am lookin' forward to learnin' everything y'all are teachin' me. And right now, that looks like a whole lot."

"Bubba, do you remember how I told you I was looking for a key to help me open up some doors that are often closed to me? Well, it seems you have helped me open a pretty big door. Bubba, while you do have a lot to learn, do not underestimate yourself. You will get better over time. When I hired you I was looking for more than great observational skills. Technical training can be mastered over a short time, but integrity and kindness are ingrained over your lifetime. My advice is to make mistakes as fast as you can. It's the best way to learn. Based on the facts as I have laid them out, what do you think is actually going on here?"

Bubba scratched his head. "I'm not real sure. From what you said, someone appears to be cozying up to the Southern Commonwealth. But at the same time, they are kind of hinting they could do them a lot of harm if they don't play along. I don't know what their motive is, but I have the sinkin' feelin' they are also doin' something similar with NAM and Ebonée."

"Excellent. You are picking this up quickly. At first, I thought maybe those other two groups were at the root of this, but I think you are right. I want to look into those other two organizations immediately."

CHAPTER NINE

"And above all, watch with glittering eyes the whole world around you because the greatest secrets are always hidden in the most unlikely places. Those who don't believe in magic will never find it."

—Roald Dahl

The next time Ki and Bubba visited the Southern Commonwealth headquarters, they were greeted by the head of Human Services, Miss Sarah Jane Campbell. Ki was surprised to see a woman in an administrative position in the Southern Commonwealth. Suspecting there was more to this story, she made a mental note to investigate her further. Though she stood at a little over five feet tall in her stocking feet, Sarah Jane's blonde hair—stacked in an updo—combined with her stiletto heels brought her stature to just shy of Kianna's six-foot two frame. And, although she carried herself in a way that was almost as pleasing as Peggy Sue, she somehow did not feel quite as authentic. Her manner was slightly forced, but was only noticeable if you were paying attention. As they walked down the hallway, Ki noticed that there was another woman sitting at Peggy Sue's desk.

Sarah Jane said, "Miss Peggy Sue and Mr. Tamba are waiting for you in Conference Room A." Then, motioning toward the woman at the desk, she said, "We had to bring in a temp to fill in for Peggy Sue today because of your investigation. I trust you won't take up too much of her precious time?"

Ki responded, "I will take whatever time it takes to do my job, but no more than necessary."

With a pinched and strained smile, Sarah Jane said, "You are the boss, as far as this goes. Do what is necessary, but it would be appreciated if you could expedite the process. It is hard to even temporarily replace such a talented and valuable asset to our Commonwealth family." With the same tight-lipped smile, she added, "I am sure you understand."

"Oh, I do understand. Does that mean I can take as much time as I want with Mr. Tamba? You did not mention his importance to the Commonwealth family. I gather he ranks somewhat lower on the hierarchy here."

Sarah Jane flushed with indignation. "No, he does not. It is just that Mr. Tamba is here at the behest of Colonel Tom, since he is his personal manservant, and the good Colonel has arranged for Mr. Tamba to be at your disposal for the day. I take my directions directly from Colonel Tom."

Ki nodded. "That is most gracious of him."

Bubba beamed a big smile at Sarah Jane. "Thank you kindly, Miss Sarah Jane."

Sarah Jane beamed at Bubba in a pointed acknowledgement. "Why, Mr. Bubba, you are most welcome. You are a gracious man, aren't you?" She cut her eyes at Ki, then did a quick curtsy and left them as they entered Conference Room A.

Tamba was sitting quietly in a chair on one side of the table staring into space, his hands folded neatly on his lap. On the opposite side of the room in an upholstered armchair sat Peggy Sue, flipping through a periodical about the perfect garden in the South. Both of them looked up to acknowledge Ki and Bubba's presence with a polite nod. Bubba turned to Ki and said, "Shall we start with Miss Peggy Sue? I am sure Miss Sarah Jane would be most appreciative."

Ki wanted to start with Tamba, but, if she was being honest, it was only because it would irk Sarah Jane. When she thought about it though, she reminded herself that would be betraying the second commitment of compassion to all others. She recognized the ease with which Bubba navigated the niceties of this pretentious society. It was one of the reasons she sought someone like him for her assistant. But what made Bubba different was that it flowed from an expansive and kind heart, not from a patronizing or opportunistic spirit. This is why she knew they were a good match.

Swallowing her pride, Ki nodded. "That would be fine Bubba. Tamba, would you please find a seat outside the conference room? We will call you when we are finished with Peggy Sue."

Tamba silently rose and left the room as Peggy Sue joined Ki and Bubba at the table. Peggy Sue embodied Southern gentility. She greeted both Ki and Bubba with an open smile and made direct eye contact.

"It is so good to see you again. I must say, I was impressed by the two of you when you were here last. Your presence just fills up a room."

Ki had to remind herself that Peggy Sue, like everyone else, was the product of her upbringing and the culture in which she was immersed. Although, Peggy Sue's words rang of sycophancy in Ki's ears, she knew Peggy Sue was genuine. While effusive, her intention to be kind to others was clear, and ultimately there was nothing wrong with that. Ki struggled to control her cynicism and found herself softening to Peggy Sue's way of being.

Ki said, "Thank you, Peggy Sue. That is a first for me and quite a compliment. I appreciate your sitting down with us today." Ki then placed a small tape recorder on the table and turned it on. "Unless you have an objection, I will be recording our sessions for future reference. It will save Bubba from having to take rather copious notes." She looked at him with a slight smile and continued. "I have some follow-up questions from our previous visit, and there are some areas where I believe your perspective will be invaluable."

Peggy Sue nodded agreeably, so Ki went on. "One of our objectives is to provide a more secure work environment. As the first person most people see when they enter the building, you are the 'face' of the Southern Commonwealth. And as the receptionist, I am sure you are the conduit for all that flows through these halls. Because of your unique position and perspective, I think you can give me some good insight on the inner-workings of this organization. What is your perception of the Southern Commonwealth's operations?" Peggy Sue looked a little concerned. Ki went on to say, "By this, I mean, how would you do things differently if you were in charge?"

Peggy Sue fidgeted in her chair. "Oh, I'm not qualified to talk about such things. I wouldn't even know where to begin. It's not my place to change the Southern Commonwealth."

Ki touched her shoulder. "I understand your reluctance. But, you see how the gears in this machine operate and where things can get gummed up. I am just looking for guidance in helping to ensure the cyber protection of the Southern Commonwealth. Bubba and I are charged with helping to improve the image and safeguards of this institution of governance. An essential part of that is listening to people such as yourself and gleaning the insights gained from working in the trenches day in and day out. I know it may feel as though I am asking you to dish dirt on your employers, but I cannot fix vulnerabilities if I do not know where they are. Does that make sense?"

Peggy Sue lit up. "It certainly does! I told a little white lie when I said I wouldn't know where to begin. I am bursting with ideas, but no one ever asked me for my suggestions before. First of all, there should be some sort of 'pre-reception' process so that by the time they get to me, I know who they want to see and what the purpose of their visit is. That would allow me to make their experience here all the fuller, richer, and more meaningful. Second, when children under five are brought in, they need to have some type of restraint system to allow their guardians to exercise greater control of them. We have had some very precious artifacts broken because parents had no control over their younguns. The third thing I would love to see put in place is some type of background check on some of the seedy characters that show up on our doorstep. The security guards catch a good bit of that, but not all. There are even some visitors that don't look suspicious on the outside, but after spending time with them, their lack of character becomes quite readily apparent."

Ki smiled. "I'll be sure to share those wonderful suggestions with Sarah Jane. Thank you. Your third recommendation is a perfect segue to my second question. You certainly have a great instinct for assessing who people really are on the inside, so we were wondering if you have noticed any 'seedy' individuals in the last month."

Peggy Sue turned her eyes upward and to the left with some obvious concentration. "I do keep a daily journal, sort of a 'Dear Diary' thing. I'll have to double-check my entries, but I do recall two gentlemen that gave me some cause for concern. They had come to see Colonel Tom, and as I recall, they were here for well over an hour. I can look for any details I noted on them if you would like."

Ki said, "Yes. Thank you, Peggy Sue. I will need their names and any information you have on them. Bubba, make a note for us to speak to

Colonel Tom about these gentlemen, and also check with your father about any security camera footage during that time frame."

Bubba turned to Ki. "I'm way ahead of you Miss Ki. I'll speak with my daddy before we leave today."

Ki looked directly at Peggy Sue and said two words. "Colonel Tom."

Then she waited in silence. Peggy Sue's face fell sullen. Ki's instinct was to let Peggy Sue's mind fill in the blanks. She knew that a protracted silence is uncomfortable to most people, so you could often get more from someone compelled to fill the void. They inevitably reveal even more than you might ask for. It appeared it was working now on Peggy Sue.

Peggy Sue sat silently for nearly a full minute. You could see the internal struggle showing on her face, but Ki let her stew in it until finally she said. "Can you assure me that this conversation will not be shared with Colonel Tom?"

Ki nodded. "Most assuredly."

Peggy Sue released a sigh. "This is really uncomfortable to speak about, but here goes. Colonel Tom has been propositioning me. Not overtly, mind you, but he has acted inappropriately a couple of times. He often uses inuendo to convey his desires, but it has been quite clear and uncomfortable to me. There was one time when I dropped by his house at his request regarding some minor task, and I found him in a state of complete undress. Though he would, and did, say he was caught unawares, he knew when I would be coming by, so I can't believe it was a coincidence. It appeared to be planned. To say I was shocked would be an understatement. I left without a word. I would never want to do anything that would cast a shadow on the man, but I have been more nervous recently when I have been alone with him. And considering his position and my position, I don't care to broach the subject with him. I'm just too embarrassed."

Ki said, "By any chance did this happen a couple weeks ago in the late afternoon. I believe it was on a Thursday?"

Peggy Sue's face showed shock. "Yes, it was! How on earth did you know that?"

"That's not important, but it does answer some questions for me. Thank you for taking time out of your busy schedule to meet with us. Bubba, would you accompany Miss Peggy Sue back to her desk and retrieve the information she has regarding the two visiting gentlemen? And on your way out, please send in Tamba."

When Tamba entered the room, she motioned for him to have a seat across from her. "Good afternoon Tamba."

The mellifluous tones of Tamba G. Prather's voice were pleasing to the ear. He would have been a very successful narrator for movies and radio. "Good afternoon, Miss Smythe."

Tamba was born in Gullah country on the South Carolina coast and, although he rarely shared it with strangers, he was proud of his heritage. His relatives were one of the reasons that the South became as prosperous as it did during the middle of the 19th Century. The Gullah peoples were rice farmers from Sierra Leone on the west coast of Africa, and when they became slaves in South Carolina, they brought their skills and talents for rice farming with them. They were prized by plantation owners as high-quality slaves. As a result, they were given more liberties than other agricultural slaves, and that resulted in the communities where they lived becoming more unified and bonded, creating a persistent culture and dialect that carried forward through the decades they had been in existence.

Ki said, "Tamba, if I am not mistaken, you are Gullah, are you not?"

Tamba smiled. "Yes, Miss Smythe. How did you know?"

Ki shrugged her shoulders. "Elementary. First of all, your accent is distinctive. Second, your first name is a traditional Gullah name."

"Very good, Miss Smythe. What else do you deduce?"

Ki seized the opening. "Since you ask, I suspect that you are not who you appear to be. You put on a good show as the faithful manservant to Colonel Tom, but for the life of me, I have a hard time buying that."

"And why is that, Miss Smythe? Do you find it difficult to believe that a black man would choose to be in service to a white man in this day and age? With all due respect, I believe you are projecting your feelings on to me. You see Colonel Tom as arrogant and ostentatious. You see me as an 'Uncle Tom' and perceive that as abhorrent and an unimaginable indignity. Suffice it to say, I have chosen my role here, and my reasons, frankly, are not any of your concern."

Ki was shocked. His statement was clear and to the point, and what he said was true. She could not reconcile his actions with her worldview. Attempting to resolve this apparent conundrum, she said, "Marain Jagu." Watching his facial expression and body language, she could detect no visible change. She was beginning to accept that she could be wrong about him although her instinct told her otherwise.

Tamba rubbed his chin. "Are you referring to the leader of the political organization Ebonée?

Ki said, "Yes. Do you know him?"

Tamba shook his head. "No. I have seen him on television promoting his agenda of black power, but that is it. Why do you bring up his name?

"Honestly, it was to see your reaction."

"Did I disappoint you?"

"As a matter of fact, you did disappoint me. It seems I will get nothing from you, so I will release you back to your duties with Colonel Tom . . . unless there is anything you might feel compelled to tell me."

"Not at this time. I have nothing to add. Good luck with your investigation."

Bubba entered the room just as Tamba was leaving. He had some notes in his hand and said, "Did I miss the interview?"

Ki smiled and said, "Yes, but that is quite alright." After Tamba left the room, she said, "Nothing was revealed and that, in and of itself, was very revealing. What did you discover from Peggy Sue about her journal?

"Well, she was correct. There were two gentlemen here to see Colonel Tom a few weeks ago and she noted that one of them never said a word but the other was quite talkative. She wrote down their names. The quiet one was Covek Veechkol, and the more gregarious visitor was Marron Sincère. What made them stand out to Peggy Sue was how glib Marron Sincère had been. There was something about him that was well-polished, but it came off as a carefully cultivated veneer, as she put it. The irony of Peggy Sue's observation and the visitor's last name was not lost on Ki. There had been no stated purpose for their visit, so before she and Bubba left, Ki needed to ask Colonel Tom why the two of them had called on him. As if on cue, there came a knock on the door and Colonel Tom stuck his head in.

"Am I interrupting anything? It appears that you have wrapped up the interviews. I must say that was quicker than I thought it would be. Thank you for expediting the process."

Ki sat back in her chair. "Your timing is impeccable. We were just getting ready to come see you. We had a question about a couple of visitors you met with a few weeks ago. Marron Sincère and a Covek Veechkol. Do you recall that meeting?"

Colonel Tom scratched his chin and appeared deep in thought, and then his face lit up. "Yes! I do remember them. Mr. Veechkol wasn't too fluent in English, but the Frenchman was quite conversant. They were here to make a donation to the Southern Commonwealth Foundation. A most generous donation, I might add."

"Was there anything else they wanted? Did they ask you many questions about the Southern Commonwealth?"

"We spent most of the time making small talk and I gave them a tour of our offices. That was about it."

Bubba spoke up. "Before we leave, I'd like to say howdy to my daddy. Would that be okay?"

Colonel Tom gave Bubba a hearty slap on the back and said. "Nothing would please me more." Turning to Ki, he said, "I look forward to getting reports on your progress."

With that, he left the conference room and Ki and Bubba went to the Data Services building to find Franklin Smith.

After Franklin and Bubba hugged and greeted each other, Ki asked Franklin about the security tapes for the day the visitors had come to donate money. Franklin went to his monitor and keyed in the date in question. There the two of them were. Ki did not recognize the one called Covek Veechkol, but the Frenchman she recognized right away. It was the same man who was watching her across the lawn at the party where she had met Penelope Lee. At the very end of their visit, he looked directly into the camera's lens and winked, just as he had done at the party.

CHAPTER TEN

"We are like water, aren't we? We can be fluid, flexible when we have to be. But strong and destructive, too." And something else, I think to myself. Like water, we mostly follow the path of least resistance."

—Wally Lamb

When Ki and Bubba returned to the office, they looked at the investigation board they had created. The last bit of information relayed by Peggy Sue took the investigation into deeper levels. It had led to the review of the security footage, which added two new people of interest to their analysis: Marron Sincère and Covek Veechkol. Ki also now had a reason to believe she knew the nature of the personal incident Colonel Tom was unwilling to share, but clearly troubled him. His conduct with Peggy Sue would have been embarrassing, but as Colonel Tom asserted, it was not particularly salacious. They also realized there was a lot more going on than what appeared on the surface. The obvious concern was data hacking and possible extortion, but the incorporation of other political entities seemed to imply more than mere blackmail and information mining. It appeared to be too layered for a simple answer.

"Bubba, I believe it is time to expand our investigation."

"You mean to other people at the Commonwealth?"

"No. Beyond their walls. There are two other political parties, and they seem to be targets of our unknown hackers as well. Either that or one of them is very cleverly deflecting attention from themselves by making themselves look like victims too."

"Miss Ki, I am relatively new to Atlanta and the whole political scene. Who are these NAM and Ebonée groups?"

"Certainly, Bubba. NAM is an acronym for New Africa Movement. They are looking to emulate the direction that the African Continent has been experiencing over the last seventy years. Africa's economy is exploding and is very likely to become the new economic center of the world. Part of the key to their expansion is having embraced an egalitarian point of view."

"Sorry, Miss Ki, but what is egalitarian?"

"It basically means equal. In Africa, they have put in an enormous effort to equalize all aspects of their government. That runs counter to most models of power structures. It is the ultimate integration experiment. Not only have they practically eliminated corruption, but their wealth distribution and other social programs have made abject poverty a thing of the past. Their economic plan is a flexible blend of capitalism and socialism."

Bubba scratched his chin. "Ya know, we learned about that back in high school civics class, except the teacher didn't quite explain it the same way."

"The Southern Commonwealth is not all that keen on a lot of their ideas. It threatens their power structure. Speaking of power, the other group is Ebonée. It is a group that encourages racial segregation as well as acts of insurrection. They want to change the balance of power so whites are subjugated to blacks. Sort of a role reversal from the days of slavery. Both parties, however, are nothing more than an annoyance to the ruling power of the Southern Commonwealth."

At that moment, the buzzer on the street door went off, informing them someone had entered the front office. Ki glanced at the video monitor and saw a very distinguished looking Caucasian gentleman accompanied by a large, plainly dressed black woman. They were a study in contrasts. She had a massive head of unruly dreadlocks and wore a light grey sweatshirt with matching sweatpants. An expansive ecru canvas purse was slung over one shoulder. He had shockingly white long hair pulled neatly back into a ponytail, and he sported a neatly trimmed white beard and mustache. He wore a black kimono style shirt and black loose-fitting pants.

Both she and Bubba walked out front to greet them and introduce themselves. Ki spoke first. "Hello. Welcome to the Smythe Detective Agency. I am Kianna Smythe and this is my personal assistant Bubba Smith. Bubba, this is Obatala and Daniel Horatio Tinkiya. Daniel, do you prefer I call you 'The Ghost'?" Both of the visitors revealed a bit of shock and disappointment they did not fully have the element of surprise in their arrival. "Am I right in assuming you are here because of the security issues in your computer network at the New Africa Movement?"

The couple stood there looking at Ki with their mouths open.

Daniel spoke first. "How on earth do you know who we are and what we want?"

"It is my job to know."

"Have we met before?" Obatala asked with deep suspicion.

"No, we have not. But I am familiar with both of you. As for your cybersecurity problems, my firm was recently hired by The Southern Commonwealth because they also were breached. During our investigation we came upon some information that suggested it was likely the same thing was happening at NAM and Ebonée. In fact, I was just about to call your office to discuss this very issue."

Obatala perked up and came in close. "Why do you think we share their problems?"

Ki sat down in the lounge area and motioned for everyone to join her. "Several reasons, but primarily because whoever is perpetrating this crime gave them two gifts. Bubba, would you be so kind as to fetch the two documents 'presented' to The Southern Commonwealth?"

While Bubba was retrieving the documents, Ki put a kettle on for tea. She spoke reverently as she went through the ritual of gathering the necessary accoutrements. "I think tea is a great equalizer. We share something communally, and that helps to put everyone on an equal footing."

Bubba returned with the documents. "Here you go, ma'am."

"Thank you, Bubba."

She then passed them the first document showing the agenda for the Ebonée riots and protests. "I am guessing you are not unfamiliar with this?"

Daniel spoke up. "Oh my! We received an email from this mystery hacker with two attachments and that was one of them. There was also a cryptic comment. The other document had information about Colonel Tom's personal schedule and agenda."

Ki smiled. "As I thought. Let me guess. The cryptic comment was 'Enjoy!'?"

Obatala said, "Exactly right!"

"Let me share the second document I received from the Southern Commonwealth. This is one you may not know about." With this she handed them the coded message.

As soon as they saw it, they sat back in shock.

Daniel was shaking his head. "Are you telling me someone hacked into our system and gave them this? I had no idea it was even lifted from our computers. This is very sensitive information. I am afraid to ask, were they able to decode it?"

"The head of decryption services said they were unable to crack the code, and I am inclined to believe he was not deceptive in his answer. I will want to know more about this at a later time. The only reason I shared this with you is because I believe in order for me to solve this crime, I need to have the cooperation of all three organizations. You all seem to be trapped in some sort of political triangle with this hacker working every angle. I must honor the privacy of my clients, so I cannot share with you anything more about what I have uncovered so far. But, should you be willing to hire me—and I will be approaching the head of Ebonée as well—I will be able to protect each of you and find out who is causing this mischief. In the interest of full disclosure, I have not yet attempted to decode your missive, but I intend to. It certainly is complex, so I expect it will take me several hours to crack it."

Obatala sized up Ki. "You have no idea how complex it is. Very talented cryptographers have been unsuccessful in deciphering it. I do not know that you will fare any better."

"We shall see. But let's get down to the matter at hand. I am sorry to be abrupt, but time is of the essence. I believe you need my help, and I would like to have access to you as an advocate and not as an adversary. Are you willing to hire me to work for your interests as well?"

Daniel and Obatala glanced at each other and asked for a moment to talk. They stepped back out into the lobby, and after several minutes Daniel returned to Ki and Bubba.

"When we came in here, we were scoping out your place. You're only a couple of blocks from our offices, so your proximity gave you one up on our other options. But after speaking with you and discovering you are already on the case, Obatala and I concur it is a foregone conclusion we need to hire you."

"Great. Bubba seems to have read the handwriting on the wall as well because he has a contract ready for you. Please read it over and sign it before you leave. Bubba will set up a time for us to come to your offices for a formal interview and analysis. Right now, I need to pull our third party into this investigation. I am going to pay a visit to Marain Jagu over at Ebonée. Bubba, please stay here and hold down the fort. I need to see him on my own."

****

The offices for Ebonée were in one of the segregated black communities in the Atlanta Area SEZ. The building was a simple five story modern glass and steel box design. There were large African tribal print banners on the corners of the structure hanging from the roof ledge, covering the side of the building from top to bottom. Across the top floor was a sign in eight-foot-high simple block letters spelling out EBONÉE. An expansive and exquisite karesansui style raked gravel garden graced the courtyard entrance to the reception foyer. Clean. Elegant. There was a certain Wabi-Sabi feel to the space that Ki appreciated, and she lingered there taking in the ambiance.

The Ebonée organization was a proponent of segregation. They did not mind being separated from the whites, but they did resent the uneven balance of power. They wanted that power to shift to the black population. African-American freedoms were severely curtailed in the Southern Commonwealth, so Ebonée was an advocate for greater autonomy. As an organization they were not afraid to use violent protests in order to express their deep resentment for white power. A coup d'état was not off the table as far as they were concerned. Their leader, Marain Jagu was not opposed to systemic racism as long as the people of color held the greater power in the equation. A favorite banner cry of Marain's was "turnabout is fair play!"

Kianna walked up to the reception desk and addressed the receptionist. "Excuse me. Is Marain Jagu in residence today?"

The woman behind the desk was statuesque with closely cropped hair and very dark skin. She was elegant in her dress and in her manner. She smiled. "Yes, he is. Do you have an appointment?"

"No, I do not have an appointment. However, I do have an urgent matter I need to discuss with him. It would be in his best interest if he saw me as soon as he is free."

"Why would it be in his best interest?"

Ki took a beat of three seconds to calm herself. "I am sorry, but I am not at liberty to discuss that with you. This is not a threat. I simply have some information that is of a sensitive nature and will be of great import to Mr. Jagu."

"The best I can do is to connect you with his personal secretary. She can set up an appointment for you to see Mr. Jagu."

Ki remained at the reception desk as the receptionist made a call, blatantly eavesdropping on her conversation with the personal secretary. "Hello, Betty? This is Lola, down at reception. I have someone here who needs to set up an appointment to meet with Mr. Jagu."

"She is a woman."

"I would say definitely mixed-race. Not particularly dark-skinned, but passable."

"No. She did not say what it was concerning. She said she wasn't at liberty to discuss it, but she did say it was urgent."

"Like I said, she won't tell me."

There was a pause.

"Alright. I'll tell her."

She then hung up and turned to Ki.

"Mr. Jagu is not available right now. His secretary is Betty Lown. Here is her card with her phone number. You can call her and try to set up an appointment for later in the week or maybe next week."

She extended the card. Ki took it and gave it a glance, noting the office was on the top floor. She put it in her pocket and headed toward the elevators. The receptionist caught up with her before she reached them and put her hand on Ki's shoulder. Ki almost overreacted, but she restrained herself.

Turning, she faced the receptionist and said calmly but forcefully, "Lola. I decided I was going to expedite the process and talk directly to Betty at her desk."

Lola looked frustrated. "I am sorry, but you need a visitor's pass to access the upper floors."

Ki smiled a big smile. "Would you be a dear and get me one of those passes so I can adhere to your protocol?"

Lola was growing exasperated. "You can't get a visitor's pass unless you have an appointment, and you have said you don't have an appointment."

"Lola, I am sorry to be such a pain in the ass, but it is urgent I speak with Marain Jagu today. Trying to get through your well-intentioned filter is only delaying the inevitable. Do me a favor and let Betty know I am on my way up to speak with her."

Lola went running back to her desk as Ki pushed the up button on the elevator. The doors were opening just as two large, well-muscled black security guards appeared and were moving toward her. She dodged in to the elevator and the doors slid shut seconds before they reached her. She pushed five on the keypad and the elevator ascended leaving the security guards flustered in the foyer.

When the elevator opened at the fifth floor, she had to use some logic to know where to go. Although Betty's card had the suite number 501 on it, she was not familiar with the floorplan. She suspected that Marain Jagu's office would be toward the front of the building overlooking the raked gravel garden. Recalling the layout of the first floor, combined with the entrance, that would mean it would be behind the bank of elevators. Then she remembered there was a button in the elevator labeled 5A with a key slot beside it. That meant the back panel of the elevator was actually a door and it would open up on Jagu's reception area. Quickly going back into the elevator before it closed, she pushed the hold button and pulled out her lock-picking tool from her pocket. Within a couple of seconds, the back panel of the elevator did indeed open to a large, well-appointed office waiting area with beautiful African art bedecking the walls and exquisite sculptures around the room in cases and on pedestals. Across from that was Betty's desk.

Smiling, she approached Betty. Betty, however, did not look happy. In fact, Betty appeared to be very frightened. She was reaching under her desk and immediately, an alarm started to sound. Ki thought, *Oh crap!* and realized she had truly pushed the envelope to the breaking point. She heard the side door to the office open, and the sound of heavy footsteps running toward her put her on high alert. Turning around, she recognized the security guards from downstairs. From a door within the office there appeared two equally massive guards with Tasers and cattle prods. They looked like they meant business. The day-to-day life of a bodyguard can be one of ennui and monotony. In most cases, they are there on the off chance something happens, but they rarely see action, so the rush of adrenaline they felt now was a welcome respite from their mundane lifestyle. Big smiles on their faces told her they were looking forward to finally getting to do what they signed up for. It was equally obvious that they did not realize what they were up against.

Since there were only four attackers, Ki moved to the center of the room in order to allow space to maneuver. There were two behind her and two in front. As the two in front reached for her, she took one each of their outstretched hands and went from standing tall to crouching small. She then used their momentum to flip them on their backs. Nimbly and delicately she then stood with one foot on each of their chests, twisting around to face the other two guards. They had pulled cattle prods out and were coming in fast. She moved slightly toward them, which they did not expect. Once they reached her position, she guided the force of their propulsion down toward the two prone guards who were starting to stand. Both cattle prods found targets in the bodies of the two rising guards, and as the tools did their jobs, she was down to two guards. She knew what was going to happen next. Boys do love their toys, and now that the cattle prods were useless, she knew the Tasers were going to come out. She manipulated the remaining guards' positions in such a way that they thought they were cornering her. One on either side of her, they went into their stances, and she calmly stood her ground. It was very likely their training taught them to work as a team, so all she had to do was watch their eyes for the sign she was looking for. When she saw it, she dropped to the ground as the Taser probes left their ports and flew toward their new targets: each other. Both guards became ineffective, overly-muscled, quivering masses. Slumped over the other two she'd already felled, the four of them made a nice display all piled up in the middle of the room.

Ki walked up to Betty.

"Hi, Betty. I am Kianna Smythe, a private eye here in Atlanta. I believe Lola from downstairs called to announce me. I would like to make an appointment to see Marain Jagu at his earliest possible convenience."

Betty was dumbfounded. She sat there staring, and then pointed speechlessly over Ki's shoulder. Ki turned around and saw Marain Jagu leaning against the door frame of his office, his arms folded on his chest and a big smile on his face, taking in the bizarre tableau.

He smiled approvingly. "Hello, my Mullata sister. What is it you have to tell me that is of such urgency?"

Ki smiled back. "I am here to let you know you need to hire me. And you need to hire me soon."

Marain fit perfectly with the design of the office. It was almost as though he and his clothes were an extension of the office décor. His clothes were the blackest black she could ever remember seeing, and they were obviously custom tailored for him. His commanding presence was palpable and undeniable. Usually, Kianna was the tallest person in the room. She now was the second tallest. He had probably four inches on her. His dark skin and shaved head suited his roughly handsome features. He oozed a self-confidence and a calm that was authentic and made people around him feel comfortable more than intimidated. She felt an immediate physical attraction, but she was cautious to not display any of that attraction in front of him. She knew it could severely bias and compromise her investigation.

The look on his face she read as bemused judgment and his response to Ki was polite but firm. "We will see about that." He smiled and then bowed slightly motioning for her to join him in his office.

When she entered the office, she couldn't help herself from gasping out loud. What she saw took her breath away. Tranquility enveloped her like a soft and comforting blanket. She had expected there to be a window in his office overlooking the raked gravel garden. While she was correct, what he had done with the space was totally unexpected. Using mirrors, lenses, and projection, the garden appeared to be a part of his office. Even though he was five stories above the actual garden space she felt as though she could walk directly onto the gravel. When Marain sat at his desk, he appeared to be sitting in the serene garden, and it imbued him with a subtle elegance the Japanese refer to as Wabi Sabi. Needless to say, the effect was impressive for any visitor sitting across from him. This was a powerful man.

CHAPTER ELEVEN

"Protest is when I say I don't like this. Resistance is when I put an end to what I don't like. Protest is when I say I refuse to go along with this anymore. Resistance is when I make sure everybody else stops going along too."

—Ulrike Meinhof

"I can see that I need to have my bodyguards learn Aikido. You are very skilled, and I am suitably impressed." His voice was so mellifluous she felt she could listen to him all day long.

Ki smiled. "Probably not necessary. They are not likely to come across someone in the South with my level of training. I am impressed you recognized the discipline. It is not the most commonly studied of the martial arts."

Marain looked pleased. "I guess that means you weren't proposing I hire you as a consultant because of your Aikido training. Why don't you tell me who you are and, more important, why I 'need' to hire you and 'soon'?"

Ki nodded. "Quick question. Have you experienced any unusual cyber activity recently?"

Marain's face revealed she had hit a nerve, and a good minute passed before he said, "Now that you mention it, we have."

Ki pressed him, seeing he was not interested in volunteering information, "Would you please confirm my suspicions? Would that have been in the form of a suspicious email from an unknown source?"

Marian registered his shock and hesitantly shared, "Actually, yes. We received an anonymous email containing two attachments. One was a coded message from NAM. We have not been able to break the code as of yet, but we are working on it. The second attachment was the personal schedule and agenda of Colonel Tom Whitehead of the Southern Commonwealth. The most unusual thing I got personally was a message asking me if I was ambidextrous since I brushed my teeth with my left hand but wrote with my right hand."

Ki smiled. "Did the email with the attachments have a message saying 'Enjoy!'?"

"Yes, it did." He smiled, pleased to have encountered a woman who appeared to be his intellectual equal.

"It's the reason I am here. Both NAM and the Southern Commonwealth got attachments in a similar email. NAM got the Whitehead Schedule and a list of planned protests and dates from Ebonée. The Southern Commonwealth received the coded message from NAM and the protest list from Ebonée. Someone is clearly trying to create conflict. There is every indication that the level of these cyber incursions is only going to increase and could possibly turn into extortion or blackmail. Whoever is doing this has access, not only to your computers, but to extremely private aspects of your personal life as well."

Jagu frowned. "How is it you know of these things?"

"Because I am being employed by both of those organizations to uncover the source of these emails, to discover their motives and endgame, and to shut down the incursions before they get any worse. I believe the only way I can truly be effective is to have the cooperation of all three of you. If I am in the dark on what any of you are experiencing, I'm missing vital information that affects the others."

Jagu ran his hand over his head while he spoke. "Two things. One, I have discovered only recently one of the biggest weaknesses of our organization is our cybersecurity. So, it is not a big surprise to find someone has been perusing our databases. This is something I plan on remedying very soon. Two, if I were to hire you, would you be sharing information about Ebonée with NAM and the Southern Commonwealth?"

"I would not divulge your internal communications with anyone other than my personal assistant and then only what is necessary for him to assist me effectively. In order to track down this perpetrator, I need to see patterns and look for digital footprints I can track back to their source. Does that answer your question?"

"Miss Kianna, I want to thank you for being so tenacious in making me aware of this internal problem regarding our computers and a common external threat. I am inclined to hire you, but I need to discuss this issue with my board of directors. Would you be available to meet with them in the near future?"

"Thank you for your consideration and taking some time out of your busy day for us to talk. By the way, one of the issues our potential extortionist could use against you is your spy, Tamba, who works at the Southern Commonwealth. Here is my business card. Have Betty call and set up an appointment for me to meet with your board."

Jagu's face went from placid to shocked. "How did you find out about Tamba?"

"To be honest, I did not know until now. I strongly suspected it, but you just confirmed it. Our hacker will have no problem discovering that and many other secrets. I recommend you act expeditiously and convene an emergency board meeting."

When they stepped out of Marain Jagu's office, the security guards were coming to. Ki waved at them and bowed slightly to them. They did not look happy.

****

Marain Jagu took her advice and was able to schedule an emergency board meeting for the next day. Ki was invited to address the board and showed up a half-hour ahead of schedule because the last time she came, it did not exactly go smoothly.

Ki walked up to the reception desk and noticed the look of recognition on Lola's face. Lola immediately came around from behind the counter and reached out and shook Ki's hand. "I am so sorry about yesterday. I am so, so sorry! I was only trying to do my job. Can you forgive me?"

Ki demurred. "Lola, it is I who should be apologizing to you. My urgency got the better of me and I did not conduct myself professionally. I should have called in advance. Why don't we call it a draw?"

Lola smiled. "That works for me. Mr. Jagu told me if you were to come early to give you a visitor's pass and to personally see you up to his office."

As they walked to the elevators, Lola said, "One of the security guards told me you are very skilled at martial arts. Is that true?"

Ki nodded. "You could say that."

"He said he is still in pain."

"I am sorry to hear that. In Aikido the goal is to subdue one's opponent, not wound them. Unfortunately, the impact of a counter move varies based on the speed and energy of the attacker. And the guards definitely were keen to do their job. It is a lot like most of life. You only get out of something what you put into it."

Lola chuckled. "Here is the key to access Mr. Jagu's office through the rear of the elevator. I understand you are already aware of it. Good luck with your meeting."

"Thank you, Lola. Be well."

When she exited the elevator, Betty was waiting for her. "Good afternoon, Miss Smythe. Mr. Jagu is waiting for you."

Marain Jagu was sitting in a bound lotus position appearing to be in the middle of his Zen garden. The optical illusion was quite captivating. His eyes opened to take her in, and a smile crept across his face.

"A pleasure to see you again, Miss Kianna Smythe. Thank you for being available on such short notice. Please have a seat."

Ki smiled and nodded to him. "Mr. Jagu. When you introduce me to the board, my formal name is fine, but it would make me feel more comfortable if you called me Ki."

"Isn't Ki the Japanese word for tree? I like that." He paused and then continued. "It is decided. I will comply with your wishes provided you do me the honor of calling me Marain. It is easier and is also far less formal . . . and I would like to get to know you on a more informal basis."

"Marain. It has a nice ring to it. I too would like to get to know you on a more informal basis. We seem to share a set of common interests. In particular, the Japanese culture. What is it about their lifestyle that resonates with you?"

"There are a number of aspects I find appealing. I like the clean and simple philosophy of Zen. We tend to become so complicated in our lives. Obfuscation is everywhere in society. Too much dogma. I also admire the homogeneous society in Japan. If the culture decided that smoking was bad, the whole society would stop smoking. Obviously, that is not true across the board, but there is a definite unity of culture I enjoy. It mirrors my attitude toward segregation."

"Homogeneous. That is an interesting way to describe it. You don't have a problem with the racial bias that can be found in Japan? Someone who is a mixed race with an American parent and Japanese parent can suffer extreme prejudice. Those children are labeled 'hafu' and suffer a significant amount of bullying. As adults there are many doors that are closed to them in Japanese society. That is utterly unfair to them."

"On the contrary. The purity of race is, to me, a point of pride. Look at Hawaii and the indigenous people there that are still fighting to preserve their culture and social identity. They ban intermarriage where mixed births will dilute their precious heritage that is so endangered by genetic intermingling."

Ki frowned slightly. "And yet you embrace this culture where you are seen as a Gaijin or 'foreign devil' or 'outsider'? I am a perfect example of the failures of this purity test here in the Southern Commonwealth. My mother is black and was raped by a white man. I am the product of that union, and I am considered by many here in this segregated society as a 'half-breed' or a 'mongrel' who does not fit into this great society you envision. Even your organization does not recognize my humanity. I am treated as an object, not a person. I believe there is only one race. The human race."

"Miss Smythe . . . sorry . . . Ki, I understand your dismay, but individual cultures like Japan have created very meaningful traditions that are unique and held in high esteem in the world community. Much of that is a result of that homogeneous culture. Japanese Gardens are a singular response to the Chinese Garden that influenced its creation. They absorb something from outside their culture, adapt it, and make it their own."

"Marain, I too appreciate the Zen philosophy and loss of dogma, but the reality is quite complicated. I do not think we can cherry-pick our philosophies. In the Zen approach to the world, there is no recognition of differences. All are one."

Marain slightly frowned. "You make good points, but there needs to be a way to get to common ground. Why is it so difficult to find a path forward in our society? It is like herding cats. I can say that in my political pursuits, I aim to have Ebonée be representative of disenfranchised individuals and cultures throughout society. When I refer to segregation, I envision being an advocate for the BIPOC population. Of course, I am referring to those who *identify* as black and indigenous, as well as other people of color."

Ki's brow furrowed. "Are you not simply exchanging one form of systemic racism for another? It strikes me as simply vindictive to be lashing out with a similar paradigm that only switches poles without resolving the core problem. I have found that the energy you put into the world is the energy that comes back at you. Would it not be more expedient to literally embrace your fellow humans?"

Marain rubbed his chin. "As you say, what you put out into the world is what comes back to you, and I am simply representing the response to the negative energy that keeps coming at me from the Southern Commonwealth. How can they learn what pain they are inflicting unless they get a taste of their own medicine?"

"I admit that it is complicated. Your response is normal and understandable, but I sense that it stems from a position of resentment and indignation. That is definitely not the love and the reconciliation that yields the common ground you are seeking. My fear is that your efforts, if successful, will only exacerbate the strife and trauma that lies just below the surface of this age-old conflict. I think that 'eye for an eye' could also be 'I for an I'. Egos and identities are the real culprits here."

"Ki, I certainly did not expect our conversation to take this turn, but, you are a worthy debate partner. Besides being beautiful, you have an amazing mind. I would like very much to discuss this further at another time, but right now the board is ready to convene."

Marain had a private entrance to the conference room, and they walked in directly from his office. There were thirteen chairs around the table. Marain's seat was at the head of the table, and eight of the remaining chairs were filled by warm bodies. Four chairs were empty, and Ki stood beside Marain. On the wall, however, was a monitor with four faces projected in quadrants. Ki could not help but notice she was the only woman in the assemblage. She also had the lightest skin of anyone in attendance as well. She couldn't help feeling self-conscious. Sexism and racism seemed to show up throughout all segments of their society.

Marain rapped a gavel three times on the table. "Thank you all for making yourselves available to attend this emergency board meeting. Without any further ado, I would like to introduce Miss Kianna Smythe. She is a private investigator who is offering her services to us. She has been working with two of our political rivals on cyber intrusions, and in the course of her research, she discovered it was highly likely the Ebonée database has been targeted as well. After she shared her findings with me, we became keenly aware that this definitely is the case. Miss Smythe, would you care to elaborate?"

Kianna smiled broadly. "Thank you, Mr. Jagu. Let me first state that you can choose not to trust me, but the cyberattacks on your databases are likely to escalate very soon, and it is also likely the personal lives of board members will be vulnerable as well. I feel sure that you will eventually face extortion and blackmail. Everything you do, write, and plan will be leaked to your political opponents. In fact, it has already started."

The gentleman sitting the closest to her asked, "What is the nature of this information that has been leaked so far?"

"The Southern Commonwealth received a detailed list of your planned protests with locations, dates, and times, as well as a coded communication from NAM. NAM, on the other hand, received the personal schedule for Colonel Tom Whitehead and the same copy of your planned protests. In other words, this perpetrator is playing one party against the other but pretending to be looking out for the interests of each group individually. No good can come of this."

One of the board members, a gentleman named Bakari who was attending virtually, spoke up. "I couldn't agree more. If whoever this is starts to delve into personal affairs, it may become embarrassing, but that would be the least of it. If anyone has done things that are illegal or immoral, this person could easily control them, as Miss Smythe has said, with the use of blackmail and extortion. A real Pandora's Box of troubles."

Another virtual member who had probably the darkest skin of anyone there spoke up. The monitor showed his name as Asani Tendaji. His voice was nearly as melodious and pleasant as Marain's.

"I will play the devil's advocate here. Are we simply making a mountain out of a mole hill? Nothing untoward has happened yet. This could very well be some hacker simply having some fun at our expense. I say let sleeping dogs lie and don't succumb to paranoia."

Ki shook her head. "I could not disagree more. There is an old adage I like to remember, 'The motto of the wise is, be prepared for surprises'. It was one my mother embraced, and to good effect. Another was, 'An ounce of prevention is worth a pound of cure.' If you do nothing, and nothing bad happens, everything is good. If you do nothing and something bad happens, the consequences could be dire and could threaten the very existence of Ebonée. I am being the advocate for common sense."

The rest of the board was nodding their heads in agreement. One of the gentlemen sitting at the table said, "I move that we have a vote on whether or not we move forward on this issue and, if we do move forward, that we retain the services of this lovely Mullata detective."

Another man at the table stood up. "I heartily second that motion. I also want to take this moment to thank her for bringing this to our attention."

Marain Jagu hit the gavel on the table and said, "We have a motion, and it has been seconded. We will vote to either accept Kianna Smythe's proposal for investigating the intrusion into our affairs or to table the issue for the time being. All those in favor, signify by raising your hand." All hands went up, although she noticed the single dissenter on the board rose his hand more slowly than the rest.

After they adjourned, Ki mingled with the men and took the opportunity to acquaint herself with the board members individually. Marain was reading the contract she had brought with her and was marking some of the agreements embedded therein. Unfortunately, the virtual attendees had signed off immediately. Kianna wished she could have spoken to Mr. Tendaji to explore his perspective. She would have to consult with Marain later to get some details about this particular board member.

CHAPTER TWELVE

"To cultivate equanimity, we practice catching ourselves when we feel attraction or aversion, before it hardens into grasping or negativity."

—Pema Chodron

Bubba had set an appointment for a more in-depth interview with The Ghost and Obatala at the NAM headquarters. The building housing their headquarters was a repurposed grocery store that had gone out of business a few years back. Carpeting, cubicle partitions, and private meeting rooms converted this vast open space into a functioning office. The drop ceiling made it feel more intimate, but even these attempts at formalizing the space paled in comparison to Ebonée's offices. Ki noticed that these buildings— the architecture and furnishings she noted in each—spoke to the nature of the group housed there. It seemed the outward appearance was designed to reflect the inner workings. Their décor choices were imbued with the ideals and principles of that organization and the people involved . Ki thought of these architectural artifices as being akin to the way personal style in clothing gives cues to the personalities of individuals and reveal how they see themselves.

When Ki and Bubba entered the building from the massive parking lot, she immediately received another insight into NAM. Their raison d'être was equanimity, and the décor as well as the diversity of the personnel spoke to that aim. Everywhere she looked, there were people of all races, including mixed races, mingling together. She and Bubba fit in here like water would fit in the sea. At the Southern Commonwealth, she felt like she was not a part of the fabric of that place. She was apart from it. Her black gene pool could not compete in that environment. Bubba, because of his white skin, just disappeared, as she knew he would. And based on how she was received as a Mulatta, Ki knew Bubba definitely would not receive a warm reception at Ebonée's offices. The overall atmosphere there was uncomfortable to her and all because of the amount of (or, rather, the shortage of) melanin in her skin. Regardless of how she was treated, she knew she was considerably more than her skin. Visiting all three of the groups she was working for helped to clarify the unease within her. She was better defined by her personal stories. Her experiences. Her traumas. Her joys. Her relationships. Race was going to be a prevailing issue in this case, and as someone who saw the value of each individual for their innate worth, this dynamic was quite triggering for her.

The NAM receptionist was a man of mixed race. He was very welcoming and asked if he could be of any assistance.

Ki smiled at him as she handed him her business card. "Well, yes. We are looking for Daniel Tinkiya and Obatala. I am Kianna Smythe, and this is my personal assistant, Bubba Smith. We have an appointment with them today at 10:00 a.m."

He reached over the counter and heartily shook both of their hands. "Welcome to NAM. I am Joe Fishbourne, and they said you would be coming by this morning. Please allow me to escort you to their cubicles."

Joe led them through the maze to Daniel's cubicle. Daniel stood to greet them and asked them to follow him to Obatala's workspace. Ki took note of the fact that there did not seem to be any difference in the sizes of these offices. She knew Daniel and Obatala were high up on the NAM hierarchy, but they did not have enclosed offices with views. Clearly, they weren't concerned with status in this organization. The four of them retreated to a meeting space with a modest conference table and some comfortable chairs. Daylight streamed in from several skylights that accessed the distant roof above their heads. All of the decor in the room was neutral in tone. The colors, the design features, and general ambiance were, by their very nature, statement free. But that, in and of itself, was a statement.

Ki settled back in her chair and, through her body language, claimed the space of head of the table.

"Obatala, I would like to start with you. I am going to ask some personal questions in an effort to get to know you better. Outward appearances rarely are a good gauge of who someone is—what motivates and inspires or scares and enrages them—and these are important insights for me regarding the people I work with."

Obatala sat there with a bemused look on her face. "What is there to tell? I'm forty-five years old and I graduated from a local college with a degree in political science. Upon graduation, I helped to establish NAM with Daniel. We both strove to employ a commonsense approach with the New Africa Movement here in the Southern Commonwealth. He and I have been partners for the last twenty-three years. I believe in equal rights for everyone, and I am challenged by the society surrounding me."

Ki nodded her head. "Yes, I got all that from your bio. But, I want to know more about you as an individual. You were adopted by a white family. Am I right?"

Obatala looked shocked. "How on earth did you know that?"

"Well, I noticed in your cubicle a few pictures of a white couple and black girl at different ages. It was not a big leap to gather that girl was you.

I am curious. Do you consider yourself more a part of the white community or the black community?"

Obatala smiled. "Being raised in a white household, I really didn't think about it. At first, I did identify with my white family. We didn't socialize a great deal, but the few friends my parents had were mixed couples or people of a mixed race. That was my normal. When I got older, society informed me in subtle, and at times not so subtle ways, that for reasons I could not comprehend, the color of my skin was an important factor in determining my worth. In the integrated school I attended, my black friends called me an Oreo. I was black on the outside, but I was white on the inside. I was confused and, to be honest with you, I am still confused to this day. When I see people of different cultures and races collaborating and confronting issues together, I am totally at ease, because that is the way things should be, and that's the way it was for me. That is important to me. As I work on the frontlines, side-by-side with people of all skin colors to bring unity and peace, I am still baffled by how racial prejudice has such an ongoing stronghold."

Ki nodded and let her continue, as she seemed to be eager to share.

"I learned a long time ago I needed to be comfortable in my own skin. I am not here to meet the expectations of other people. They accept me as I am or they don't, but if they don't, that is their problem. I treat people with respect and dignity regardless of whether I get the same from them. That often takes people off guard. I have found that responding in kind to someone treating me poorly only confirms for them how they perceive me. That creates a dead end in our communications. I think it boils down to the energy you put out is what is reflected back at you. I'm not saying I have changed them, but I have changed the way I hold them, and that seems to make a big difference. More bridges get built and fewer walls."

Daniel bowed slightly to Ki and waited for Obatala to signal that she had finished. "I'll jump in, if you don't mind. I was adopted by a black couple. Even though I am white, I have always identified with the black community. I was immersed in a primarily black culture and grew up with mostly black friends, which essentially created the opposite dynamic from what Obatala experienced. In fact, that was how I received my nickname, The Ghost. The interesting thing was how my friends usually saw me simply as a person and not a person of a particular color. They came to know the authentic me because we shared trials and tribulations as well as adventures together. In other words, we had a common story. In college I met Obatala and she opened my eyes to the complexity of the cultures surrounding us. I grew up during the period when Atlanta was first designated as a Special Economic Zone. It took this area quite a while to settle into a rhythm of acceptance regarding segregation outside of its political boundaries. I worked in a restaurant that was trying to bridge that divide. There were three separate dining rooms. One for "colored", one for white, and one in the middle where races could mingle. At first that middle room pretty much stayed empty. But, in time, things changed. It took nearly ten years to establish a definable cultural middle ground between those disparate views of integration and segregation.

"Of course, a lot of people have always thought of Atlanta as an island of northern influence. It does tend to be more cosmopolitan in its perspective, so it was inevitable that it become a sort of political demilitarized zone. When the Southern Commonwealth was formed, Atlanta was large enough it could not successfully be assimilated into the culture they wanted to establish. That is how we became this odd duck of a cousin to Southern gentility."

Ki replied, "Thank you Daniel, and thank you Obatala. Let me bring you up to speed with where Bubba and I are in our investigation. I have met with Marain Jagu and the board of directors over at Ebonée. They unanimously voted to hire our firm to investigate their security breach and data leak. It has become clear to me that each of you—NAM, Ebonée, and the Commonwealth—is being targeted by the same entity. At this point, I do not have any leads for a suspect. Do you have any thoughts as to who might be behind this?"

Obatala leaned forward. "If it wasn't for the fact that both the Southern Commonwealth and Ebonée are going through the same thing, my thought would be it was one of them. Neither group really cares for our message or what we do here. And yet, it doesn't make sense that either of them would reveal important information about their own group. It seems they want to sow discord in the Southern political realm. I honestly have no idea who would have such motives. No one has come up on our radar."

Ki nodded. "Yes, it puzzles me as well. I do not know of any group with such an agenda. Although, one of the reasons I have been so public about coming to each of you is the hope that they will see me as a threat and attempt to rope me in and possibly expose something about themselves that I can use. That reminds me, Bubba, please make a note to see if our computer software has recorded any attempts to breach the firewall.

"Yes, Miss Ki. It will be the first thing on my to-do list when we get back to the office today."

"Okay. Here is what I am going to need from NAM: remote access to your mainframe, a list of all of your donors and board members with their contact information, and a detailed account of any threatening communications you have received in the last year. I have already received all of that from the Southern Commonwealth and Ebonée. Bubba and I will start collating all of this information as soon as we get back in the office to look for patterns. Any questions for me?"

Daniel and Obatala shook their heads. Obatala said, "I am going to slip away to gather some of this information for you to take with you. I'll also set you up with our tech people, and they can show you how to access the mainframe."

Ki smiled and shook both of their hands. "Thank you for taking the time and providing us with the information. I am likely to have further questions once I have gone over the data. Expect to hear from me in the next day or so. Again, thank you."

****

Once they got back to the office, Bubba checked the computer, and as Ki had predicted, there had been several attempts by someone to break through their firewall. The attempts had not been successful, but they had left no clues to indicate where the attack originated. Whoever was doing this was very skilled. Ki knew it was simply a matter of time before her defenses succumbed to this intruder's efforts. She considered taking her system offline, but that would prevent her from accessing her clients' systems. Her cousin in Marietta had installed the existing security software for her, and she was a genius at what she did. She was going to have to trust her work. The biggest concern she had was remotely accessing NAM, the Southern Commonwealth, and Ebonée. The hacker could have installed a "back door" subroutine she might inadvertently download into her own system. She made a note to have Bubba set up a call to her cousin so she could ask for her advice. In the meantime, she started sorting the printed documents from all three organizations.

Essentially, she was looking for commonalities between the organizations that might point in a particular direction. These patterns could lead her to some insights into the identity of this hacker. The first thing she looked at was donors and quickly hit paydirt. It wasn't definitive proof of anything, but she noticed three major donors with no physical address, just a post office box in a specific zip code in Atlanta. The most curious thing was the post office box numbers were sequential. That was a big red flag.

Then, when she examined the mailing addresses for the board members of each group, the zip code for these post office boxes appeared on that list as well. Bingo. Now she needed the photographs of the board members so she could see whom she was actually dealing with. However, she did not find what she was expecting. Her theory was that this was the same individual for all of the occurrences, but she saw three distinctly different people. In fact, each was what one could call the quintessential representative for the organization they were attached to. The Southern Commonwealth member was a white man named Marquis Carruthers who rivaled Colonel Tom in his almost cartoonish style. The NAM representative was a mixed-race woman whose picture included a photo of her black husband and adopted white son. She was the embodiment of egalitarian inclusion. And finally, the Ebonée seat-holder was none other than the man who was the "devil's advocate" challenging her during their meeting: Asani Tendaji.

CHAPTER THIRTEEN

"Self-defense is not just a set of techniques; it's a state of mind, and it begins with the belief that you are worth defending."

—Rorian Gracie

It appeared this was not the work of a lone hacker, but rather the coordinated efforts of a sophisticated organization. They had not only hacked the politico's computers, but seemed to have operations embedded in the Southern Commonwealth, NAM, and Ebonée. Kianna had identified at least six people involved: the man at the gala who winked at her, the investor with the winking man who visited Colonel Tom, the man blackmailing Senator Marquis Lee, and a board member with each group. The infiltrations provided avenues for these spies to contribute to the functioning of each group, appearing to support them, making them privy to much more than just raw data. She surmised that extortion was their likely endgame, but it seemed as though there were deeper ulterior motives, though she hadn't yet worked out what they were. She realized that through her queries she was likely raising alarm bells within this nest of vipers. Since she had laid out her concerns to the board of directors at Ebonée, and at least one of the hackers' was present, she knew it was only a matter of time before they made their move. And sure enough, before long she received a cryptic email that confirmed her suspicions.

The communique she received was confusing in its content, but clear in its message. They had done their homework on her because they crafted a challenging code that would test her skills. It simply read:

CEASE AND DESIST!

go play learn nine (1 day)'(33.753087, -84.383704, anon)

ignore at your peril

There were no attachments in the email, and her computer security system gave her no warnings, so at least her data was safe. When she tried to find out where it had come from, it was to no avail as the transmission had been routed through numerous servers located in twelve countries.

Obviously, she was being threatened. She must stop investigating or she would come to harm. Also, she quickly deduced the numbers were the latitude and longitude of a location. She understood *anon* to be Middle English for "soon" or "presently," and not an abbreviation for *anonymous*.

The rest of the message, however, was unclear. When she broke down the message into its components, she came closer to parsing its meaning. The word "go" could mean either the verb or the name of the popular board game. *Nine* presented a challenge because it could mean a time of day or a quantity. But if she looked at them all together it pointed toward engaging in a game of *Go*. There was a Go parlor in the Asian section of Atlanta. Her gut told her she needed to visit this Go parlor by 9:00 a.m., roughly one day from when she opened the email. While the last line was clearly a threat, she found it confusing. Was she not supposed to ignore the ceasing and desisting part or the game of Go? It was not very clear. One could argue they were inextricably linked. And there was no chance she would cease and desist her investigation. After doing some more research on the three organizations she gleaned information that confirmed visiting the coordinates provided in the email was an imperative.

After her cousin told her she had nothing to fear from remotely accessing the mainframe computers at NAM, the Southern Commonwealth, and Ebonée, she spent the rest of the day looking for additional areas where the organizations overlapped. She discovered that the only other overlaps, besides the donors, were in hiring the same physical security company to guard against burglary and fire. The company was ubiquitous, so there was really no surprise they all used the same one. In fact, she used them as well.

Ki tried, unsuccessfully, to dig deeper into the donors and board members who were red flagged from her earlier research. According to public records searches, they simply did not exist. They had no Commonwealth Identification Numbers and no physical addresses, only virtual ones.

Kianna asked Bubba to set up appointments for them to meet with each of the three organizations in order to update them on progress and what she felt they needed to do to safeguard their secrets. As he began picking up the phone to make phone calls, she remembered to say, "But do not schedule anything for tomorrow. I will be spending the day at the Atlanta Go Parlor."

"What is *Go*?" he asked with confusion and intrigue.

"It is a board game popular in Asia. It is, at the same time, a simpler and a far more complex form of chess. It is estimated to be around four thousand years old, possibly the world's oldest board game. It is a game I played as a child, and then as teenager and as an adult I played at a competitive level. I still dabble with it on occasion."

"So, is this for fun or is it something regarding work? Sorry, maybe that is none of my business."

"Strictly work, Bubba. Strictly work."

She then read him the cryptic note, to which Bubba responded, "I am going with you to those coordinates. I don't like the sound of that last warning because I smell a rat."

Ki smiled at the confidence developing in her cohort. "Of course, Bubba. I do not think I should go into any of this without backup from this point on. In fact, I definitely need you with me at the parlor tomorrow. I will be focused on my game, so you will be paying attention to the people I play. I trust your instincts. Take good notes."

Bubba grinned. "Sounds like a challenge, but I think I am up for it."

"I know you are. Oh, and Bubba, I think it wouldn't hurt to bring your gun."

Bubba could not hide his surprise or his glee.

Ki cautioned. "Don't get too excited. The last thing we want is for there to be a need to use it."

Bubba nodded in agreement, but he felt good because he knew he would be better able to protect his boss.

"For now, we need to gather all the advance insight we can about the coordinates they sent. Remember, expect the unexpected! I am not a big fan of technology; however, I am not averse to using a helpful tool if I can. I have a device I have used on numerous occasions—you may be familiar with it: the 'Fly on the Wall' that uses a portable 3-D retinal projection system that is synched up with smart glasses. It will allow me to bring you in with a tag-along that hooks you up with my device."

Ki pulled out a small cube from her bag and two pairs of frameless glasses. She set the cube on the table and handed one pair of the glasses to Bubba and put the other pair on. "Okay. Let your eyes focus on the image as it appears in the lenses. That image will be projected onto your retina. I will access the universal mapping system that is linked to the Atlanta Surveillance System and Satellite Downlinks Software."

Then Ki spoke, articulating loudly and pointedly, "Computer, access the following coordinates: 33.753087, -84.383704."

The address it read back was 47 Piedmont Avenue, Special Economic Zone Atlanta, State of Georgia, Southern Commonwealth.

Bubba had heard of this device, but had never used one. They were way out of his price range, but he had a knack for using high-tech systems, so he picked it up quickly. As the search produced its results, he saw a three-dimensional layout of the street and buildings located at the address. He could see people walking on the sidewalk and cars driving down the street. This was a real-time representation of what was happening at this address. Overhead satellites were synchronized with surveillance cameras in the metropolitan area. Though there were a few areas out of visual range, the computer was designed to extrapolate the appearance of these areas. If a person moved out of the surveillance zone, the computer projected likely movements of that person, which meant what you saw was not necessarily accurate, but it did give a reasonable estimation of behavior.

Bubba glanced over and saw Ki putting on some very thin and translucent gloves. When she reached out to the 3-D map, she was able to enlarge the image and move it so they had the street view of a parking garage at that address. It was as if they were standing on the sidewalk adjacent to it. She then moved the map in such a way that it felt as though they were walking into the garage. She could see into some doorways with a couple of dark places that weren't completely on the refreshing scan. She zoomed into one of those areas, and sure enough, there was the foot of someone who knew they were out of view of the surveillance. Ki smiled. "Looks like you were right, Bubba. That looks like a potential ambush. Let's take these things off and talk about a tactical plan."

****

When Ki arrived at the parking garage, she knew she would be facing at least four assailants. Her surveillance revealed four different shadow areas that were suspect. What she didn't know was if those areas contained more than one assailant. But forewarned is forearmed, and she was prepared to encounter some level of assault; but what happened was not so much an ambush as it was a showdown.

There were four attackers, as she had expected, but they all came right out in the open and positioned themselves around her at some distance. She also realized immediately what kind of fight this was going to be. Watching their moves, how they maneuvered themselves and what they wore, she knew they were not skilled in Aikido. However, these were not amateurs. Not by any means. She figured they were not likely to make the initial moves, so she had to somehow goad them into coming to her. She knew her best move was to do nothing. But if she was going to do nothing, she was going to do it with style. She knelt on the floor and closed her eyes. She then reached into her bodice and pulled out a blindfold. Placing the blindfold over her eyes, she simply knelt there with a beatific smile on her face.

They all came at her in a rush. Each arrived in her zone separately, and she discerned the pattern was clockwise. Anyone watching the scene that unfolded would have thought she was a leaf blowing in the wind. She seemed to know where and when each attacker would approach her before they made their move. She never let her knees leave the garage floor. At one point, one of the assailants came at her face with a long wooden rod, but she did not react until he suddenly shifted his attack to her abdomen. She then redirected his motion to her right, and his wooden rod went flying into the abdomen of another attacker who was closing in on her. As she did this, she bent over backward and grabbed onto the sleeves of the man coming at her from behind and used the momentum of his lunging toward her to hurl his body over her head into one of the concrete pillars. Quietly, she slipped her personal low-profile bokken from the concealed pocket in her loose-fitting pants. As the fourth man charged her, she waited patiently for him to be in exactly the right place before she gently raised the bokken to connect with his solar plexus. Using it like a fulcrum, she sent him flying over her into the same pillar where his partner was lying prostrate on the ground. Apparently, they'd had enough and realized they were no match for her because they scattered like rats leaving a sinking ship.

When she took off her blindfold, she was shocked to see Bubba hurtling past her, his body twisted so that his back was toward her. She saw the bullet come through his left shoulder as he aimed and fired his revolver at the rifleman who was hiding in one of the surveillance shadows. The rifleman was hit directly in his chest, and he collapsed on the ground. Bubba landed at her feet like a limp rag. He was smiling in spite of the blood flowing from him. He knew that he very likely had saved her from certain death.

Bubba looked up at her smugly, his expression saying, *Aren't you glad I brought the gun?*. Instead he muttered, "You okay, Miss Ki?"

Ki grinned back at him. "Bubba, you did great."

"Thank you, Miss Ki. I do think, however, we need to get this wound of mine tended to. It hurts like the dickens."

Ki lifted Bubba from the ground and helped him to the car. On the way to the ER, she asked if he could tell her what happened.

"Like we talked about, I came down here 'bout an hour afore you, put on the rig you were usin', and hid in one of those shadow spots. You were doin' pretty good handling those guys, and I could see you didn't need any of my help. So, I figured I should look at a bigger area in the garage; that way, in case there were any surprises, I could warn you. That's when I saw this guy with the rifle step out of the shadows. I knew you couldn't see him.

So, as he fired, I threw myself in the path of the bullet and took a bead on him. I told you this old country boy knows his way around a gun. Now, what about all this blood leakin' out of me?"

Ki laughed at how much Bubba managed to say while wincing with pain.

"Bubba, I can't thank you enough! Thankfully, this looks like just a flesh wound and you will be on the mend quickly. I do not want you to push yourself, but if you are up to it, I think today makes it clear I will need some backup tomorrow. Hopefully it will be a little less exciting than today's adventure.

****

While waiting to be checked in to the ER, Bubba asked her about her fighting technique.

"Miss Ki, I noticed that those guys were doin' somethin' different than the stuff that you do. Were they any good? I know you beat them and all, but do you have any comments?"

"Yes, Bubba, they were quite competent in their own way. However, they were not in the same league as I am, so the result of the fight was a foregone conclusion. I have had much more training in hand-to-hand combat than they have. Remember, I expect you to eventually learn how to use it."

"You told me once Eye-kee-do is Japanese. How do you spell it?"

"It is spelled, 'A-I-K-I-D-O'. In Japanese it is referred to as shugyo. That basically means Aikido is a focused physical and spiritual training that develops true wisdom and perfects human character. If you have been paying attention, you will have noticed that this aligns with my personal philosophy. *Ai* means harmony; *ki* means universal energy; and *do* literally means to live. In other words, to live in harmony with the universal energy.

My path of learning is long. I consider myself a beginner even though I have been training for nearly twenty years. There is always more to learn."

"Wow! I will never be able to catch up with you!"

"Bubba, the best time to plant a tree is twenty years ago. We can only be here now. Do not try to be who you are not. Be who you are, and you will be fine. If we live in the past, we fill our heads with regrets and self-pity. If we live in the future, our hearts become filled with striving and worries. That is what is meant by the phrase, 'Be Here Now'. It is an easy philosophy to profess, but there is a lifetime of practice in achieving it."

Bubba was clearly beginning to succumb to the sedative properties of the pain medication administered at the ER and could only manage to mumble, "Huh?"

Ki laughed and determined that was a lesson for another day.

CHAPTER FOURTEEN

"If aliens exist, they might play chess, but they certainly play Go."

—Unknown Chess Master

The next day at the Go Parlor, it was clear as to what was going to happen. When they arrived, she saw the competition schedule posted on the bulletin board behind the reception desk. She would face nine players with forty-five minutes of play time for each of them.

Whoever was ahead at the end of the round would be declared the winner of that heat and would move on to challenge the next player. In the first round, she was given a nine stone handicap. If she won, she would lose one stone, and one for each subsequent win. If she lost, she would have all of her remaining handicap stones taken away. She was a very capable player, and she easily won against her first opponents. At the end of the first round, a shadowy figure handed her a sealed envelope with instructions to not open the envelope or any others she received until she left the premises. She was also told if she were to lose a game, she would not be given an envelope. Ki noticed the number of the game she had just played was in bold print on the front of the envelope.

The room was relatively silent during game play, but everyone was courteous and respectful. The players were of different genders, races, and ages. None of them matched the pictures of the donors and board members of the three political organizations. Still, she had a sinking feeling one of these people was the mastermind behind the cyber intrusions. Everyone played at varying levels of skill, but Ki had no difficulty in winning most of her pairings. However, there was one game that stood out for her. The player she encountered in the second round used some excellent strategies, but he also made some very obvious errors. It was almost as though he was intentionally trying to lose. At the end of each game she was handed another sealed envelope identical to the first, but numbered to correspond with the round she'd just completed. The entire time she played she kept mental notes regarding the players. Bubba was there with his left arm in a sling but still able to keep copious written notes. He really put his all into it.

Bubba had kept quiet the entire time and, although he didn't know the rules of the game, he was very attentive. When she finished and they were seated in the foyer of the parlor he asked, "Miss Ki, is this envelope thing a part of the tradition of the game? It seems strange."

"No, Bubba. I think that particular bit of subterfuge is my main reason for being lured here today. Our perpetrator is using this as a means of communicating with me while remaining anonymous. I am anxious to read them, so let's get back to the office and analyze them. I imagine there is some sort of code involved."

****

Once back in their private office space, she laid out the envelopes on a large clear desk. She tore open the #1 envelope, pulled out the paper that was inside, and was perplexed. She realized this was going to require some really focused thinking. The words scrawled across each note were not words, but rather strings of letters with no discernible pattern. Some had capital letters, and punctuation showed up haphazardly. The first thing she did was set all the envelopes in consecutive order, and then pulled the paper out of each envelope and labeled it by the number on the envelope from which it came. She quickly discerned the messages were out of sequence.

At the top of each cypher note was a single clue. On the first note the word POWER was written in bold letters. On the second note was the word DEVIL. The third note was titled CATHOLIC. The fourth note was longer - #OF FORCES IN THE UNIVERSE. The fifth note was EGO. The sixth note was PATTERN. The seventh note was FORTUNE. The eighth note was CREATOR, CREATION, LOVE. And the ninth and final note was HEAVEN.

"Well, Bubba, what do you think?"

Bubba scratched his head. "I think this guy has got way too much time on his hands. That's what I think."

Ki laughed softly. "Granted. But other than that, we work with what we have, and what we have is a pretty simple puzzle. He could have confounded us with something really obscure, but this is pretty easy."

"Well, to you maybe. Why don't you walk me through it?"

Ki had to admit she enjoyed the challenge of these types of puzzles. She practically beamed at Bubba when she said, "Okay. First of all, each of the titles gives us a clue for their proper order. Most of them can be represented as a geometric symbol. Some of them are obvious and others require a certain amount of logic. We will start with the first envelope we received. It said POWER. Go was a Chinese invention, so I am leaning toward Chinese numerology here. The number representing power in Chinese is six, so we can draw a hexagon on this sheet. These words will each be the sixth word in his missive. What do you think EGO represents?"

Bubba smiled. "Well, that's easy. Number one."

Ki frowned. "Too obvious. My guess is two. There are two basic ego types, namely yin and yang, another Chinese ideology. Plus, the egoistic mind is a dualistic mind and separates the world into the observer and observed. Therefore, I think this makes the fifth envelope number two. She drew a single line and the number two."

Bubba thought about it and nodded his head. "So, what is the first envelope?"

Ki scanned them all and pointed to the one that said CATHOLIC. "The word CATHOLIC means universal. Taking the prefix *uni*, that takes us to *unity* or *uniform*. She drew a circle on the third envelope and wrote the number one. Okay, your turn."

Bubba rubbed his chin and pointed at the fourth envelope with the words #OF FORCES IN THE UNIVERSE.

"That's an easy one. It's the only one already in the correct order. If I remember my science class correctly, there are four forces in the universe: gravity, magnetism, strong nuclear force, and the weak nuclear force. You're next."

Ki laughed heartily. "Good for you, Bubba! I think you are dead on." She drew a square and the number four on that envelope. Alright, if we are going to do easy, I choose the DEVIL on the 2nd envelope. That would have to be five with a pentagon. Agree?"

Bubba agreed right away. "Yep. Ole' Beelzebub himself. HEAVEN has to be seven. That number shows up everywhere in the Bible." He was so confident that he reached over and wrote seven and drew a rough heptagon on the envelope.

Ki smiled. "Bubba, you are showing real promise. I bet your daddy would be proud!"

"Shucks. Thank you ma'am."

"You are welcome. CREATOR, CREATION, LOVE has to be the trinity. Father, Son, Holy Spirit." She wrote down a three and a triangle on the eighth envelope.

Ki turned her attention to the remaining clues. "Okay, that leaves just two envelopes. One of them is FORTUNE and the other is PATTERN. Of the two remaining numbers, I'm inclined to think FORTUNE is the number 8 and an octagon. It is common to find eight-sided mirrors in Chinese homes for good luck."

Bubba chimed in, "So, by process of elimination the last one is nine, which makes sense because, if my memory of math class serves me, the number nine has lots of patterns associated with it. I don't remember what a nine-sided figure is called."

Ki said, "Nonagon"

Jotting the figure on the envelope, Bubba rubbed his hands together. "Alright! Finally, we can figure this thing out."

Ki shook her head. "Not so fast. While we do have the proper order, now we have to apply an unknown substitution code to decrypt the message. I cannot tell you how much I enjoy figuring out these kinds of cyphers."

After laying out the segments from each note in proper order, she studied the first part of the coded message.

Krwx Zlyy Yzcshr,

Dlxys ed woo, L gwjs se ywc L wkzlxr ceax yvlooy wjk wulolslry lj Wlvlke. Shws gwy w trxc lzixryyltr klyiowc shws cea ias ej lj shr iwxvljm mwxwmr. L zays ywc, L hwtr jrtrx yrrj wjcshljm nalsr olvr ls. L wz yexxc wueas shr zwxvyzwj. Hly ljsrjs gwy ejoc se geajk cea, wjk L xrmxrs hly oeyy dxez zc rzioec. Hr gloo ur zlyyrk, uas L ke jes uowzr cea lj wjc gwc.

"Well, that just looks like Greek to me." Bubba said, scratching his head.

"I think this calls for a substitution code where each letter in the alphabet is substituted by another letter, although sometimes a cryptographer will have one letter stay the same. You figure it out by using logic. For instance, in this note we can immediately discern the letter L is a substitute for the letter I or i. It shows up as a single letter and it is capitalized in the middle of sentences, so it is reasonable to deduce that this is the personal pronoun *I*. For the most part, any single letter in a cryptogram of this sort will be either an *I* or an *A*. Our friend has helped us out considerably by keeping context spacing, punctuation, and capitalization consistent with what we would expect to see in standard correspondence. I have seen codes done where it is simply a continuous string of letters with no punctuation or spacing, which is much more difficult, though not impossible.

"Our mystery perpetrator must want us to read this pretty badly because he . . . or she . . . went easy on us. There are some basic assumptions we can operate with. For instance, this is in the form of a formal letter. Unless I am mistaken, this starts out: Dear Miss Smythe. I can deduce that *k* is *d*; *r* is *e*; *w* is *a*; *x* is *r*, and so on. To confirm that, we can look for other clues. Based on what I have seen so far, we should see a number of *shr* combinations because that is the word *the*. Another combo should be *shws*, which translates as *that*. Given those clues, I think you can create a decryption key so we can translate this note. Let me know if you have any problems."

Bubba scratched his head. "Thanks a lot. I think."

Bubba plunged into the challenge, and when he presented his work to Ki, the whole message read:

Dear Miss Smythe,

First of all, I want to say I admire your skills and abilities in Aikido. That was a very impressive display that you put on in the parking garage. I must say, I have never seen anything quite like it. I am sorry about the marksman. His intent was only to wound you, and I regret his loss from my employ. He will be missed, but I do not blame you in any way.

You are also proving to be a skilled investigator. You saw through my ruse from the beginning. You probably have no idea yet regarding my overall plan, but I suspect that in short order you will be solving that puzzle as well. Needless to say, my plans are having to be modified as we speak. Don't get me wrong. I enjoy the challenge, but you have forced me to work considerably harder to achieve my goals. Then again, I have always felt that nothing moves forward effectively without resistance, so I encourage you to try and thwart my intentions at every turn.

At some point, I would relish the opportunity to sit down and speak with you regarding my objectives. I sense that you have the intelligence to grapple with the ideology that I am trying to manifest here in the Southern Commonwealth. Many people would consider me and my actions to be "evil". However, nothing could be further from the truth. My aims are for a stable and comfortable life for everyone in society. Unfortunately, you have to break a lot of eggs to make a delicious omelet. I believe it is referred to as collateral damage.

A couple of thoughts to leave you with: 1. Please straighten the picture on the eastern wall of your office. I have a touch of OCD and it disturbs me. 2. Although your cousin has done an admirable job at protecting your data from my prying eyes, you are by no means keeping me from knowing your secrets.

Your admirer,

Mänsklig Chelovek

p.s. good luck in deciphering my name. ;) it gives a hint as to my ultimate aims.

After Ki read it, she exclaimed, "Well, that is intriguing. Bubba, what do you make of it? Oh, by the way, excellent job in decoding his missive. Thank you."

"Miss Ki, you are more than welcome. And thank you for giving me a chance to prove myself in other areas. I want to be of use to you as more than just a gopher. As for what I make of it, well, parts of it are a real head scratcher. But I'll tell you what is pretty damn clear. For one, he's a bright fella. He is also well informed about things he really shouldn't be. And finally, he seems to be a big fan of yours."

Ki smiled. "Right on all counts, Bubba. What do you think about his statement regarding his changing his plans?"

Bubba chuckled. "Yep. That's interestin'. Real interestin'. If I were to make a stab at it, I'd say he's lyin' like a rug. He dresses it up real pretty, but I'm guessin' he would much rather you back away from what you've uncovered."

"Very astute, Bubba. That is exactly what I thought too. I do not suspect he is willing to so easily abandon the plans that clearly took a lot of time, energy, and thought. My guess is he is probably trying to steer us off his trail to preserve it. Also, he has far less insight about what I know than he is claiming. But, that being said, how did he witness the fight in the garage, how does he know about my cousin, and how on God's green earth does he know about the crooked picture in the office?"

Bubba shook his head. "Yep. Those are the head scratchers I was talkin' about."

Ki was staring off into the distance when she said, "Bubba, I wonder if we've actually seen this guy. It would be just like him to put himself into my life somehow without me knowing about it. In fact, now that I think about it, I'm pretty sure I know how and when. The Go games. I will lay odds to even he was one of the participants in one of the matches."

"Do you really think so? Which one? How can we tell. If he did, he was very sneaky about it."

"I'm thinking we might have a clue from the envelopes and what they reveal. Look back through the messages and see which envelopes have his name in code."

Bubba searched and cross-referenced. Once he had it, he said with a degree of intrigue, "Now that is interesting. Envelope 2 and 1 which are labeled DEVIL and POWER. I'd say, that's a clue right there. What do you think?"

"I think you are right. Now, pull out the notes you took during the game and see who I played during those games?"

A big grin crept onto Bubba's face. "Boy, howdy. Also interesting. They were the only two Caucasian men. The second one was late fifties to early sixties and the first one was by my guess, mid-40's. I'll betcha that one of those guys is our Mänsklig Chelovek."

Ki beamed. "I know who it is! It was player number two. He played a deceptive game. He was a much better player than he let on. He made obviously intentional mistakes. No doubt about it. He was Mänsklig Chelovek. The funny thing is, he seemed familiar to me at the time, but I was focused on the game. Now I know why. He is the same person who winked at me at the gala where I met Penelope Lee, and he is also the one who winked at the camera at the Southern Commonwealth. He was wearing a disguise those times, but his eyes give him away. I wonder if he has been inserting himself into my life in other ways because there is still some additional connection I cannot quite put my finger on. It is driving me crazy, but I will figure it out given enough time."

CHAPTER FIFTEEN

"I think that [there is] this fundamental right to privacy and the philosophy that govern-ment shouldn't be intrusive."

—Tim Cook

Ki and Bubba met at the Atlanta Botanical Garden to determine next steps in their investigation.

As they found a bench to sit in one of the garden areas, Bubba exclaimed, "We know what he looks like! But how exactly does that help us?"

Ki sighed and spoke pensively. "It will require some patience on our part, but I have a plan. Right now, however, we need to speak with our clients."

Bubba nodded his head. "Agreed, but I'm a little concerned about some of the things we can't figure out about this guy. How in blazes does he know some of the things he knows? It's one thing to have a place bugged, but what he seems to know goes way beyond that."

"It is a concern for me as well. It is why we are meeting out of the office. Now that we know he has eyes on us, we must be diligent in our pursuits. He has shown his hand in some respects, and we can use that to our advantage. If we know he is watching us and our clients, it should be fairly easy to feed him false information."

Bubba laughed. "That there is a great idea!"

"Yes, but Chelovek is no slouch. He could see this ploy coming a mile away, so we have to move carefully, not overplay our hand. We want to lace enough truth into what we give him so he does not detect deceit. We also need to let our clients in on these strategies and make sure there is a consistency within each group in what they are communicating."

Ki and Bubba decided it was wiser to meet with each group separately, starting with Ebonée, then NAM, and finally the Southern Commonwealth before bringing them together. But Ki's priority was to have Kelly, her code-writing genius cousin, make a secret visit to each campus, off the radar and out of view of technologically prying eyes. Ki also restricted their personal visits going forward to outdoor public venues. Bubba met with his father to bring him into the loop on their off-grid maneuverings. Ki personally visited the NAM headquarters and the Ebonée offices speaking with their data people directly, giving them the same directives around communications. Over the span of about a week, Kelly purged all three of the systems of the numerous malware programs that had been surreptitiously installed by Chelovek. One of the most insidious was designed to send all the data to three separate hard drives he had in a secure location each time an automatic save was activated. Kelly also closed down several backdoors Chelovek could use to enter the systems undetected. Once that was taken care of, Ki felt more confident in using their computers to dig deeper into what was going on, but first, they owed the heads of each group an update on the status of the their investigation and the work she had done to secure their operations.

First up was Ebonée, and this time she felt compelled to have Bubba accompany her. She was curious to see how Marain would react to Bubba's presence. Marain was the black equivalent of Colonel Tom, although far more eloquent and elegant in his demeanor. He was polite and amenable on the surface, but he clearly held Bubba in contempt, and his disdain was only thinly veiled. The off-hand comments and snubs were telltale signs of his deeply held prejudice even though his tone was coated in saccharine.

As they walked the beautifully cultivated grounds they spoke with a casual demeanor per Ki's instructions, and they kept their heads tucked and spoke in hushed tones. She explained they were still gathering intelligence regarding how this computer snoop was getting some of the more personal information, but they had been able to disrupt his access to their corporate data by letting her cousin protect the hard drives. Until she knew more, she felt it was warranted to be overly circumspect. She laid out the protocol she felt would best protect them from future intrusions.

"Ki, it sounds like you have all your bases covered, including getting the white point of view through your assistant."

"Marain, Bubba has become much more than a 'white point of view.' He is a valuable team member, and he has saved my life once already. We are becoming friends beyond our roles as colleagues."

"Sorry, Ki. I meant no offense. Let's change the subject. Tell me what you have discovered regarding our nemesis?"

"Thanks to Bubba's help we know what he looks like and his name. He goes by the name of Mänsklig Chelovek, which I am sure is a pseudonym. I did an internet search and found nothing about a person with this name, but I did find that *mänsklig* is Swedish for *human*, and *chelovek* is Russian for *human*. My thought is he is playing all the parties against each other in order to sow discord and perpetuate the belief that the government is not capable of protecting the interests of our citizens."

"How was he able to so easily penetrate our cyber security?"

Bubba smiled and said, "In your case it was not difficult since you were using off the shelf security software. That's pretty much designed to do nothing more than keep your friends out. Thanks to Ki's cousin Kelly, you now have *top* shelf protection."

"Thank you." Marain said to no one in particular, avoiding directly acknowledging Bubba's contribution.

Ki, continued, attempting to break the tension, "Have you been able to contact that board member I brought to your attention?"

"No. He is a real mystery. Apparently, the only contact he has ever had with us has been virtually. I hate to admit it, but he used a great deal of money and what we now know was a fictional resume to get a seat on the board of directors. He has now disappeared. My suspicion is that Mr. Chelovek has pulled out of Ebonée. Now that our new systems are locked down and his board spy is gone, I think it's safe to say he got all he was looking for. Does that mean we will soon be able to sever our ties with your company?"

Ki shook her head. "I wish that were true, although I do enjoy your company. I'm afraid we have uncovered a massive nest of vipers. We still do not know how he is accessing the very personal and sensitive information that did not come from your organization or your computers. Something else is going on. Besides, we have not been able to access the personal computers of the existing board members. I would be very surprised if this web of deceit hasn't exposed them as well. Since he sat on the board with these people, even if only virtually, he knows how to get to them. Chelovek is crafty and connected and has proven to be very thorough indeed. In other words, we have just begun to fight."

Jagu was deeply troubled as Ki shared her findings. "All right, Ki. You have convinced me. I feel very vulnerable right now and I do not like that feeling. Please let us all do our best to resolve this situation. Do you think you need to go into the board member's computers at this time?"

"No, but it may come to that. Let me explore one other option that may resolve the situation once and for all. It will not be without some personal risk, but it could be a permanent solution to our dilemma."

Marain smiled and threw his head back. "That would be fantastic! I look forward to the day. If we can be of any assistance regarding your safety, do not hesitate to ask for my assistance. I am growing to care for you. I do not want to see you come to any harm."

Ki didn't let her emotions betray her, but she found herself longing to pursue a deeper relationship with this man. "I will bear that in mind, and believe me, if I think it is necessary, I will NOT hesitate to call you in. However, for right now, I feel confident in Bubba's ability to have my back."

Before they left Marain's grounds, she slipped him a handwritten note in a sealed envelope. She came in close and whispered in his ear. "Destroy this after reading."

****

When they got to NAM's headquarters they followed the same protocol as they did at Ebonée. However, there was no manicured landscaping for a leisurely stroll. Their building was in a commercial zone, so their options were limited to standing conspicuously in the parking lot or taking a walk through the neighborhood. Ki opted to walk through the neighborhood. The "Ghost" was unable to join them as he was tied up in a meeting, so Ki led Obatala along tree-lined sidewalks, carefully scanning her surroundings for signs of surveillance. She had been exploring some theories around Chelovek's means for accessing their personal spaces and would be testing her theory soon, but for the time being, they had to exercise extreme caution.

As they walked, Ki and Bubba detailed what they had learned about the hacker and his potential motives. Ki shared with Obatala the same fears she had about what was going on at Ebonée. Although it looked like they had stopped the penetration of their cyber security, there were too many loose ends, and their board of directors could indeed be compromised. Chelovek was proving to be a worthy opponent, so it was not safe for Ki to make any assumptions. She mumbled to Obatala, "This code of yours that was discovered by Chelovek concerns me. If he cracks it, he could easily use it to send false information to your people and stir up chaos."

Obatala smiled smugly. "I have little concern along those lines. It is a very unusual code."

"That may be true, but this man is a code master." Ki described the multi-layered code Chelovek sent her. She also explained that she felt he was pulling punches because he clearly had the capability of much more complex subterfuge. She cautioned that it takes a great deal of intelligence to fake simple-mindedness and make obvious mistakes in such an artful way. He was likely quite capable of creating an impenetrable code."

Obatala looked sullen. "I see your point. Do you have any recommendations?"

"Yes. We can determine if he has already cracked it by planting some false information that would be too tempting for him to resist. If he shows his hand, we will know you need to create a different code. I can help you with that; but, for now, I recommend we pretend that we don't suspect anything. If you don't mind, I would like to try and decipher the message he stole from you. I do not, however, want any help from you. I need to get a sense of just how impenetrable it is."

Obatala nodded. "That sounds fine to me. Knock yourself out. I guess I need to get to work on a backup regardless."

Bubba spoke up. "I am goin' to stick my nose in here by sayin' y'all prob'ly don't wanna waste your time puttin' together something y'all are going to have to change again. This Chelovek fella is as slippery as an eel in a vat of Vaseline. Just remember he's figured a way to see what's goin' on without usin' your gonkulaters." Seeing their confusion, Bubba clarified, "That's a personal term of affection I use for computers."

"I'll try to remember that. That term could come in handy someday to obfuscate a message."

Once they had made their way back to NAM headquarters, they bid Obatala farewell and slipped her a sealed envelope, relaying the same message she had passed to Marain.

Their next stop was the Southern Commonwealth.

****

Colonel Tom and Franklin greeted Ki and Bubba in the gardens surrounding the faux-columned mansion. In spite of herself, Ki was susceptible to the tranquil façade that belied the passive-aggressive interior landscape of the Southern Commonwealth.

Colonel Tom, in his ostentatious manner, proved to be the consummate showman. Ki had to keep reminding herself that his bon vivant demeanor was merely a veneer to cover a self-involved, manipulative man. Colonel Tom played the role he did because it worked for him. The people in his political bubble were drawn to his charismatic and jovial style.

Franklin, on the other hand, was down to earth and authentic. He was far closer to being the ideal Southern gentleman. He was polite but not obsequious, and you could trust that whatever he told you was the honest to God truth.

Bubba, hugged his father robustly and said, "Hey, Daddy. Good to see you in the here and now."

"Likewise, Bubba! How have you been? I suspect you and Miss Ki are making some progress with our hacker friend?"

"Oh yeah. Miss Ki, do you want to fill in Colonel Tom and Daddy?"

"No, why don't you take the reins this time and let them know where we stand?

Ki had dual purposes for handing off to Bubba. She wanted to create an opportunity for him to step up and show his father and Colonel Tom that he was growing in his position, and it allowed her to more closely observe their expressions and make some mental notes.

When Bubba was finished, Colonel Tom was the first to speak. "So, as much as I would like to put this all behind us, it sounds to me like we ain't close to being done yet. It sounds like you think we are only scratching the surface? That right, Miss Smythe?"

"That's right, Colonel Tom. He knows we are on to him and he is smart enough to go to ground. Since my cousin has straightened out your computers, we are definitely in a more secure place. But I do not think it prudent to let down our guard at all. We are still vulnerable, and one of Chelovek's deadliest tools is silence. As Bubba related to you, he knows details about movements and conversations that happen in private. I have some suspicions about how he is pulling that off, but I need to dig deeper. Colonel Tom, I do need a private word with you, please."

"Why certainly, young lady. That would truly be my pleasure."

Ki and Colonel Tom left Bubba and Franklin on the front lawn and wandered into a secluded part of the garden to a paved parterre. The wisteria climbing the posts helped to frame views of a tranquil pond surrounded by weeping willows replete with a pair of graceful and regal swans. The whole scene was very reminiscent of a Maxfield Parrish painting. Ki had to tip her hat to the skill of the landscape architects who designed these grounds.

When she spoke, she whispered and kept her head facing down toward the ground. "Colonel Tom, please allow me to be blunt. I would appreciate it if you would do the same with me. A simple nod will suffice."

Colonel Tom nodded.

"Wonderful. I do not believe it is a stretch to presume the private act involving Miss Peggy Sue was sexual in nature. And, you are quite confident there were no witnesses to the indiscretion?"

Colonel Tom nodded.

"Thank you. I am going to hand you a sealed envelope with instructions on next steps. This is for your eyes only. Based on what you have confirmed, I have a plan I am proposing for how to smoke out our Mr. Chelovek. I will be in touch soon."

Colonel Tom nodded a final time understanding his predicament quite clearly, and then turned on his heels to retreat to his office.

CHAPTER SIXTEEN

"Appear weak when you are strong, and strong when you are weak."

—Sun Tzu, *The Art of War*

When she and Bubba got back to the office, Ki tackled the NAM code. She looked at the message Chelovek had lifted from NAM's website. Of course, it made no sense at all. It read: *ihtewttconomonoontainuehttautscerbliwvomrfawen.*

There were no patterns that made any sense because it was one continuous string of letters. With no punctuation or capitalization there was no guide to syntax. All the possible Caesar Shift ciphers didn't work. Regardless of how many times she shifted the alphabet, the message was still nonsense. The Enigma Code didn't make sense because that would be way too complex for such a small organization. They would have to have their own personal Enigma Machine. After several attempts she realized that the playfair cipher wasn't a candidate because the 5 by 5 grid did not yield any results and there were no X's in the message. It obviously wasn't the pigpen cipher because there were no graphic symbols. But when she tried the transposition cipher, she knew she had hit pay dirt. To NAM's credit, it was a clever variation on that old standby—it was a tri-letter variant. She turned the string of letters around to read:

newafrmovwilbrecstuattheuniatnoonomonodcttwethi

Breaking it up into three letter increments gave her this message: *new afr mov wil ber ecs tua tth eun iat noo onm ono ctt wet hi*. She was able to work out what the first few were, but she was confused by the latter half. Then it occurred to her to account for likely two letter words. Now it read: *new afr mov wil be rec stu at the uni at noo on mon oct twe thi*. She translated this to: *New Africa Movement will be recruiting students at the university at noon on Monday October 23rd*. Success. She immediately sent Obatala and the Ghost a direct email message saying:

> I hope your recruiting effort at the University on the
> 23rd of October was very successful.
>
>
> Yours, (not so secretly),
> Kianna Smythe
>
>
> p.s. *agasirahsuoseht*

She had spent the better part of a day breaking this code, but felt it was well worth it. She had shown NAM they did not have a secure code. If she could break it, she felt certain Chelovek could as well. Now they needed to run a test to see just how extensive his surveillance was. She would need to discuss with them the best timing for that particular exercise.

****

When Colonel Tom got home, he started a small fire in the fireplace in his bedroom. He then went to his bedroom closet and shut the door. He pulled out the note given to him by Kianna. In the perceived privacy of his personal space, he muttered, "That uppity black negress is quite skilled at her job; but, a woman, let alone a damn blackie, has no business telling me what to do."

Pulling a pen light from his pocket, he read the note and memorized it. Following this, he crumpled the note and threw it into the fireplace where the flames consumed it. Then, following the directions in the note, he took out a blank pad of paper from his writing desk where he jotted down a to-do list for the next day.

There were personal tasks that were mundane, such as picking up some small items at the store, filling his car with gas, and scheduling a haircut. But the note from Kianna Smythe had also told him to include scheduling a private meeting with Bryan Merrits—the head of his Public Relations department—regarding an outdoor rally to be held in Atlanta. He left the pad on his desk, and then after watching some boring television movie, he retired to his bed and fell fast asleep. He slept so soundly that he didn't notice the light on his writing desk turn on by itself at 2:00 a.m. After a short while, it also turned off by itself.

The next day, Colonel Tom called Brian's secretary and set up a meeting in the conference room in the southern wing of the Commonwealth's headquarters. Following Miss Ki's directions, he met with Bryan and told him to organize an impromptu rally outside their Atlanta offices to promote the Southern Commonwealth's agenda to what he considered to be a mostly unenlightened crowd. He had pretty much accepted that the Commonwealth's mission needed some image finessing in order to turn around the political intrusion from the snooty progressives and what he had come to call the Northwest Territories. The event was to be scheduled at the end of the week at noon, and lunch would be provided for those attending. He also told Brian he planned on making an appearance as well.

****

Marain Jagu was not quite sure what Kianna Smythe was up to, but he did trust she had a well-considered strategy. So, doing as he was told, he took a walk downtown and went to the local shopping district, found a restroom, walked in, and found a random stall. There he read Ki's note and memorized it. He tore the pieces to shreds and then flushed them down the toilet. Upon exiting, he went to a men's boutique shop and bought himself a very distinctive set of ebony cufflinks. After paying the clerk, he went back to his office.

Ki's note asked him to go to the most secure place on the grounds and meet with the head of Human Services and have a feigned spontaneous conversation regarding people under their employ who would not be averse to being involved in a violent and armed demonstration. He explained he had received some information regarding a rally the Southern Commonwealth would be staging at their Atlanta offices. He wanted some of his people to be present to counter protest. The Human Services director gave him a few names, which he wrote down. He then thanked the director for his time and went back to his office.

He summoned the first two people on the list from the director. Ten minutes later they showed up at his door.

"Gentlemen, please come in and make yourselves comfortable."

They were both large and intimidating. These men would be perfect for what Ki had in mind.

"Gentlemen, thank you for taking the time to see me on such short notice. I will get right to the point. I want you to help me to make it clear to our southern white 'landlords' in no uncertain terms that we are not in the mood for any of their antics. They are conducting a rally at their headquarters here in Atlanta, and it is open to the public. Gentlemen, you are part of that public and I want you to voice opposition to their sanctimonious political rhetoric. And I do mean by any means necessary. Do I make myself clear?"

The larger of the two men smiled. "We understand perfectly, sir. You can count on us."

****

Obatala took out the note Ki had given her, and she sat under a large evergreen shade tree in a public park about two miles from the NAM offices. It was the most secure place she could find, and Ki had been adamant about it being out of sight of any surveillance devices. She located the security cameras in the park and made sure there was no coverage from where she sat under the spruce tree. The foliage was a perfect foil for her to secretly read the handwritten note. After memorizing Ki's directions, she folded the note and stuffed it into her bag. Back at the office, she put the note through the double crosscut shredder.

Without conveying any of the subterfuge, she went to Daniel's office and asked if he had a minute.

She said, "I received a message from our lady detective. It probably won't come as a surprise to you that she cracked our 'super secure' code. It took her less than a day."

Daniel frowned. "To be honest, I am not surprised. She is one smart cookie. What do you think we need to do?"

Obatala sat and sighed heavily then told Daniel, "I think we should consider letting her create a new code for us. But I think we can also take advantage of this situation in some way. I have an inkling of an idea, but I'm not ready to share quite yet."

Daniel looked her in the eye. "The only caution I would put forth is she would be privy to our communications if she creates the new code. It's not that I don't trust her. She has proven herself to be helpful and reliable up to this point. But she could be a potentially weak link in our security. At first blush, I am inclined to support your idea. Let's talk about it later."

Obatala conceded. "Thanks, Daniel. We will discuss it with her later. Oh, by the way, some information came in through my private newly secured email that I need to share with you. According to one of our insiders, the Southern Commonwealth is planning a public outdoor rally at their Atlanta headquarters. It is open to the public and she felt it wouldn't hurt to check it out. I was wondering if maybe the two of us could attend together. If the press is going to be there, a little free publicity surely wouldn't hurt."

Daniel nodded in agreement, "Sounds great to me. Let me just pencil that into my calendar."

****

Chelovek said to himself, "All things come to those who wait." He was looking forward to attending this outdoor rally by the Southern Commonwealth because he knew all three politicos would be present. He didn't know what was going to happen, but he knew the potential for conflict was great. He just may be the one to light the fuse. Yes. This was exactly what he wanted to see occur.

Mänsklig was early and only the fourth person to sign in for the rally. Just for fun, he signed in with his real name: Frank Brown. He smiled to himself as he wrote it down. He chose the vegetarian option for lunch, found himself a seat, and settled in to wait for the fun to begin. After ten minutes, Obatala and The Ghost showed up and sat in the front row, just two rows in front of him. As with most of these types of events, it was going to start a few minutes late in order to allow late arrivals time to show up while not being disrespectful to early attendees and just-in-timers. And it had the added benefit of building anticipation. Two minutes after the designated start time the two thugs from Ebonée made their entrance and, as he predicted, they took seats in the back. Shortly after they sat, Marain Jagu made his entrance. Things were definitely shaping up.

The weather was perfect. A light, refreshing breeze danced across the lawn, and the warmth of the sun finished it off nicely. At five minutes past noon, the panel filed in and sure enough, there was Colonel Beauregard Thomas Whitehead in his costume. Of course, the press had been notified, and Colonel Tom loved to play his role to the hilt. In spite of Chelovek's disdain for politics and any form of state control, he had to admit he felt drawn to the caricature of this bombastic yet refined Southern gentleman. Colonel Tom knew what people expected, and he was sure to turn in a stellar performance.

Since this was the Southern Commonwealth's show, the moderator immediately introduced the great Colonel Tom Whitehead, which garnered a smattering of polite applause. Chelovek turned his head slightly to see if he could glimpse the response of the two black thugs. Emotionless, with their arms folded across their broad chests, they made no move to applaud this ostentatious white bigot.

Colonel Tom cleared his throat and gazed out on the audience of about seventy-five people. It was as he expected. It was a group of mixed races. It just made him uncomfortable to be around these people. He truly did not understand how people of color could mingle with normal people. The differences seemed so profound that if it weren't for the Southern Commonwealth's goal to bring a stable political and social environment to the South he would not show up for these things and have to stomach the degradation. Regardless, here he was trying his best to assert the Commonwealth's vision while simultaneously hating the compromise it would require. The public relations people were good at what they did, but he wished they could leave him out of it. He did, however, understand the power of personality, and if there was one thing he brought to the table, it was showmanship.

"My fellow citizens, thank you for joining me here today in the great city of Atlanta, in the glorious state of Georgia. It is so good to be here in this Special Economic Zone where the Southern Commonwealth is experimenting with the possibilities of racial integration in businesses and residential areas. Let me hasten to remind you we can't make these changes without the efforts of fine upstanding citizens like yourself. Our goal in the Southern Commonwealth is to find a way for our communities to come to a better understanding and tolerance of our differences in order to grow as a nation. Each state has its own approach and Georgia is one of the pioneers on this front. Believe me when I tell you the SEZ we created in Atlanta is the pride of the Commonwealth."

Chelovek raised his hand.

Colonel Tom looked relieved to be freed from this performative nonsense. At least the person raising a hand was white and a man. "Yes, sir. Do you have a question or a comment?"

Chelovek cleared his throat. "Well, Colonel Tom, a bit of each. First the comment. I do believe you are being a tad insincere in your commentary regarding Atlanta being the pride of the Southern Commonwealth. History seems to indicate in the not so distant past, when Atlanta was actively resisting your segregationist policies you said, and I quote, 'Atlanta is nothing more than an island of progressive liberal politics that is an embarrassment to the Southern Commonwealth'. My question, good sir, is what is your true agenda here?"

To Colonel Tom's credit, he was expecting something like this. Without hesitating or hemming and hawing, he responded.

"First of all, thank you for such an insightful question. You have definitely done your homework. I acknowledge that I have made some disparaging remarks in the past, which I now regret. As some great philosopher once said, the only constant is change, and I can testify to that. If we are going to heal those wounds of the past, we need to find our way to a truth that is palatable to all the parties involved. Truth, I have found, lies somewhere in the middle between two points of view. Would you not agree?"

Chelovek had done his job as an instigator and now he sat back to watch the conflagration rage.

The Ghost stood up and, pointing his finger at Colonel Tom, shouted, "What a load of crap! Your precious SEZ is just a stopgap to eventually force the evolution of a segregated society here in Atlanta. On top of that, you don't even mention the fact you reek of patriarchal dominance!"

Obatala's voice boomed, "Right on, brother! Ya'll are just a bunch of power hungry white men trying to control everyone that will let you push your way into their lives. As my white brother Daniel said, I never hear you say anything about women in your proposed Eden. Women are capable of far more than just washing your dishes and clothes."

A tall white woman stood up and yelled, "If you read your Bible, you'd know why men need to be in charge!"

A large black man in a suit and tie bellowed, "But who says they need to be white!"

Marain Jagu walked to the front of crowd. "Give that man a cigar! Power should be in the hands of the majority and the majority of people in the South are black. Whitey has had his day!"

The two black men accompanying Marain suddenly stood up and started pushing chairs over, and the biggest of them said, "I do believe this shindig is *over!*"

The reporter from the Atlanta Sun Journal was absolutely loving this turn of events. She had thought this was going to be another boring political speech and her article would be showing up on the inside pages, buried deep in the paper. Now she could see this confrontation turning into a front page story, above the fold. She quickly scurried over to Marain and Obatala and pulled them aside to get some quotes.

"Obatala, my name is Cyndy Lou Gastoon from the *Atlanta Sun Journal.* I liked what you had to say. Could you elaborate more for our readers regarding where the New Africa Movement stands on some of these issues?"

"Certainly, Cyndy. Colonel Tom was quoting Heraclitus when he said the only constant is change. I would like to challenge that oft quoted truth. I personally believe there are five more constants we need to consider, namely the following: First, life's unfair. Next, people will hurt you. Third, yesterday is gone. Fourth, you are not in control. And finally, you will die someday. Looking at the first four of these truisms, while they may be true, they only become problematic if we are fatalists. Yes, life's unfair. But, there is a spectrum of fairness, and to accept the most patently unfair practices perpetrated by others is to succumb to a power that is mostly derived from a lack of resistance. The second truth is that people will hurt you. But it is also true that people can defend themselves and in so doing, we can reduce the amount of pain we will experience. Thirdly, while it is true that yesterday is gone, the lessons of that past should inform you in your journey. In other words, learn from the past so you don't make the same mistakes. Finally, you are not in control. No matter who you are, be you a political behemoth like the Southern Commonwealth or an everyday citizen, you are never in control. But, and this is a very big but, you do have influence, and by rising up in resistance, you have the power to influence how things unfold and how your life unfolds."

Cyndy smiled and said, "You forgot one. The one about everyone dying."

Obtala laughed. "I'm going to reserve judgment on that until that day arrives."

Cyndy then turned to Marain who stood nearby, nodding his head in agreement with Obtala's final statement. "Mr. Jagu, would you like to express the perspective of your organization, Ebonée."

"Certainly, Cyndy. Thank you for the use of this platform. Obatala, my honorable sister, you and I may disagree on many things, but I can tell you this, I do not disagree with what you just said. I would only add to it from my own perspective. Enough is enough. The Southern Commonwealth threw us a bone in setting Atlanta up as a Special Economic Zone. It was a way of quelling an inevitable uprising of our city's proletariat. It is no secret, I do not have a problem with segregation, but rather I have a problem with who has the power. You are black, so I am sure you can see my point. The power should be in the hands of the dominant population, and here in the South, that dominant population is black. I have said it before, and I will say it now. Turnabout is fair play. The aging white aristocracy needs to be taught a lesson that will help our current captors and jailors understand what it is like to be on the receiving end of a lopsided power struggle."

Mänsklig Chelovek was quite pleased with himself. Mission accomplished. The event had made the news, and now the discord would spread through the more than willing assistance of the media. Seeing Obatala and Marain Jagu being interviewed made his heart rejoice. He quietly rose and left as the raucous din of raised voices escalated and the Southern Commonwealth's security forces tried to restore order. As he walked away, he thought of the one thorn in his side. He really needed to have a face-to-face dialog with Kianna Smythe. He did not realize it, but at that very moment Kianna Smythe was watching him walk back to his hidden headquarters.

CHAPTER SEVENTEEN

"Man is not what he thinks he is, he is what he hides."

—Andre' Malraux

Bubba had put his carpentry skills to good use during the last few days. Based on what Ki surmised from Chelovek's ability to know what was happening in even the most private parts of her office, she had Bubba build what she called the "Black Box." The large structure occupied the middle of a large open space, away from doors and windows. Inside the wooden and drywall construction was an aluminum mesh, which acted as a Faraday Cage, blocking any electronic snooping and also simultaneously offering protection from any EMP's that may be used against her equipment. She put her desk and chair as well as her phone and computer in there. There was also room for several chairs in case she wanted to hold a private meeting safe from prying eyes and ears. It was a very simple but effective sanctuary that she felt confident would foil any type of surveillance. This is where she did research, had conversations, and conducted clandestine operations related to the Chelovek case. For the first time since taking on this case, she felt secure. It was in this Black Box that she was now spying on her nemesis.

Via the Fly on the Wall apparatus, Ki watched Mänsklig Chelovek enter the dead-end alleyway, walk to a graffiti-covered brick wall, and then slowly fade away. There was no door. There was no window. There was absolutely no sign of any place he could have gone. She knew a visit to the site in person was required to determine not only where he disappeared to, but also how he dissolved. Of course, with Chelovek, she should have expected nothing less, but how he pulled it off was truly baffling.

Ki took off the device and loaded in the mapping program that had followed Chelovek, printed a map, and stopped by Bubba's desk.

"Bubba. are you up for a mystery?" she asked, knowing what the response would be. He gave an eager nod.

Collecting her coat and keys, she said. "Grab a jacket and join me."

Bubba jumped up and was right on her heels. As they left the building and made their way to the site, Ki explained to Bubba what she had seen.

"Whoa! That there is a real puzzler."

She recognized the landmarks he had passed when she was tracing his footsteps and everything seemed normal, but when they got to where the dead-end alleyway should have been, it wasn't there. Instead, she found an abandoned warehouse with boarded up windows and doors. Nothing added up. She turned on her heels and headed back to the car.

Her frustration showing, she slowed to let Bubba catch up and said, "Sorry, Bubba. Our friend Chelovek has thrown me for a loop. We need to go back to the office and dig deeper into this conundrum."

Once they got back, they went to her desk in the Black Box, and she put the Fly-On-The-Wall device back on and replayed the recording she had made. Bubba put on the tag-along attachment so he could see what she was seeing. Everything was just as she remembered, but now that she had a frame of reference, she realized something was just a bit off. Still, she couldn't quite put her finger on it. She asked Bubba to try to bring fresh eyes to the scene, and it took them three reviews before Ki saw it. After

Chelovek turned down the alley, his shoelaces were newer when he turned down the alley that did not exist.

Ki smiled in appreciation of her worthy opponent's skills.

"I'm not sure of the specific technology he is using, but basically he has created a holographic projection of himself that implants his image into the surveillance system of Fly-On-The-Wall's software. I doubt if he realized I was following him. This is probably a safeguard against anyone who may stumble onto his headquarters. I would venture that every time he goes out, he wears the same clothes. He just hasn't updated the projection yet."

Bubba grinned. "Well, it's good to know he's not perfect. So, what's the next step?"

"I am going to do some research on that warehouse. If it is not his headquarters, it must be close by. Once I have some more information, we are going to head back there and investigate."

*****

Tax records revealed the current owner of the building, as well as those surrounding it, was an international holding company based in Hong Kong and Yemen. It was called American Novelties and Realty Clearinghouse, Hongkong & Yemen LLC. Ki started to laugh out loud, and Bubba poked his head in to see what garnered such a reaction.

Bubba said, "What is so funny?"

"Bubba, take the name of this company and make an acronym from its name."

He grabbed a pen and copied it down from her screen. A.N.a.R.C.H.Y. LLC.

As Bubba settled down, he commented, "Now that is what I call hiding in plain sight!"

Getting into the actual facility was not going to be a walk in the park. Ki was certain Chelovek's security would be on par with top secret government agencies, and the technology would be top tier and state of the art. According to the "as-built" blueprints in the tax department, the warehouse appeared to be a big empty box. There were three floors for offices above a twenty-foot-high free span area on the ground floor presumably for inventory storage. All the utilities appeared to be inactive and off-line. All the surrounding buildings were income properties leased to corporations that, on paper at least, appeared to be legitimate. It was becoming clear that in order to discover what was actually happening on the premises they would need to break into the facility.

*****

When they got to the building they went to the spot where Chelovek's electronic doppelganger had taken over. There was a door there, but it had several padlocks in place. Also, the posted signs sent dire warnings to any potential trespassers: DANGER! VENOMOUS SNAKES LOOSE ON PROPERTY! FOR YOUR OWN SAFETY, TURN AROUND NOW! ABANDON ALL HOPE, YE WHO ENTERS HERE!

Bubba let out a breath. "Lord have mercy. Those signs are definitely doin' their job. I sure ain't hankerin' to deal with no pizonous creepy crawlers!"

Ki just laughed. "The likelihood of Chelovek actually keeping deadly snakes here is pretty low, but the signs should do the trick to deter any of the local riffraff. Besides, if people ever got in, guaranteed there is nothing there of any street value that would be worth the effort. So, what do you say we pick these locks and get on with our investigation?"

Bubba sucked in his breath. "Okay, Miss Ki. I'm gonna trust you on this, but I don't mind tellin' you I'm as nervous as a long-tailed cat in a room full a rockin' chairs."

Ki made short work of the padlocks and they stepped into the warehouse. Much to her chagrin and Bubba's horror, an enormous copperhead measuring about two feet long slithered past them, and two massive diamond-back rattlesnakes headed their way. Bubba screamed and jumped on top of a pallet near the door. Ki, laughed at her assistant's lack of bravery. She bent down, reaching out to the snakes, and lickity split, the vipers disappeared into thin air. Ki looked up at Bubba and said, "Relax, you are okay. I had a feeling we were in for more illusions. Those pit vipers were authentic looking holographic projections and, to be truthful, that copperhead took my breath away."

Bubba was still looking a little piqued. "How did you know they were fake?"

"Well, several things. First of all, real snakes wouldn't be out in the open like that. They would have felt the vibrations of us coming in, and they would have sought shelter. Generally speaking, snakes are more afraid of you than you are of them."

Bubba was stepping down off the pallet. "I think you are underestimating how scared I am of snakes. If they were more afraid than me, them varmints would have grown virtual wings and flown away!"

As they found their way through the warehouse, it was pretty much what Ki expected. Dust was thick on everything. There were some empty boxes stacked on a couple of pallets. Lights did not work so they had to rely on the Maglite she always carried with her to find their way around. They carefully followed the ramp that took them up to the first floor of offices. All of the cubicle walls had been dismantled and were stacked against some of the interior walls. At least there was some light coming in from the partially painted windows. The bulk of the interior space was a series of closed office doors. They peered through the glass fronts and saw abandoned desks and filing cabinets with drawers pulled out. No signs of office equipment, just dusty, broken-down office furniture.

"Bubba, have you noticed anything off about this place?"

Bubba looked around. "No, not really. It is kind of like I'd of guessed it would be."

"Exactly. We know Chelovek has been through here recently, but it doesn't look like there has been any foot traffic in ages. There is either another entrance we missed or something else is going on."

Bubba looked back and exclaimed, "You're right! In fact, it doesn't look like you and I have been here either! No footprints at all!"

"Good catch, Bubba. I missed that entirely. This could be a holographic projection of dust and dirt."

They continued to explore the premises, covering all three floors. Each was nearly identical to the others. On the third floor up from the ground floor they found a darkened corridor. Bubba volunteered to follow it to the end, and he found what appeared to be an abandoned elevator shaft. But when Bubba leaned forward to shine his light down it, he hit his head on something. Feeling with his hands, he realized it was an elevator door. The three-dimensional holographic projection of a hole was so realistic it had even given him a touch of vertigo.

"Miss Ki, come over here. I think I found something important."

When she got to the elevator, she closed her eyes and turned off the flashlight so she would not be distracted by the illusion. In her mind, she could more easily envision the reality of the scene. As she felt down the wall to the left of where she knew the elevator to be and felt a button on the wall. When she pushed it, the elevator door opened and light spilled into the hallway. Ki shrugged and said, "In for a dime, in for a dollar. Let's see what happens if we get in."

Once they were in, the elevator door closed, and they sat there not moving. On the interior panel were nine buttons, numbered from the top to the bottom—9 through 1. Guessing that they were on the ninth floor since there was nothing above them, Ki pressed 6, which should have taken them down to the warehouse floor. Nothing happened. She pressed the button with the symbol for opening the door. With a certain amount of relief, the elevator door opened. At least they weren't stuck there. Pressing the close elevator door symbol, the doors closed.

"Bubba, I have an idea. But it may be dangerous. If you want to stay behind, I will not hold it against you. I see you brought your gun, so I imagine you are ready to use it if necessary. Is your shoulder going to give you any problems?"

"Oh, I can shoot with either hand, so I'm good. What are you thinking?"

"I am thinking this elevator requires a code of some sort. Chelovek loves doing this sort of thing. If I am right, it could deliver us right into the hands of Mr. Mänsklig Chelovek and his minions. If they've been monitoring this elevator, they know what's going on by now, and they may be waiting for us."

"You know, I've seen a movie picture or two, and if there is an elevator involved, you can pretty much count on the hero . . . or the villain . . . riding on the top of it to get the jump on their adversary. We can get there through that access panel in the ceiling and close it behind us. Let's just hope these guys don't watch as many movies as I do."

Ki nodded.

"What do you think the code is?"

"Since it is Chelovek, I am going to guess it is something near and dear to his heart, so I think it has to be: 2, 6, 2, 7, 2, 4, 9, 1."

"Miss Ki, where on earth did you come up with that number? That sounds complicated to me."

"Using the phone keypad as a guide where 2 is for A, B, & C, those numbers spell out ANARCHY. Then I included the number 1 to designate the floor of the facility. Cross your fingers."

Ki entered the code and, sure enough, the elevator started to descend. They quickly scrambled up into the recessed area and closed it silently behind them. When the elevator came to a halt and the door opened, there was not a sound in response to its arrival.

Ki peeked her head through the opening to scan the surroundings before dropping back down into the lift. Nobody.

She whispered, "Be ready for action at any time, Bubba."

A sign affixed to the wall outside the elevator read MAINTENANCE. That made some sense.

Ki said, "Bubba, if this is the first floor, it would provide access to wiring and piping and other important utility lines feeding into the facility above us. In that case, pressing 2 as the last digit would take us to the main operations area. So, working backward, if 9 was the top floor, access to the false warehouse floor should be 6. Let's give it a try."

Closing the elevator door, they decided to risk staying in the car on their ride up. When it arrived at the destination, the doors opened to a dark corridor. Stepping out, they looked back and, as expected, the holographic projection depicted an empty elevator shaft. They followed the corridor out to the warehouse floor. Once they oriented themselves to where the entry door was, Bubba turned to Ki.

"Miss Ki, we've checked out floors 9, 8, 7, 6, and 1. What do you think is on 2, 3, 4 and 5?"

"Good question Bubba. I have a feeling the second floor is main operations. Based on the actual structure of this building, I am going to guess the fifth floor is probably a parking area that provides a concealed street access. As far as floors three and four are concerned, your guess is as good as mine. Possibly offices, file storage, meeting rooms? Hard to say right now. But I believe we have pressed our luck for the time being. Hopefully we were not detected and can continue our exploration another day. All in all, I believe we have gained some important insights into our felonious friend Mr. Mänsklig Chelovek. One thing I can say with confidence is that he has a much bigger operation than what I had I thought, and is even more dangerous than I assumed.

CHAPTER EIGHTEEN

"It's still magic, even if you know how it's done."

—Terry Pratchett

Ki knew that if she were going to explore Chelovek's lair and not be discovered, she couldn't just slip in and poke around. She would need to surveil his facility to determine how it was being used and when he was least likely to be there. Was it a 24-hour enterprise? Was it a standard 9-to-5, five days a week operation? The problem was she really did not know the extent of his operations or what they were all about, and he was doing an impressive job of concealing his business. Just considering this facility and the neighboring ones, it was clear Chelovek had a vast amount of real estate under his control, and the size of the warehouse seemed disproportionate to what Ki knew of his clandestine activities. Ki thought a clue might lie in the surrounding businesses, so she decided to scour the backgrounds of the tenants abutting the warehouse.

They were all branches and subsidiaries of established national and international corporations. There was a real estate company, a home and office security business, a wireless telephone retail store, a mail-order novelty company selling high-end electronic gizmos and games, a temporary employee services company, a savings and loan bank, an investment brokerage house, and a legal services firm. There didn't seem to be any immediate correlation between them. She took a step back to see if they had anything in common. Then it dawned on her. They all provided access to different types of information. Chelovek was all about data. Depending on how much access he had to these operations, he could be like the spider in the middle of a web with his eight legs tapping into data streams of each strand of that web. Based on her observations so far, Ki's guess was he had very deep access.

Ki called Bubba into the Black Box. "Bubba, I need to get into Chelovek's headquarters, but I cannot risk running into him there. I would like your assistance in luring him away while I sneak in. Since he has eyes and ears on us in nearly every part of this office, I want to set up a meeting for us in a location where he does not have surveillance in order to force him out of his lair. I think an off-site meeting should be enticing enough that he would not trust any of his henchmen to go in his stead. He was successfully drawn to the rally I orchestrated, so I am thinking something that brings together all the major players in a remote and unlikely spot will do the trick. That will keep everyone far enough away from the warehouse without an easy route to return and give me time to explore the facility.

"Make the calls and send confirmation emails outside the Black Box so Chelovek will be privy to them. Reach out to Obatala, the Ghost, Marain, and Colonel Tom, saying the six of us will meet at whatever place you think fits the bill. Instruct them to reschedule any meetings already on their calendars. You need to convey that this is a top priority. Just remember, the location you choose cannot be under any type of electronic surveillance. If you must physically dismantle any cameras and microphones, so be it. Chelovek will need to be there in person. Have you got all that?"

Bubba acknowledged silently with a nod of his head and left the Black Box. About thirty minutes later he returned and said everything was set up.

"Colonel Tom is the only one who had any pushback, but he finally agreed. Here is the location and timing." he said handing her a slip of paper. "I hope that works for you. By the way, just thinkin' ahead . . . what do you want me to say when you don't show up?"

Ki thought about it. "Something along the lines of you heard from me, and I am in route. Say we are extremely close to cracking this whole thing wide open. Also, for Chelovek's prying ears, drop in something about how we may have figured out where he lives and, although he was deeply integrated into the Southern Commonwealth and the political lives entwined here, he is not nearly as dangerous as we originally thought. That will prick his egoic bubble. Give me about forty-five minutes after everyone arrives, then you can pretend to receive a call from me and inform everyone I was unavoidably detained and we have to reschedule. That should give me enough time to learn all I can from exploring the base of operations."

****

Bubba went to the park he had chosen the day before to scope out the grounds. There was one camera that was possibly a problem in that it had a clear view of where the group would be meeting. He was tempted to just shoot it out with his handgun, but he thought better of it and accessed its base to cut the wires. When he opened the maintenance panels for the wiring, he realized that it was a faux camera. It looked like the real thing but was not functional—another way for the city to save money. He wanted to make sure Chelovek could spy on them without being too obvious. A visual line of sight was probably not critical, but Bubba guessed he would use some sort of portable short-range listening device. Once he found an appropriate place, he sat down and relaxed to wait for the fun to start.

After about ten minutes, Bubba identified Chelovek entering the park and taking a seat on a bench some distance from him. He pulled a newspaper out of his briefcase and held it in front of him as though he were reading. After a few minutes he set the newspaper aside and pulled out a laptop and a wi-fi enhancer. He set the enhancer on the bench beside him, tucked earbuds into his ears, opened the laptop, and began typing. If Bubba didn't miss his guess, the enhancer was actually a remote microphone receiver.

The first to appear was Colonel Tom. "Well, hello there, Bubba! How are you son? You're lookin' 'bout as fine as frog hair, I do declare!"

At first, Bubba was a taken aback because this man was not the Colonel Tom he was accustomed to seeing. The costume was off. Colonel Tom was wearing street clothes and no hat or cane. "Colonel Tom! I didn't recognize you! You about gave me a start!"

"Sorry about that son, but I'm tryin' ta keep a low profile. It is amazin' how easy it is to hide in plain sight. Most people only know me from the costume I wear. Makes it easier to blend in. Are you and that negress detective doin' alright?"

"We're doin' well, sir. Makin' some real progress on this case you threw our way. I have to thank you for givin' us a chance, sir."

Colonel Tom slapped Bubba on the back. "It was our pleasure. Your daddy's a good man, son. You deserve a chance to shine. Although, for the life of me, I don't understand how you can work with a negress. The idea of it just gets under my skin."

Bubba looked Colonel Tom in the eye. "Well, Colonel Tom, I guess you and I are different that way. My daddy raised me up to not look at the outside of a person but rather the inside. It takes some time, but people reveal who they are by the way they treat you and talk to you. And Miss Ki? She is a really good person. I have nothin' but good feelin's for her. You ought to give her a chance. After all, you work with Tamba and he's colored."

"Well, Tamba, he just pulled up roots and left me. I liked the man because he knew his place. We both did. But, to be clear, I didn't work *with* him. He worked *for* me. There's a big difference. We weren't exactly sharin' recipes, if you know what I mean."

"But why not, Colonel Tom? Do you really think he's less of a man than you 'cause his skin is darker?"

Colonel Tom frowned. "I'm not sayin' that! Of course, he's a human bein'. We're *all* human bein's. I swear I don't have a prejudice bone in my body! It's just hard to teach an old dog new tricks. We get set in our ways and it's about as easy to change as turnin' the Queen Mary on a dime."

Bubba shook his head. "I am sure you think you are open-minded, Colonel Tom, but that is not how it appears to most people of color. You and I act the way we do out of a force of habit that has formed over our entire lives. It's like trying to stop breathing. Not only is it natural but it feels necessary, and we do it without thinkin'."

Colonel Tom folded his arms and said, "I treated Tamba that way because I was his boss and I expected him to give me my due respect."

Bubba countered, "My daddy works for you, and you don't treat him the same."

It was like it was the first time Colonel Tom had ever considered that perspective and stood there dumbstruck.

Just then, Marain Jagu showed up, but stood there silently not addressing the two men. Not being privy to the conversation that had just ensued, he was more than a little surprised when Colonel Tom approached him and vigorously shook his hand, saying, "Marain! I am so glad you could make it to our gathering."

"This is an unexpected hearty welcome from such a distinguished, powerful, bigoted white man." Smiling, Marain heartily returned the welcome and hugged Colonel Tom. Every muscle in Colonel Tom was as tense as a stretched rubber band. "Please don't take offense. I am a distinguished, powerful, bigoted black man. We are cut from the same piece of cloth, just dyed a different color."

Recovering, Colonel Tom shook his head. "Marain, I seek nothing but peace in the commonwealth."

Marain smiled. "My dear Colonel Tom, in the words of the great Malcolm X, 'You can't separate peace from freedom because no one can be at peace unless he has his freedom.'"

Obatala and The Ghost came into ear shot of the group in time to hear his comments. Obatala said, "Spoken like a blind man. Do you not hear yourself? Half the population of the world is women and yet you speak with the personal pronouns 'he' and 'his'. Am I missing something here? You and Colonel Tom are certainly cut from the same piece of cloth. His culture suppresses women as much as you do."

Bubba stepped into the fray and tried to lower the rising tension. "Miss Obatala, I am sure that Mr. Jagu did not mean any disrespect. We truly can become victims of our culture. They don't always reflect our personal views. Colonel Tom was saying earlier he is open to change, but you can't turn the Queen Mary on a dime. I'm not all that sure who this Queen Mary is but she must be a big ol' gal."

Everyone laughed including the lone figure sitting on the park bench about one hundred yards away.

The Ghost spoke up. "Bubba, I would say Colonel Tom makes a good point, as do Marain and Obatala. However, our individual agendas often keep us at odds and blind us to the truths of other perspectives. For the time being, I recommend we try to maintain a certain decorum while we wait for

Kianna. Can everyone agree to put aside our differences?" Heads nodded all around. "I trust she has some important news to share?"

Bubba looked relieved. "Yep. Miss Ki has made some real progress and wants to share it with ya'll. She is running a little late because of a chore she needed to attend to. She did tell me to let you know she just might have figured out where this Chelovek fellow lives. Not sure what he looks like, but she has a lead for gettin' a photograph."

Everyone agreed that was great news and settled in with idle chit chat. Bubba did not, however, sense the olive branch they accepted would last for long, and he was soon proven right. As he expected it began again between Colonel Tom and Marain Jagu.

Marain was staring at Colonel Tom and finally asked him, "Colonel Tom, I am so glad we have this opportunity to talk. My sister Obatala was, I believe, accurate in describing us as very similar in our perspectives towards women. The main difference is not, however, the color of our skin. I believe it goes much deeper than that. I believe that it lies in power. The Southern Commonwealth is holding, and has held for some time now, a disproportionate amount of that power. I can respect not wanting to concede any of it, but that does not make this right. The abuse of that power is evident to me but not to you. I want you to consider, if the shoe were on the other foot, what would be your response? I think in order to understand our pain, your race would benefit from a shift in the balance of power."

Before Colonel Tom could respond, the Ghost interjected, "Marain and Colonel Tom, I would hazard a guess you are both patriots in your own way. Is that true?"

Both of them nodded their assent.

"Marain, I would offer you something from one of the heroes you quoted earlier. Malcolm X said, 'You're not supposed to be so blind with patriotism you can't face reality. Wrong is wrong, no matter who says it.' The use of power to subjugate another person and deprive him or her of their freedom and human rights is undeniably wrong. It goes back to one of the oldest behavior codes in the world—the Golden Rule: 'Do unto others, as you would have them do unto you.' It can be found in the Bible in Matthew, chapter 7 verse 12. Even in the Lord's prayer we find it said we should be forgiven our trespasses as *we* would forgive those who trespass against us. Now, I believe you both profess to be God-fearing Christian men. The question now becomes, how do you rationalize and justify your positions?"

****

When Ki arrived at the warehouse, she had no trouble entering the space. This time the virtual snakes held no surprise for her, and she went directly to the darkened corridor and the elevator. Once inside, she descended to the second floor with expectations of finding whatever technology Chelovek was using in his campaign of deceit and control. Surprisingly, the place seemed unmanned. Her guess was the outside deterrents to people breaking in had proved so effective Chelovek felt protected without having additional security personnel. She made her way through the virginal white space to a lobby where she saw five pathways that snaked deeper into the facility. Digital displays over each entryway held signs indicating POLITICAL, FINANCIAL, EXTORTION, LEGAL, and UNIVERSITIES. Interesting. She chose the POLITICAL corridor.

Translucent embedded lighting was diffused through the wall surfaces and gave one the illusion of the entire space spreading into infinity. All the surfaces, including the sinuous ebony black corridor floor gently arcing through the space, were spotless and sterile. After several minutes of walking, she came to a hub of some sort where there were eight portals.

Beyond these doors, the floor led to what she assumed were more passages. She had difficulty imagining how all of this was laid out.

All but one of the portals had a red light shining above it. The one portal with a light turned off slid open when she approached it. Lights flickered on as she entered the space. What she saw took her breath away! The walls and floors melded into what appeared to be an infinite space. The expanse was nearly twenty feet wide in front of her with a circular dome about twenty feet high above her head. There was no definition within the space to provide a frame of reference, so the boundless expanse of the illusion was quite convincing. Just at the entry point, hanging on the wall, was a helmet designed to wrap around a person's head that encompassed the entire field of vision. There were also thin gloves with microdots on each of the fingers and thumbs. When she tried them on, the gloves automatically shrunk to fit her hands and were so light she hardly noticed she was wearing them. When she placed the helmet on her head, it too adjusted itself to the size and shape of her head. The earphones embedded in the helmet spoke to her.

"New user detected. Voice recognition setup required. Please repeat after me: 'the quick red fox jumped over the lazy brown dog'."

Obeying the voice, she repeated the statement.

Then it said, "Bio statistics now encoded in the system. State name for user."

Ki stated her name.

"Welcome Kianna Smythe. Where would you like to go?"

She really didn't need to think very hard about this one.

"Kianna Smyth Detective Agency," she commanded, and there she was! Every detail of the office was reproduced in front of her. It was three dimensional and proportional. She could walk through the entire space with the exception of the Black Box Bubba had built for her.

Then she had an idea and said, "Computer, play last recorded observation."

In what could not have been more than a millisecond she could see herself entering the Black Box and then Bubba following soon after. She could not hear a thing until Bubba reemerged and proceeded to contact people about the meeting Kianna wanted to hold. Whoever was recording this went over to Bubba's desk, and the display showed the notes he was taking on his pad and everything on his computer screen. The one good thing was the sound baffle device on the Black Box was functioning. She had thought she was probably being paranoid, but now she knew how deeply Chelovek had penetrated her privacy. A new thought rose in her mind. Knowing what she knew about him, she would need to be extra vigilant in keeping him out of her only privacy stronghold.

She then proceeded to virtually visit NAM headquarters, Ebonée headquarters, and, of course, the Southern Commonwealth. Her apartment, Bubba's apartment, the homes of Obatala and the Ghost, as well as Marain and Colonel Tom were all under Chelovek's watchful eye and ear. It turned out the only places she could not virtually travel were a few outdoor spots under fairly dense tree canopy cover on the grounds surrounding the offices and residences. Well, at least her gut instincts were correct, and it looked like most of what they had said had gone undetected because of her precautions. She had a lot to report to her clients, but now the problem was how to deal with Chelovek and his cohorts once and for all.

When she exited the room, she headed back in the direction from which she had come. No more than ten steps along the ebony path, she heard footsteps coming her way. There were two people having a casual conversation. She saw them before they saw her and noticed they were wearing uniforms. This did not bode well for her. She kept walking and acting in a nonchalant manner as though she had every right to be there. When they caught sight of her, they were clearly on high alert. They came to a stop directly in front of her. They stood firm with no intention of letting her pass.

An extremely tall and well-muscled man with blond hair put his hand up and spoke first. "Who are you and where is your security pass for this section?"

Ki thought about this and decided honesty was the best approach. "My name is Kianna Smythe and I was never issued a security pass."

The massive blonde-headed man turned to his associate and informed him. "Kianna Smythe is a priority one surveillance target for Mr. Chelovek. She has no authorization for entry to this facility."

Turning to Kianna, he said, "Miss Smythe, we will be taking you to a detention cell until Mr. Chelovek returns."

Ki smiled. "Don't be afraid."

With a simultaneously amused and confused expression, he asked, "Why would I be afraid of a tiny thing like you?"

Ki cautioned him. "Because I have no intention of complying with your request."

The shorter and stockier man moved aggressively toward her saying, "Yeah, well, that isn't an option!"

When he lunged at her, she stepped aside and pushed him to the floor just as the taller man was reaching for her. She used his energy and mass to send him into the glowing wall. Both were on the floor when she reached down and pressed two spots on their necks causing them to pass out. Easy peasy. Of course, this meant Chelovek would soon learn of her presence there. He would, no doubt, take extreme measures to lock down the facility, so getting in again was no longer on the table. But she had gotten what she came for. She now had a better understanding of his capabilities and his reach. What his motives and plans were was another matter entirely. That was going to require more personal interaction with Chelovek himself.

Ki had no problem finding her way out of the facility, and as soon as she was on the road back to her office, she called Bubba. "Bubba, how did it go with our clients?"

Bubba chuckled. "Well, Miss Ki, you heard that saying, 'birds of a feather, flock together'? This group ain't nothin' like that. Let's just say the conversation was very entertainin'. It is more like a tiger, a duck, and rattlesnake trying to find something in common. Oh, and by the way, Chelovek did show up. He kept a discreet distance, and I spoon fed him what you wanted me to 'leak' to him. How did it go on your end?"

Ki sighed. "Bubba, you have no idea. Luckily, I only had one encounter with security and, needless to say, that was never any real threat. But, I learned a lot about just how deep Chelovek's operations extend. I must admit, there have been times I worried I was being overly cautious . . . paranoid even. Now I realize I should have been even more careful than I was. Contact our clients and have them come to our office as early as possible tomorrow morning and set up enough seating for everyone in the Black Box. Also, I discovered that our Black Box is the only thing keeping Chelovek in the dark. It is a priority we protect its sanctity."

"Good to know, Miss Ki. See you come the morning."

"Oh, and Bubba, don't do *anything* in your apartment you wouldn't mind having on the front page of the local paper. His surveillance is that good!"

CHAPTER NINETEEN

"There is no greater agony than bearing an untold story inside you."

—Maya Angelou

Before everyone arrived, Ki quickly checked out the Black Box and found nothing awry. However, her inner voice told her she needed to make a more thorough examination. Now that Chelovek knew that she had penetrated his inner sanctum, it only made sense that he would find a way to reveal her secrets by somehow compromising the sanctity of her electronically invisible room. After an exhaustive investigation of the outer and inner surfaces of her Black Box she still found nothing. That did not quell the inner voice. Redoubling her efforts, her search found something so subtle she could understand how she missed it. On the roof of the box she found a dab of black paint no bigger than a millimeter. It was not exactly the same shade of black as the rest of the paint because it was still drying. Using her pen knife she probed the spot, and sure enough there was the head of an ultra-thin wire penetrating her secure room. She debated on whether she should leave it in and use it to pass on false information to Chelovek or if she should just pull it out and send him a clear message of defiance. Considering everything she needed to discuss with her clients, it was too late to create a false narrative, so she opted for dismantling his camouflaged surveillance. She also realized that her own security system must be compromised because there had to have been an intruder in her office, but she never was notified. Something else to examine, but for the moment she had to focus on the gathering now assembling.

Bubba took one look at the group of people crowding into the middle of the Black Box and decided it was the most surreal and unlikely group of people ever to choose to meet with each other. The five of them listened to Ki with rapt attention as she shared with them what she and Bubba had discovered. First, she described the warehouse and the sophisticated holographic projectors concealing the elevator shaft and the virtual venomous reptiles. Then she told them about the descent into the bowels of the facility and the research into the surrounding companies. Finally, when she revealed she had infiltrated the facility while they were meeting in the park, they waited on the edge of their seats for her to tell them what she planned to do about their foe.

"Before we discuss how we move forward on this, I have one last thing to share with you regarding what Chelovek knows about each of you. Before I left his facility, I visited each of your personal residences virtually. Not only could I see every corner of your living space and even hear the creaking floorboards and groaning pipes, but he has full control of all electrical outputs and the electronic devices in your homes. He can turn on your computers and their cameras, answer your phones, shut off your lights, and even change the thermostats. Believe me when I tell you, your lives are not your own."

Marain spoke in a hushed voice, "Well, that must mean he can hear us right now."

Kianna reassured him. "No, he can't. When I viewed the recording that was made of this office and Bubba entered into this secure room,

I could hear nothing. I am calling this space a Black Box. It is a giant Faraday Cage, which keeps out electronic signals and also protects my equipment from electro-magnetic pulses. In addition, there is a sound baffle installed to dampen any vibrations from the walls. So, what initially felt like paranoia to have Bubba build it actually paid off."

Obatala spoke up. "How on earth is Chelovek doing this?"

Kianna smiled. "Great question, and it is one I have been pondering since we started this investigation. The computer hacking was easy enough to thwart, but his being in a position to literally look over your shoulder while you are typing your password, makes it moot. When I did a search on what commonalities your operations shared, one of the things that popped up was your security company. I dismissed this initially because it is ubiquitous. Probably 90 percent of businesses and homes use them. My best guess is that, when they installed the systems, they put in 'extra' security in the form of microdot lenses and sensitive acoustic systems, as well as links to your devices. After extensive investigations, I discovered he is a silent partner behind that security company and one of his tenants near the warehouse is the second largest security company in the region. He is using them to supplement what he already has in place. That company is probably leaking data to Chelovek like a sieve leaks water."

Colonel Tom shook his head. "So, you're tellin' me this Chelovek fella has seen everything I've been doin' in my house?"

Kianna nodded somberly. "That does not mean he is always watching you personally. But he probably has technicians who are assigned to you, and they observe your daily activities. Plus, he can record events as well. Do you now understand how he is able to extort people so easily? That said, I am sure he reserves extortion only for special projects. I think in each of your cases he was just beginning to launch his campaign to manipulate your operations. I would say we caught it just in the nick of time. It does not mean, however, you all are out of the woods quite yet. He can still very effectively disrupt your plans to his advantage. He still has his tentacles reaching into our lives, but I am forming a plan to extricate him fully and also shut down his entire international operation."

Marain shifted in his seat. "Well, Miss Ki, I am sure I am speaking for the rest of us in saying thank you for the extraordinary diligence, perceptivity, and investigative skills you have brought to bear." Everyone gave her a small round of applause. "But the question now is, what are we going to do about it? It seems to me the scope of his operations is massive. In some ways, he may see us the way a picnicker sees a few ants. We are like a minor pest he can ignore or easily eliminate."

Ki understood his concern, and began trying to assuage their fears. "Marain, you have cut to the chase. We need to act, and act soon. Make no bones about it. As I said, if we play our cards right, we can bring his whole international operation down around him. I want to go over my thoughts with you and then get your feedback on whether it sounds feasible. Before describing the plans, however, there is one critical thing you all need to remember. We must all work together. Considering the fact there are tensions and conflicts—underlying as well as those on the surface—between you all, is that something you think you can do?"

Everyone nodded their heads, but some more tentatively than others.

"The reason I ask this is simple. I am aware that because you come from very different backgrounds, you may find it difficult to trust each other. There is a saying I heard a long time ago I will share with you. 'Your enemy is someone whose story you have yet to hear.' We cannot afford to have any enemies amongst us, so I want each of you to share your story of who you are. What is it that has formed your life and helped to create you? This is important. Do not take it lightly. I want us to start right now. Daniel, would you please go first?"

Daniel sighed. "I normally don't talk about my past because I am not seeking sympathy, but I do think understanding is essential here. I am fully on board with what Ki is saying. Stories are important, and I think this is a way to that understanding. If you were to walk a mile in my shoes, you may find your perspective on the world shifts. As some of you know, I pass for white because of my skin color, but I am black on the inside. Physically it is true. I am white. I am of Caucasian ancestry, but how I present to the world is not how I feel inside. Being the adopted child of a black family, I admit my perspective may differ significantly from most of you. Of course, the possible exception may be Obatala with her being raised by a white family.

"I find myself being treated in society as though I am white. My white skin grants me access to a number of opportunities the Southern Commonwealth's social matrix prohibits for people with black skin. There was one time I applied for a job inside the SEZ of Atlanta where integration is allowed. I filled out some paperwork and mailed it in. Subsequently, I was asked in for an interview. A friend of mine who was black applied for the same job, except he was far more qualified than I was. His name 'sounded' black and the requested photograph he sent got him a rejection letter stating the position was already filled. That was not true. I know this because they were still interviewing candidates. When I showed up for my second interview, there was not a single black face in the thirty or so candidates waiting their turn. Integration may be 'allowed' in the SEZ, but it is definitely not practiced.

"In my youth, there was an incident that bothered me on a very deep level. When I was twelve years old, I was staying with a white friend's grandparents in Sarasota, Florida. We were in the car driving to their friend's house to go swimming in their pool. There was a large muscular black man on the curb waiting for our car to pass before he crossed the road. As soon as the car passed, he started to cross the road. My friend's grandfather slammed on his brakes and backed up the car. He rolled down his window, and in an angry voice said, 'Get back on the curb nigger!' This black man was very polite and respectful and said, 'Sorry, sir. I forgot my place, sir.' He did as he was told, and as the car drove away, my friend's grandfather said, 'Goddamn niggers think they own the world.' I can't begin to understand why there isn't a race war when people can be treated this way simply because their skin is a different color. If the situation were to be reversed, I can only imagine the bloodshed. It is one reason Obatala and I formed the egalitarian movement of NAM. That is a small part of this black cracker's story."

Obatala raised her hand. "I can go next. As a black female raised by white parents, I saw distinct differences between my home life, my school life, and my life 'at large' in the community. At home I was raised with very little reference to the color of my skin. Of course, I noticed the difference, but I was told by my parents the color of my skin, while it was darker, was no different than having different color hair. They said people can have blond, brown, black, white, red, or gray hair, and that was just the color of their hair. They lied to me when they said the color of someone's skin was just like that. They believed and embodied that philosophy, and while it is an ideal to aspire to, I learned the hard way the world does not agree. They emphasized to me that underneath the skin I was just the same as everybody else.

"I was in for a rude awakening when I went to school. I attended an integrated school here in the Atlanta SEZ, so there were white and black children in classes together, but I was the only black child with white parents. Classmates would call me an Oreo, like the cookie. Black on the outside and white on the inside. I ended up being ostracized by most of the black as well as white students in my school, and they segregated themselves by race. My friends were mostly mixed-race children, though there were a couple of black kids and a white kid that were more open-minded and welcoming. I couldn't help but notice my teachers engaged in the same divisive practices. Cultural clustering appears to be part of how today's societies behave.

"In the larger world I quickly discovered that having black skin meant you were treated differently in white-owned stores and facilities. I was constantly watched and monitored by salesclerks and security guards. Sometimes I would sit in a chair outside a store at the mall and observe how differently white and black customers were treated. Can you imagine what it is like to constantly live in this judgment? How would you feel to be treated as though you were some sort of low-life criminal and to realize that *everyone* whose skin was dark was considered unwanted and untrusted? Most white people have no clue about how their black brothers and sisters are treated every single day. People buy into a myth that has been perpetrated on an entire people. It makes me cry to see such blatant behavior." After wiping away tears, Obatala continued. "The creation of NAM was my response to so much of my experience. If you ever want to know if Daniel and I are promoting a pipe dream, I challenge you to spend some time at our organization's headquarters. Like any group of people we have our occasional differences, but those differences are due to poor inter-human relationships and is divorced of any blame being put onto another person's skin color."

Bubba spoke up. "Listenin' to you two, I never realized just how blind I've been. My life has been pretty good, and all them black and white problems you were mentionin' were things I would read about and dismiss because it wasn't part of my world. I was too focused on my day to day livin' to notice. That stuff never affected me. My school was segregated both race-wise and also sex-wise. And not only were all the students white and male, the teachers were too. That was our world. We got our social cues from television and movies. Like most people, even the movies I watched were pretty much the same as the life I was leadin'. My savin' grace is I was fortunate enough to be reared by a man who taught me important lessons on how to respect women and that I should treat all people regardless of color in a way I would want to be treated. That there's a good tool. Not everybody treated me right, and sometimes it pained me to do so, but I would try to give them the benefit of the doubt. As far as segregation goes, that was just how things were and I never really thought about it much because it didn't usually affect me directly. Recently, however, Miss Ki and I were heading back from the Southern Commonwealth's national headquarters and we stopped at a restaurant. It was in a black county and, as such, it was segregated by a county mandate. Being white, I couldn't be served. Miss Ki ordered a couple of to-go boxes while I waited in the car. It made me understand what it was like to be excluded because I was white.

"I do remember one time my buddies and I were out cattin' around and there were these black teenagers about our age. I said maybe we could invite them to hang out with us and one of my friends said, 'I ain't no nigger lover. They got their place and I got mine. That's the way it is and that's the way it's always gonna be.' We didn't mess with 'em, but neither did we go out of our way to make them feel welcome. If anything, it was just the opposite. I still feel bad I didn't treat them kindly. I have to say, hearin' these stories so far is lettin' me feel the guilt of my ignorance. I know it ain't goin' to change nuthin', but I am sorry."

Marain Jagu raised his hand. "I would like to go next. Kianna, I must start by saying I think this is a very good exercise and it is very clarifying. My situation is different from everyone here, but then again, that seems to be the unfolding theme. I grew up in a segregated black community and attended Percy Julian High School. Reluctantly, I have to give a nod and a thank you to Colonel Tom for his government's establishment of segregated communities. When the Southern Commonwealth established this modified apartheid, they 'allowed' these communities to establish their own businesses and banking, and most important, their own educational systems. By being independent, blacks were able to create an identity outside of the systemic racism that was rampant among privileged white men. They were no longer reliant on an identity that suppressed them within their own community. They never felt they were lesser than anyone else. Our black brothers and sisters also received a far better education than we had ever had in our long history in this country. Knowledge is power and the segregated black population residing in the South are probably the best educated people in all of the Americas.

"The Southern Commonwealth has many troubling social issues—what I would certainly deem serious problems—but the ones that have impacted me the most are not the overt racist paradigms. I get that. I am a racist myself, but I have become such as a response to the way I am treated in mixed society. In the black community, I feel very comfortable. The greatest pain I felt was when I was working in the service industry of the white communities. Granted there are better paying jobs in that sector, but there is a cost to working there, and it is high. I was treated as less than human. As far as the white community was concerned, I served a function, but it was like I was invisible. When I was addressed, it was to demand a service. I may as well have been a machine. It bred in me an overwhelming desire to educate these people. I wanted, and still want, to teach them what it is like to be on the receiving end of such treatment. I know intellectually they are merely exhibiting a certain momentum of behavior. It's how it is and it's how it's been, and of course, unless something changes, it is how it will be. However, in my heart of hearts I know to be shunned and ignored is not how people should be treated. I want to scream at the top of my lungs, 'LOOK AT ME! ACKNOWLEDGE ME!' I am just so angry." Marain stopped abruptly and sighed heavily before continuing. "Well, as Bubba might say, 'Stick a fork in me; I'm done!' Oh, and Bubba, as an aside . . . I don't mean you any disrespect. I really like you and you treat me with respect. Thank you."

Bubba smiled. "No disrespect taken, sir. And I like you too."

Colonel Tom was fidgeting in his seat and all eyes were on him. "Well, it seems I have moved from the catbird seat to the hot seat. That's my way of sayin', I guess it's my turn. First, I want to state what I believe to be the obvious. I am not who I appear to be. As the head of the Southern Commonwealth, I am the persona that represents their philosophy—the face of the organization. In reality, I am merely a caricature modeled after a cross between Colonel Sanders and Mark Twain—though a younger and slightly more handsome version." Colonel Tom flashed a quick smile. "The truth is I am not a Colonel, never was a Colonel, and never intend on bein' one. In fact, I have never served in the military or even been to a military base. In other words, for the purposes of this confab/parlay, I am going to drop the whole persona thing. You are going to get the whole, unvarnished, raw version of who I am and what I personally believe. This doesn't happen often, and if anyone were to blab what I am going to say, I would adamantly and vociferously deny it. That bein' said, here we go.

"I grew up in Mobile, Alabama, makin' mud pies with my little sister and fishin' in the swamp. My family wasn't well off, but we did scratch out a livin' best we could. We lived in a segregated white county, and I attended all-white schools, but boys and girls were mixed. We learned enough to get by in our readin', writin', and figurin'. But we also had lessons in manners and the Bible. In our manners class we learned about treating girls and colored folks with respect. I found out none too soon that what we're supposed to do was not what most people actually do most of the time.

"But anyways, the only colored folk I had to deal with was mostly people waitin' on me in restaurants or plumbers and other service people like yard maintenance. I never socialized with the colored. It just wasn't done. And to be honest, I was always very nervous around the colored, and please don't take this as an offense, but I still am. I guess we fear what we don't know. People would talk about how it was just in a negra's blood to be dishonest, and you had to be careful around 'em. I couldn't even imagine bein' friends with one. It makes me nervous inside to even think about it. I wouldn't know what to say cause they speak almost a whole different language when they're talkin' amongst themselves. Besides, I had an uncle on my Daddy's side of the family that was beat up by a couple a Negras. Thinkin' back on it, I couldn't exactly say that he didn't deserve it. I don't even think of myself as bein' particularly racist, but after hearing you just now, I may need to reassess that perspective.

"Hearin' your stories here today has opened my eyes and ears a whole lot more. My head kinda feels like its goin' to explode. I definitely feel a lot closer to you all, so I think Miss Ki's suggestion was worthwhile. But I am also not sayin' I have suddenly become a liberal, progressive integrationist. In fact, it ain't likely I will change much. Regardless, it is gonna take some time really thinkin' about what you've all said. And I will add this. My respect for all of you personally has gone up a great deal."

Ki said, "Well, thank you all for your honesty. I know this can be a difficult and traumatic experience, but I believe it was necessary for us to bond and act as team when we need to and believe me, we will need to. Again, thank you. Now it is my turn. Some of this will be old news to a couple of people here, but not all of it.

"Let me go back to my very beginning. I am the product of rape. My mother was assaulted by a white man thirty-six years ago. She is a black woman who, at the time, worked in the healthcare field as an RN. The primary thing she remembers about him to this day is that he was so arrogant and self-focused. He felt if he wanted something, he had the absolute right to fulfill his desires, regardless of his impact on others. He did nothing to hide himself other than to fall off the radar. She reported the rape and gave a description of the man to the authorities, but they never seemed to follow up on the case. This was fairly common in those days when the Southern Commonwealth was becoming established. White men thought they could act with impunity and often did.

"My mother never tried to hide any of it from me. In fact, one of the reasons I am a private eye is because there still burns in me the desire to find and meet my father. Regardless of what he did and his cavalier attitude, he is a part of my roots. I believe we need to connect with our past because it informs our present and can influence our future.

"In school, I had a similar experience to Marain. I had an excellent education, but I bore the skin color of a mixed-race person. I learned that if there is someone in your group who is different, many children feel a need to degrade and humiliate that person or persons. I believe that insecurity drives a lot of bullying. You can be higher than everyone else in two ways. One is by being the better person. The other, less honorable way, is to lower everyone around you so that, by comparison, you are superior . . . at least as far as your ego is concerned.

"My philosophy was still forming, but I began to understand that the things that defined *what* you were, did not define *who* you were. Your character and morals counted for more than the color of your skin. Fortunately, my mother was there to guide me and advise me. She also instilled in me the idea that I should know how to protect myself, so she let me take Aikido lessons. Aikido really appealed to me because it is not based on attacking so much as redirecting your enemy's energy. Before long, word got around that you should not mess with Kianna Smythe.

"The other important attribute I received from my mother was my heightened sense of awareness. Once you learn to focus and observe, it is incredible what is right in front of you. The world tends to be filled with people who are paying more attention to their egos and thoughts than they are to what is happening around them. It is very helpful when you are investigating crimes and such."

A hush fell over the group as the impact of each of their stories hit home. Walls had started to crumble and bridges of empathy were starting to form. Ki knew the true test of these newly formed bonds would be severely tested in the next couple of days. If they could provide a unified front, there was an excellent chance of success.

CHAPTER TWENTY

"In preparing for battle I have always found that plans are useless, but planning is indispensable."

—Dwight D. Eisenhower

After the meeting, Ki gave Bubba a large note with block letters that said in plain-as-day language,

Human Human,

Meet me for a Go game at the go parlor tomorrow at 10:00 a.m. We need to talk.

Kianna Smythe

Bubba read the note and said, "Are you sure this is going to work?"

Ki nodded. "No question about it. I am certain the fact that I broke into his facility has driven him crazy, and he knows he has lost his leverage and advantage due to my informing the three major political parties of his capabilities. He, no doubt is desperate to communicate with me. He *will* be there. As soon as you walk out of this Black Box, you will be back on his radar. And yes, he would get the message just as clearly were you to flip him the bird, as I sense you would rather do. However, we need to take the high road."

Bubba laughed. "Miss Ki, you do know me. Probably better than I know myself."

Bubba took the note and placed it on the open desk in the office. He smiled into the thin air and did a slight bow. He thought, *That'll get his attention.*

****

The next day at the Go Parlor, Ki entered at exactly 10:00 a.m. and, as she expected, Mänsklig Chelovek was sitting in the foyer, smiling from ear to ear. There was a quiet confidence about this man that in someone else may have come off as arrogant or off-putting, but on him it felt authentic.

"I cannot begin to tell you how happy I am you decided to meet with me, Miss Smythe. I can tell by your note you have deciphered my name, so I must presume you have some idea about what I am up to."

Ki smiled and made a polite bow, much the same as Bubba would have done. She sat down next to him and said, "I'm not sure how I should address you, but I think we can dispense with the formalities, so how about Mänsklig?"

He replied, "Yes, my dear. Mänsklig suits me fine for the time being. Now, should I refer to you as Miss Ki as Bubba does? Or would you prefer some other moniker?"

"At this point we do not know each other well enough, nor have you earned the privilege of being that familiar with me. Kianna is what I prefer. I wanted to have this meeting for us to get to know each other better. You have me at a disadvantage. You have a great deal of data about me, though I caution you, that will only inform you to a degree. People are so much more than statistics. However, I have yet to compile even a cursory profile on you as you have quite successfully scrubbed the internet of any personal information. You appear to be a non-entity."

Chelovek smiled. "You are quite correct, Kianna. It was one of the first actions I took in setting up my operations. As you have already surmised, data is my stock and trade. Think of me as an information broker. Intimate private and personal data can be particularly lucrative. It seems very, very few people are without some secret they need to keep from other's eyes. In addition, people are willing to spend enormous sums of money for information they would like to discover." Chelovek paused and look intently at Kianna, "Take yourself, for instance. Wouldn't you like to know who the man was that raped your mother. I heard you say as much not that long ago."

Kianna was shaken to her core but managed to conceal that and deny him the satisfaction of eliciting a reaction from her. She would not allow herself any weakness in front of this vile predator. As she smiled coolly, her mind raced with questions. *How did he know this about the rape of her mother? Had he compromised the security of her secure room? What was he trying to accomplish? Was she just second guessing herself?* She wasn't sure what to say next. Luckily, Chelovek let her off the hook.

"When you were talking about segregation with Marain Jagu in his office you opened up to him. You see, Kianna, I have much more than mere data on you."

Ki breathed a silent prayer of relief. "You have me there. However, I am still at a loss when it comes to who you are. Perhaps we could play a game of Go, and you can level the playing field just a bit by telling me something about you. Does that sound fair?"

"Absolutely. A game of Go would be a luxury for me."

"And I will make a deal with you. I will answer one question for each timed round where you best me. A quid pro quo, if you will."

With a slight deferential bow of his head, Chelovek said, "I accept your terms. Let's play."

The host of the Go parlor set them up in a private room with a view of a *tsuboniwa*, a small Japanese garden. The warbling song of a Carolina wren and the trickling rhythmic splashing of water falling from the bamboo spigot into the washbasin created a tranquil atmosphere.

Chelovek's opening moves were not unexpected. His forays into her territory paralleled what he was doing with his surveillance strategies. It was also obvious to her that he was not holding back as he had in their previous game. She only won by one space, but she did win.

"Alright, Mänsklig. Time to settle up. What is your real name?"

Chelovek beamed a smile. "There are very few people that know what I am about to reveal to you. Ever since you came to my attention, I have been anxious to connect with you. I admire you in many ways. I consider you a worthy opponent. So, here goes.

"My real name, Frank Brown, has mostly faded from my memory. I can barely remember the person I was in those days. I was so young. I was so angry. I was searching for my identity, and I sought refuge and comfort wherever I could find it. Over thirty years have passed since those days of innocence and frustration. I can see the gleam in your eye, and I will save you a lot of time. Knowing my real name will not help you learn any more about me. You will need to keep winning our games."

The next game of Go found Kianna leaning in to Chelovek's style and handily beating him by five spaces. For the first time, she saw the faintest look of concern in his face. But he proved true to his word and after bowing to her, said, "Congratulations, Kianna. Next question, please."

"What was your childhood like?"

Chelovek look puzzled. "I am not sure I understand why that would be of any strategic importance to you, but fine. They are your rules. Let me start at the beginning. I was an orphan, and I was given up for adoption in the year 2060 by a mother who was abused and raped by a husband filled with a burning rage that he could never sate. It was not until many years later that I discovered her act of putting me up for adoption was an act of kindness, not abandonment. My mother's sacrifice spared me a home environment that would have been fraught with conflict and struggle. But as I said, I did not really know any of that until much later in life. I only knew what I felt, and I felt abandoned. Unwanted and unloved. I was consumed by an emptiness that defied description. The years crept by without solace. I would make friends in the orphanage, and then they would be adopted or placed in a foster home, which left me alone once again. I thought I was fated to always be left in the wings. Unfulfilled. Enough of this memory lane. Let's play another round."

Ki was taken aback by the candidness of his disclosure, and even more, she was overwhelmed by the aggressiveness of Chelovek's opening play. He did not intend to lose again. But Ki knew that the best defense for this type of strategy was a good offense. It is hard to attack when you are busy defending yourself. It was what Chelovek was trying to do to her, but she refused to take the bait, and sacrificed some territory in order to best him. In the end, the game was a draw.

"Well, Mänsklig, I was impressed by your play. I seriously felt challenged for a while there. Good job. But with a draw, it takes us to another round, and I will not be so lenient this time."

Chelovek was not nearly as loquacious as he had been at the beginning of their first encounter. He just smiled, nodded his head, and cleared the board. Ki was on attack from the very beginning this time and, although her opponent was wily and clearly an excellent player, she won the next round by two spaces. She could tell that Chelovek did not like to lose; however, he was, at the very least, a gracious loser and bowed to her again in his defeat.

"Next question?"

"I would like to know more about your mother."

A quiet descended over Chelovek, and for a moment his eyes took on a faraway look. He said with a soft voice, "I find I become emotional when speaking about my mother. Let me collect myself." After a couple of minutes, he came back from whatever private place he retreated to. "All right. I am ready."

He looked directly at Kianna, engaging her fully as he began. "After I was released from the orphanage, I researched the scant records on file regarding my birth mother. I was determined to hunt her down and confront her with those choices she had made, and I wanted to somehow hold her accountable. I fully intended to unload my anger, pain, and resentment on her. Oh, how I anticipated the sweet taste of righteous indignation and a final retribution. Although I had a deep and palpable yearning for love, that love was always unrequited. You cannot fill a bottomless hole, but the burning need to be recognized and honored felt infinite as well.

"When I was finally discharged from the orphanage on my 18th birthday, beyond all odds I found her on my first try. But it turned out to be a bittersweet homecoming. She was still alive, but barely. She was in the last throes of stage four ovarian cancer. Her illness was a final slap in the face for an arduous existence. She had been taken in by a volunteer hospice center for the homeless and was dying from her cancer. She was unresponsive to my presence. The palliative care she was receiving kept her out of pain, but also made her blissfully unaware of the real world. I was denied a final audience with my creator. What closure I finally received I learned from a volunteer who had become close to her. He said she deeply regretted and yet celebrated her choice to put me in the orphanage. It had pained her deeply to lose a part of who she was, but she could not bear to expose her child to the life of misery and abuse that seemed to be her lot in life. Her entire life had been a constant series of disappointments. The safety net that society had woven to catch the downtrodden was full of many gaping holes, and my mother had somehow managed to slip through most of them. This was the beginning of my hate affair with the state. It is said the road to hell is paved with good intentions, and it is a wide and well-paved road indeed that is laid by politicians and government officials."

At this point, Chelovek went quiet again. Ki could see his self-control in holding back the memories of that time and the anger that was residing just below the surface. He gathered himself and said, "I am ready for the next round. You are a formidable opponent. But to see how good you really are, I want the next game to be rapid timed. Three seconds per move."

Ki paused but then nodded her head.

Without time to analyze and plan the game, it went by much quicker. Chelovek and Ki both had to really think on their feet. At the end of the game, although it was close, Chelovek was the victor. He smiled a broad and satisfied smile. "Finally! Now, my question to you is something that has had me puzzled ever since you started this skirmish between us. The only thing your clients have in common is my intrusion into their affairs. I personally find all three political groups despicable. How can you reconcile these disparate parties without throwing up your hands in frustration? To me they are like squabbling youngsters."

Without any time for reflection, Ki responded. "Mänsklig, I do what I do because I am excited by the challenge of solving a puzzle and you are, by far, the most challenging puzzle I have come across in my life. You are the glue that drew these groups together. I concur they have disparate philosophies and paradigms, but what they have in common is their humanity. Imperfect, yes, but they are each well-intentioned regardless of their different filters. If I expect everyone to see the world the way that I do, I will be living in a state of constant disappointment. Let's play two more games, and I think the last one was one of the most exciting I have ever played, so let us amp it up a notch. This time why not do it at a quicker pace. Two seconds between moves. Ready?"

Once the board was cleared, the sharp clicking of stones on wood was akin to a dueling pizzicato symphony between ebony and ivory. The resulting tableau was a beautiful freeform Rorschach Test with Kianna taking another win by a single space. She expected him to respond in some negative fashion, but, surprisingly, he seemed quite sedate. Ultimately, this was a part of his enigma. Based on what she had observed about him, this seemed out of character for his narcissistic personality. It made her suspect he had some other card up his sleeve that he had yet to play. "My question to you this time is a follow-up on the actions you take in support of your political views. Why do you support anarchism?"

"Thank you, Kianna. Finally, a question I feel comfortable answering. Philosophically speaking, I consider myself an existentialist. As you probably already know, there are three defining attributes that describe an existentialist: belief in the rights of the individual, a passionate approach to life, and that all meaning is derived from context. After I learned about existentialism, I felt as though I had found meaning to my existence, and I could finally accept myself. The beauty of being an existentialist is that one can hold a broad spectrum of beliefs simultaneously. There are atheistic existentialists such as Nietzsche. There are theistic existentialists such as Kierkegaard. Truly a broad range of paradigms, from Sartre to Heidegger and Arendt to Camus. Once I understood this, I felt like a whole person. Not that it eliminated or even resolved my conflicts, but at least now I have a focus to my life. I have a purpose.

"As I matured, my political paradigm shifted and evolved. At first, my response to politics was one of apathy. True, I resented politicians, but I felt I had no control over them. I saw them as essentially vile creatures with personal agendas that only superficially addressed the needs of their constituents. Everything seemed to pass a filter of their self-interests. When I researched the matter more deeply, however, I was intrigued by the development of the United States and the writing of the US Constitution. I saw it as a metaphor for my life—at best, I was treated in a cavalier manner; at worst, I felt abandoned, isolated, and oppressed, struggling to be free. The words in the Constitution took on a new meaning for me and they seemed relevant. So, I went down the road of becoming a constitutional originalist. In time, however, I saw that approach didn't really fulfill my own personal needs, and I recognized the Constitution kept certain people in control while not extending its ideals to other groups of people. So I settled into defining myself as a libertarian or, more specifically, a social libertarian that allowed people more self-regulation. Initially I was content, but my life was still being ruled by elected officials who were only interested in maintaining the status quo. Grift and self-interest were rampant, and I knew I wanted to effect real change.

That is when I finally settled on my current position embracing the modern definition of anarchism. I had eventually come to reject the whole idea of the state taking care of the people in society and embraced the idea that collectively, independent people would form rules and governance that grew organically in their own communities. I want to be an advocate for humanity. I changed my name from Frank Brown to Mänsklig Chelovek. This better reflected how I saw myself. I was a human being. Period. Titles and political offices simply became the trappings of different social paradigms. I became an island of freedom in a vast ocean of sycophants suckling at the teat of the state. I wanted to free my fellow humans from that ignorant subservience. I wanted to wake them up to the possibility of freedom if only they would open their eyes and ears. To do that, I needed to shake up their cozy little world.

"This new man, this Mänsklig Chelovek was a true anarchist. People, in their blissful corporate media-ruled ignorance tend to define anarchists as radicals who want to sew purposeless chaos and disruption through random acts of violence. Bombings, riots, and other such terrorist activities were incorrectly thought to be anarchist calling cards. Is such activity anarchy? Absolutely. It creates chaos. But, does that cause meaningful change? Of course, but it is like using a screwdriver as a scalpel for a delicate operation. Left to their own devices, I know that political factions would simply disintegrate over time. The state is in a constant process of evolving and my primary aim is to not wait for that inevitable evolution, but to guide it. I have settled on a surefire way of choosing the method of its ultimate demise."

Ki sat with rapt attention through Chelovek's revelation. There was a lot to digest and, to be honest, she wasn't sure how to process it quite yet. "Thank you for sharing Mänsklig. I would love to discuss it more, maybe at another meeting?"

"Certainly."

The final game unfolded like a river flowing through a verdant valley. It followed the normal course of the streambed and responded to the obstacles placed in its way. As dams were created and the flow diverted, each player responded with strategies that met their overall plan from the beginning. It was all natural and, although each player created challenges, each player also responded eloquently in kind. When all was said and done and the liberties and conquests were counted, the game was a draw.

Ki and Chelovek cordially bowed to each other. Ki spoke first. "Well played, Mänsklig. Your moves were subtle and effective. I can also see you held nothing back in this game. Perhaps I should have told you upfront that I had won the Ing Cup in Japan ten years ago. Sorry about that."

Chelovek laughed. "You definitely surprised me with your skill. I too am embarrassed. I probably should have told you I won the LG Cup six years ago. Well, regardless, I suspect we should soon meet somewhere neutral and confess both our deepest secrets to each other. Did you have a particular place in mind?"

"No, I do not, but I will get back to you. I really need to give it some thought. I do not want to be in any place you have under surveillance. You can understand that, I am sure."

"Certainly. Why don't you just leave a note on your desk outside of that damnable Black Box of yours. Touché on that contraption by the way. You were the first in the world to ever thwart my surveillance. Of course, you can count on me to gain entry in some way."

They each bowed deeply and went their separate ways.

CHAPTER TWENTY-ONE

"Change happens by listening and then starting a dialogue with the people who are doing something you don't believe is right."

—Jane Goodall

It took some thinking, but finally Ki figured out the best place to meet with Chelovek. She didn't want to tell him ahead of time because, if he knew even a little in advance, he could set up surveillance. She wanted this meeting to be on her terms as much as possible. At 7:00 a.m. on Thursday morning she wrote on a sheet of paper in large block letters the clues she knew would intrigue and challenge him. It was disconcerting, knowing someone was watching her every move as she laid the paper on Bubba's desk.

Jupiter∑3:4285185(1492)2784(bigO)262NWX31212PM

It was pretty simple, but it was also fun for her. She couldn't help but be a little excited to see what he thought of it. She saw him as her intellectual equal and, as much as she loathed his behaviors, she did have respect for his mind and his craft. Less than an hour after exposing the note to Chelovek, she set out for the destination and had no traffic difficulties. She pulled into the intersection she had designated shortly before noon. She parked the car on the side of the road, and six minutes later Chelovek pulled up. He got out of the car, ambled up to Ki's side window, and tapped on it lightly, whereupon she rolled it down. He bent down and smiled. "Sorry I'm a minute late. I guess the stop lights in Bainbridge threw me off."

"Hop in the front seat and join me. Did you like my puzzle?"

Once he was seated, he said, "Yes, I did. You gave me quite a challenge initially, but I unraveled it after a few minutes . . . obviously. Jupiter was a bit of an obfuscation until I remembered that Thor was the Norse version of that Roman God, which told me we were meeting on Thursday. The rest of it was about route numbers and travel time. Now the 'bigO' threw me off until I consulted the map. I got a chuckle out of that one. Fun. Kianna, my dear, you do entertain me."

"Yes, it was fun. Now, sit back and relax, and I will take us to our destination."

Chelovek laughed. "Kianna, I would not normally be inclined to go to an undisclosed location with just anyone, but you have so captured my attention and piqued my curiosity that I simply can't resist. And, by the way, smart play there in having us connect away from our actual meeting spot. It's clear you have discovered my eye-in-the-sky toys."

"I'm just covering my bases. The motto of the wise is, 'be prepared for surprises'."

"Well, Kianna, you can never be too careful. Especially with someone like myself." He smiled.

****

The hike to the cave entrance was not particularly strenuous, but the elevation change was enough to wind both of them. When they finally arrived, Chelovek sat on a rock overlooking the cliffs and countryside and said, "I just want to take a breather before we go on, if that's okay."

Ki wiped some sweat from her brow. "Sounds good to me."

With the skill of an adept magician, Chelovek slipped a tiny, two-centimeter black plastic cube out of his jacket pocket and pressed the adhesive surface to the rock where he was sitting. He positioned it in a manner where one end was pointing toward the cave and the other was pointing up to the sky. He took off his glasses and cleaned them with a cloth before putting them back on. Then he stood up and said, "Let's get this show on the road."

Letting Chelovek think he was getting away with his subterfuge, Kianna stretched and said, "Follow me, Mänsklig."

As they entered the cave, Bubba, who had been secreted in the back of Kianna's vehicle, made his way up the hill and sat next to the device that Chelovek had placed on the rock. He pulled a roll of wire mesh from his backpack to cover the cube. Then he took his lunch from the pack and settled in to enjoy a sandwich and wait for the cue from Kianna that they were returning. Mid-bite, he felt a sharp prick in his neck, and then felt the world fading away as he slipped into a state of unconsciousness.

Making their way into the darkening environment, Ki turned and fished out a small headlamp from her backpack and handed it to Chelovek. Once they were about a quarter of a mile into the cavern, she pulled out a couple of small tri-pod seats and an electric lantern. "Make yourself comfortable, Mänsklig. I feel secure here. Does this suit your needs as well?"

"It does indeed. And I must say, I am intrigued by your style. Very unpredictable."

"I want to set some ground rules first. Each of us can ask the other five questions. The person responding must answer truthfully and to the best of his or her ability. I want this to be a dialogue versus a discussion. In other words, we are not trying to sway the other person's thoughts, but rather we talk about who we are. If this goes well here, I am hoping to elevate this to a discussion where arguing our positions may lead the other person toward embracing our point of view. My first question is: how do you define truth?"

Chelovek was quiet as he considered the question. "Very interesting question. Not what I expected at all. Truth for me is related to honesty and authenticity. Things that are authentic to me are things that define me as a person. Since my root philosophy is that of an existentialist, I firmly believe all truth is derived from context."

"Could you give me an example of what you mean by context determining meaning and truth?"

Chelovek smiled. "Before I answer, is that your second question, or is it a follow-up question?"

Ki laughed out loud. "I would have to say follow-up question. We can count it as my second question provided that was your first question."

"You are good." he said through a chortle. "Okay, an example . . . say a lamb's belly is slashed open and the intestines and internal organs are ripped from the body cavity and eaten raw. Given two different contexts, we would have two different meanings, ergo two different truths. In the first situation, there is a Satanist with a knife, and he is making a sacrifice to the Devil. The ritual calls for him to eat the organs of the offering raw. In the second situation there is a Golden Eagle that has grabbed a lamb from the flock, and it flies the dead carcass to its aerie to feed its young. In the first situation the meaning of this act is sacrifice and obedience to a belief system, and the *truth* it speaks to could be characterized as evil. In the second situation, the meaning is nurturing and care for a newborn and the *truth* it speaks to is love. Very different meanings and very different truths.

"If that is too obtuse, here is an example that is more relatable. It is against the law to steal. It doesn't matter what is stolen; it is against the law. However, if you embrace a 'military' mentality and go strictly by the law, someone who steals a loaf of bread to feed his starving family is guilty of the same crime as a person who steals money from an elderly woman who now cannot afford to buy food. The context should define the meaning of the law."

Ki rubbed her chin and nodded her head. "I see. You present an interesting case. Now my second question. What is the scope of your organization?"

"Now that is a question that I was expecting, which led me to not expect you to ask it. Even your predictability is unpredictable! How wonderful. I could simply say international, but I suspect that would only require additional follow-up questions on your part. I will put it this way: my operation in Atlanta is just one of twenty facilities of its kind around the world. I am normally found in my Beijing office, but I am spearheading my newest pet project in the Southern Commonwealth. Our cash flow comes in through a number of fronts—mostly extortion and blackmail, legislative influence and lobbying, data mining, site and cyber security, and finally investments and brokerage houses. I say all of this knowing that given enough time, you would have figured all of this out. Does that sufficiently answer your question?" Chelovek hoped she would not press further, and she didn't.

"Yes. Thank you. My third question is a little more esoteric. What do you think keeps people from reaching their full potential?"

"Outstanding question, my dear. The simple answer is fear. There are *so* many fears. Fear of the unknown, fear of failure, fear of success, fear of death, fear of intrusion, of 'others', of exposure. It is the most powerful tool in my arsenal. Without it, I would not be in business. The rampant insecurity of so many people literally fuels my business and my future plans. Next question."

"My fourth question is, what do you think are the two greatest evils in the world?"

Chelovek laughed out loud. "Kianna, you will never cease to amaze me. My answer is short and simple. Apathy and power. When people stop caring, they may as well stop living. It is our entanglement in the world that gives us satisfaction and growth. Without it you may as well be a potato. Power, on the other hand, feeds the ego and gets out of control over time. It can never be sated. It is a void with no bottom. In fact, it is my own personal demon. I personally use power as a tool to disrupt the apathy that surrounds me, and I can testify to the pull and grasp it has on me. You asked me for honesty? Well, here it is. Power is my Achilles heel."

With a slight nod of the head, Kianna said, "Mänsklig, I appreciate the apparent honesty and sincerity you gave me in your responses to my queries. I am, however, going to reserve my last question for just before we leave. Now it is your turn to ask five questions. I will give as good as I got."

"I must admit that I really liked some of your questions and I am curious about how you think. Your answers may help me frame our discussion in a more influential light. So, the first question is, how do you define truth?"

"I am going to quote my associate Bubba by using one of his quaint but wonderful colloquialisms. He once told me that truth is about as slippery as an eel in a vat of Vaseline. Like you, I lean toward existentialist thinking, and I believe that truth is influenced greatly by the context in which it is framed. However, in order to truly understand, it is critical to apply not only the filter of intellect, but also the filter of the heart. In other words, how do you *feel* about something being *true*? Myth is a good example. Myth is used to teach a lesson and, although the words regarding the myth itself are not literally true, the lesson conveys a certain truth within its telling. The resonance of that truth filters through your heart and it literally rings true. Is that answer comprehensible? I feel as though I may be rambling a bit."

"My dear Kianna, you could not be any more lucid. Thank you. For my second question, I will reiterate your third question. What do *you* think keeps people from reaching their full potential?"

"I must say that I thought your answer to my question was insightful and a large part of me concurs. But I also believe that a significant component that impedes forward motion in achieving one's full potential is a lack of people knowing who they really are. There is often no inner vision or comprehension of that authentic person within themselves that allows them to overcome that fear. Knowing who one is and what one really values can disarm the crippling fear that controls so many of us. A large number of people confuse *what* they are with *who* they are. People identify with their race, their sex, their job, or literally hundreds of other external aspects that have nothing to do with their core being. People who know *who* they are shine with an inner light that extinguishes all those fears that you mentioned earlier. Next question?"

"Your response has wetted my desire to commence our discussion. But that will have to wait. As you probably guessed, my third question is, what do you think are the two greatest evils in the world?"

Kianna was expecting this question. Chelovek's response had helped her a great deal in coming up with an unfolding strategy for dealing with him. Her response needed to be honest but not tip her hand. She needed to touch on power but focus more on her idea of the second evil.

"Well, Mänsklig, I would have to say that you and I are not very far off in our responses. Power is one of my two; however, I would beg to differ regarding apathy. I find apathy to be sad and nothing more. My second evil would have to be righteous indignation. You said in your response that 'it is our entanglement in the world that gives us satisfaction and growth.'

For me, entanglement creates suffering in the world. When we become entangled with our false selves, we let those ideas own us, and when we find conflict with others regarding those perspectives, we feel threatened and defend ourselves. Enter righteous indignation, which creates conflict and suffering."

"Thank you, Kianna. Very insightful. Now for my fourth question, what is your impression of me?"

Kianna smiled and shook her head back and forth. "All right. You want honesty, so here it is. On the plus side, I find you charismatic and brilliant. Obviously, you are a genius and have an incredible intellect. My guess is you test off the scale on the standard IQ spectrum. You also know how to use that great mind for problem-solving. On the negative side, however, you are arrogant, condescending, and self-centered, plus you try to compensate for an unrequited love by using power and influence to fill the void in your heart."

"That was brutally honest. And I did ask for it. So, I guess, thank you? Okay, final question. What is it that you want, Miss Kianna Smythe?"

"That, Mr. Chelovek, is an excellent question. At the core of my being, I seek to know who I am and to be present in the here and now, not dwelling in the past or the future. In Kyoto, Japan, there is a major temple complex called *Daitokuji*. Within it, there are a number of sub-temples. One of them is *Ryoanji*. It is famous worldwide for its raked gravel garden. But, for me, its focus is a small garden with a washbasin. Water splashes into the basin, dripping from a bamboo spigot. Very serene, especially the message spelled out on the washbasin in Chinese characters that says, 'I am, and that is enough.' That is my aspiration. By the way, I am hoping that you will grant me one additional question before my final question. And you, of course, can ask one final question as well."

"Certainly. Fire away."

"What are your plans for Bubba, aside from the kidnapping, that is?"

Chelovek's chin literally dropped. "How in the world did you know about Bubba's capture? It has just happened, and we have been in this cave the whole time. You are more than uncanny in your observation skills. Your instinct borders on a sixth sense."

Kianna looked point blank at Chelovek. "If you say so, but I thought it was obvious. Your satellite surveillance and solution to my code allowed your associate to travel in advance to the location where I met you, likely by helicopter. Once the satellites locked onto my car, your team back in Atlanta conveyed our final destination to your associate. I had logically guessed that you not only had 'eyes in the sky' focused on me, but also on Bubba, so you knew where he was. I realize now, you had plans in place to take Bubba before you even left your compound. He had the assignment from me to circumvent your signal booster and transmission cube using a mini-Faraday cage. Yes, I saw you placing it on the rock near the cave entrance. I expected something like that. I had hoped Bubba would have avoided your trap, and he probably would have done so if not for being incapacitated from a distance. Am I guessing correctly that you used a tranquilizer and blow gun?"

Chelovek nodded his head.

"When I mentioned his name in my response to you regarding the truth, your pupils narrowed, and your mouth showed a minute reaction of concern. It was then I confirmed, in my mind at least, what you had done. That said, you have not answered my question. What are you planning to do with Bubba?"

"I plan on holding him hostage. The terms of his release will be forthcoming. Now, my final question for you is, what are your plans for me?"

A sly smile crept onto Kianna's face. "Unless you can convince me otherwise in our discussion, I plan on destroying you and every aspect of your operations. I presume your associate will be able to help you get back to your vehicle. I have a lot of work to do before we meet for our discussion. I will leave the place of our meeting for that discussion up to you. I also trust that, as a gentleman, which you appear to be, you will not harm Bubba in any way whatsoever. The consequences of doing him any harm will be dire indeed. And now, for my last question." Kianna gave Chelovek her most beatific smile. "Why have you entangled yourself with me to such a great extent and given me so much information? It makes very little sense to me. I had not expected you to be so forthcoming."

Chelovek was quiet for nearly a full minute. His face presented as a man in deep thought. Finally, he spoke. "First of all, I respect you. I respect your intelligence, your wit, your bearing, your acumen, and your insight. All those things that I find admirable in a person issue forth from you. I would rather have you as a partner than a foe. It is that simple."

CHAPTER TWENTY-TWO

"Each friend represents a world in us, a world possibly not born until they arrive, and it is only by this meeting that a new world is born."

—Anais Nin

Although Kianna had anticipated the move, Bubba's abduction took the wind out of her sails. She had to trust in Bubba to do what he needed to do because she could not be there to guide or assist him. In spite of her emotional response to Bubba's capture, she was grateful for all the valuable data she got from Chelovek that could help her create a plan to take him down. It was a lot to process. Normally, she was a person of decisive action, but now she felt like a deer in the headlights of a car. Her mind raced and her emotions were all over the map. She needed to calm down and absorb everything happening to her. One step at a time. Whatever her next steps were, she needed to make sure Bubba was safe. Although she was counting on using his capture to her advantage, she did not want to sacrifice him.

Her first order of business would be to gather her team of clients and fill them in on what she was planning. Each of them also needed to understand the parts they were to play in her game plan. The drive back to Atlanta gave her time to refine some of the rough edges. She had to be extremely careful now to ensure there were no slip ups from herself or any of her clients and their employees. Too much was at risk if anything were to go wrong.

****

Back in her office, she entered her Black Box and stripped down naked. Searching her clothes, she found two bugs that Chelovek had secreted onto her clothing and one in her hair. After examining them, she realized these were very special listening devices. They could store a limited amount of data and, if unable to broadcast immediately, they would broadcast once they could. In other words, Chelovek had found a way to penetrate the inner sanctum of her Black Box. If she had communicated with anyone verbally before searching herself, she would have compromised her stealth mode, and all of her plans would be for naught. Thankfully, her instinct was spot on. She set the bugs aside in a secure location, thinking they just may come in handy at a later time.

She was confident that Chelovek's assessment of her as a threat was more on the level of a nuisance than anything consequential. She hoped he would soon find out how wrong he was. She needed to maintain that illusion, but it had to be believable because she did not want to underestimate *his* intelligence and insight. The trick now was to communicate two streams of information simultaneously. One with false data that Chelovek would be sure to intercept through which to obfuscate her intent, and another channel for coordinating and communicating with her clients. She knew they had all been given the basic plans for building their own Black Boxes, but she wasn't sure if all the work was completed. The only location not in her neighborhood was Colonel Tom's Southern Commonwealth. For Ebonée and NAM, she could check on their progress by walking to their offices and not have to worry about electronic surveillance. When she dropped by the

NAM facilities, Obatala informed her it would be another two days before their Black Box would be completed. She had higher hopes for Marain's progress, and a quick call to him confirmed he had indeed finished their version of a Black Box.

At Ebonée, the main floor receptionist now knew her by sight and waved hello. Marain had given instruction for her to have full access to him, so she immediately went up to his office to visit. Marain's receptionist announced Kianna's presence, and when he came out to greet her, he flashed a big smile and gave her an unexpected hug. When they entered his office, Ki was surprised to see none other than Tamba.

Marain winked at Ki. "I would introduce you, but I believe you have both met already."

Kianna laughed. "We have indeed. It seems as though the hen has come home to roost. May I ask why?"

Tamba's beautiful voice rang out. "My time at the Southern Commonwealth had to come to an end. While my undercover work was successful, all this business with Chelovek suggested it would only be a matter of time before I was exposed. Your investigation presented a problem for me, but it became clear I would be compromised if Chelovek continued poking around. Now I can lend my talents to you and Marain without any subterfuge. It feels good to be free of that mantle of deception."

Ki nodded thoughtfully but did not respond. She quietly went to Marain and whispered in his ear. His response was immediate, and he sported an expansive smile. "Follow me. I think you will be proud of our accomplishments."

They walked through the access door to the board room and Marain motioned for them to be seated. With a sweep of his hand he announced, "Welcome to our Black Box."

Ki had to admit, this was much better than the rudimentary structure Bubba had cobbled together for her. It looked like a normal room. Obviously, there was an advantage to having the vast resources of a large organization at your disposal.

"This is amazing. A word of caution, however."

She went on to describe the efforts that Chelovek had employed to install a microwire bug in the structure of the Black Box.

"I am going to ask a favor of you, Marain. Do you think you could host a meeting here for everyone?"

Without any hesitation, Marain said, "Certainly. I admit to a certain trepidation over having Colonel Tom here on the premises. I will do what I can to make him feel welcome, although I doubt if he will ever feel comfortable in our midst. Ebonée does not have many lily-white bigots as our guests. Needless to say, he will be a bit shocked to see Tamba here."

Ki smiled. "So, I take it Tamba is going to be joining our team?"

Marain nodded. "Unless you object. He is one of our most talented and skilled field operatives."

"I believe he will make a fine addition to our group."

When Ki got back to her office, it suddenly dawned on her! She had a solution close at hand. Chelovek himself had given her the means to communicate with him via the bugs he had planted on her earlier. She got them out and placed them on her person. Then, sitting in her Black Box she pulled out her phone and called her three clients and told them she needed to meet with them as soon as possible and supplied them with details regarding the time and location of the meeting. The only fly in the ointment was Colonel Tom who had a conflicting appointment, and he was going to send a representative in his place. Chelovek was sure to be listening to this conversation, so she felt confident he would surreptitiously drop in on their meeting. What he would hear would be only what she wanted him to hear.

****

The first person to arrive was the new representative from the Southern Commonwealth. To Kianna's surprise it was someone she had recently come to know, Latitia Hicks. The senator from Louisiana was good to his word and had pulled some strings with Colonel Tom. Latitia had filled the position recently vacated by Tamba, and she was now the handmaiden and personal assistant to none other than Colonel Tom.

"Latitia! How very good to see you! I am very happy you have landed on your feet. How are you?"

"I am well. When Colonel Tom mentioned that I was going to meet with you, I was thrilled! Thanks to you, my life has taken on a new direction and meaning. I can never thank you enough."

"Do not mention it. It was only the right thing to do. Did Colonel Tom bring you up to speed on the situation we are dealing with here?"

"He did. He gave me a quick rundown of who all was involved. I do believe Chelovek was the one who was blackmailing Senator Marquis Lee. So, it seems I've actually been involved to a degree all along."

"There is another recent addition to our team. His name is Tamba and, in a way, he was also instrumental in you getting hired. You filled the spot with Colonel Tom that he vacated. He is a spy for Ebonée, but his cover was compromised."

Latitia looked at Ki with surprise and amusement. "Oh my! Had Colonel Tom shown up here today, he would have been in for a very big surprise."

Just then Obatala and Daniel entered the Ebonée board room. Ki turned to greet them and made introductions.

"Latitia, I would like to introduce you to Obatala and the Ghost from NAM. Latitia is representing Colonel Tom at our meeting here today."

Latitia walked forward and shook both of their hands. "What a great pleasure to meet you. I feel like a groupie. Here I am in the same room with Obatala and the Ghost. I have read so much about you and your organization, and I must say I am becoming a big fan."

Daniel smiled. "Please, call me Daniel. The Ghost is good for PR, but it feels more than a little pretentious when someone addresses me by that title."

Obatala's smile was broad. "I can't believe it! The world is really changing. A black woman representing the Southern Commonwealth! Somebody please write it down on a calendar. This is a red-letter day."

Latitia shook her head. "I wish. No, I am merely here to be eyes and ears for Colonel Tom. I have no decision-making power."

Obatala laughed. "Never downgrade yourself, young lady. It is a start, and it makes my heart sing. It is a real pleasure to meet you. It shows me the beginning of a possible future."

Marain and Tamba were the last to enter. Once introductions were made all around, Kianna settled down to business. They were now seated in the board room Black Box, and she handed each person a slip of paper warning them about the bugs listening in on their conversations. She planned to lead everyone through her measures for keeping Chelovek in the dark about what was in store. Before she started, and while everyone was engaged in idle chitchat, she handed everyone a thick envelope with handwritten information detailing each of their roles and the timing of the operation that would begin in two days. On the Southern Commonwealth's envelope, Ki crossed out Colonel Tom's name and wrote in the name Latitia Hicks. She then wrote a note on a small slip of paper. *See me after the meeting.*

It is critical. Once everyone had their packet, she stood at the head of the table and cleared her throat.

"Alright, I would like to call this meeting to order. I have a great deal of information to share. I have met with Chelovek twice now, and I am planning on meeting with him a third time. The first meeting, though casual, allowed me to learn more about him and his background. The second meeting was a much more in-depth conversation where I discovered how he thinks and is likely to respond to any action we take. In our next meeting, Chelovek expects a tête-à-tête in which we will each make a case for our side and convince the other to join forces. I doubt he will be able to offer any argument that would convince me he is in the right, but I am willing to hear him out.

"One of my strategies is attempting to convince him we are not worth his time or effort and to move on from this game. One of the more interesting things he revealed is that his operations are worldwide. The international operations he is overseeing are massive. He is usually in China at his headquarters in Beijing. Now, understand, what I have in mind is a desperate ploy on my part. To be honest with you, I think the biggest threat we offer is we know how to circumvent his 3-D security surveillance. I am prepared to promise we will not disclose how we foiled his spying in return for his backing off of the Southern Commonwealth, Ebonée, and NAM. This may just be the most valuable thing I have to offer him, and I hope it is enough to free Bubba and leave the three of your operations alone."

Marain gasped. "Did you say 'free Bubba'? I was wondering where that boy was. Did they abduct him? I really like that boy, even if he is white."

Kianna shook her head. "I was going to get to that. But you need to know that Bubba's seizure was not totally unexpected. I do feel confident we can negotiate his release, and it will benefit all of us.

"There is a lot to do now. As parting words, especially for the benefit of Latitia and Tamba, remember that we are very likely being surveilled everywhere we go outside of our Black Boxes. These cloaked rooms are our only advantage over Chelovek at this point." Everyone nodded and started filing out of the room. Kianna motioned to Latitia to hold up. She pulled out a pad of paper and quickly wrote a note, which she handed to Latitia.

The note read:

You have a bug on your sleeve, I believe planted by Colonel Tom. It is identical to the one Chelovek secreted on to me. It is likely that he has been compromised by Chelovek. I am going to give you a separate package to deliver to Colonel Tom. Today's meeting has been corrupted, so there is no need to keep it secret. However, do not say anything about this message or share your packet of information. Nod your head if you agree.

Latitia nodded.

CHAPTER TWENTY-THREE

"Limits like fear, is often an illusion."

—Michael Jordan

Bubba Smith awoke in a luxurious apartment. If he was indeed held hostage, they were intentional about making sure he was comfortable. From the art on display, to the wall-to-wall carpeting and the high-end furniture, he soon saw that whoever lived there invested heavily in the design aesthetic and liked expensive things. When Bubba pushed open the ten-foot tall balcony doors, he discovered he was on an upper floor of a very tall building. The view was breathtaking.

He was alert enough to know the first thing he needed to do was get himself oriented. Before he could accomplish the task assigned to him by Ki, he needed to know exactly where he was. Unfortunately, what his eyes told him did not bode well for him or Ki's plans. The last thing he remembered was being on the side of a forested hill in southern Georgia, so he expected to be somewhere in Atlanta, most likely in Chelovek's underground lair. However, when he stepped onto the balcony and scanned his surroundings, the city of Beijing, China, with a commanding view of the Forbidden Palace sprawled before him. Still, his senses told him a different story. The muffled sound of traffic and people, suffused with bird songs, the delicate smells of sweet fresh air, pungent florals, and freshly-mown hay didn't align with what he was seeing. He should have experienced an entirely different set of sights, smells, and sounds.

Something definitely was not right with this picture. Coming back inside, he sat on the sofa and tried to put it all together in his head, but still he was stumped. He went back out onto the balcony again and felt a gentle breeze, but it was blowing from the northwest, and the flags he saw on nearby buildings were flapping in a different direction. He quickly realized what must be going on. Reaching into his pants pocket, he pulled out a nickel and tossed it off the balcony. Just as he thought. The nickel hit a surface about eight feet away and slid down that surface to the invisible floor about ten feet below him. The nickel appeared to be floating in mid-air. Everything that stimulated his senses was a virtual experience. It was, by far, the most realistic projection he had ever seen. If this was a video, it was not on a loop. There was no repetition, and it was seamless. He guessed that this was live streaming from Beijing in real time. He had heard of telepresence and knew inroads were being made into that technology, but this was beyond anything he could imagine. This definitively showed that Chelovek was not just some Georgia extortion scheme criminal. This put him in a whole new league.

Bubba whispered to himself. "Whooee, Miss Ki. Y'all not gonna believe this."

He was stopped short when he heard Mänsklig Chelovek whisper in his ear, "I beg to differ, Bubba. I think she will believe all of this. Well done. You saw through the ruse in record time. I have had guests here who never pieced it together."

Bubba looked around but couldn't see Chelovek anywhere. "Well, I must say, you had me goin' there for a minute. I know this is in Beijing, but not sure why."

Now Chelovek's voice seemed to be coming from the middle of the room. "This is the view from my actual apartment in Beijing. When I am traveling, it is some small comfort for me to be in a surrounding that gives me a sense of stability in the world. I am willing, however, to project a different locale, if you prefer. I told Kianna I would make you as comfortable as possible, and I am nothing if not a man of my word. Perhaps my cabin on the shore of a pond in Maine would be more to your liking."

Instantly, the image surrounding him morphed into an eastern deciduous forest peppered with spruce and hemlock. A pristine body of water with a dock and a canoe appeared to be twenty feet away. In the distance, he could hear the cry of a loon. In Beijing, the sun was setting, but in this setting it was rising. An indicator that this too was happening in real time. Incredibly, the outdoors was not the only change. The room decor and walls took on a rustic feel, and below his feet, Bubba saw a bear rug and a scuffed hardwood floor. Chelovek's illusion matched other sensory details of that location as well.

Bubba was trying to process this when Chelovek asked, "Does this suit you, Bubba? I am going to take my leave of you for a bit; but, before I do, I wanted to make sure you have everything you need. The refrigerator and shelves are well stocked with food you like—real food, not a technological fabrication. If I'm not mistaken . . . and I'm sure I'm not . . . they should be your favorites."

"Mr. Chelovek, you certainly do think of everything. I'm guessing you probably have a computer handy. I don't rightly know how long I'm gonna be cooped up in here, so I would like to play some of my favorite computer games. Can you square that away?"

Now Chelovek's voice was coming from the far side of the living room. "I'm glad you asked, Bubba. Come over here by the side window. I have a console, keyboard, and Virtual Reality hookup. It is all ready to go; and yes, I know which games you prefer. I have them loaded and set with your current levels in all the games. You have full access to the internet if you are interested in exploring anything new."

As Bubba walked over to the other side of the room, he asked, "Mr. Chelovek, why are you bein' so nice and accommodatin' with me? This ain't what I was expectin'. Mind you, I'm not complainin' though."

"Bubba, it's complicated. I can tell you this though. It does involve Kianna and, just so you know, I am meeting with her soon to fill her in on what I am doing here. I plan on bringing her here to this space to see for herself that I am treating you right and, if everything works out, as I suspect it will, you should probably be leaving here with her soon. So settle in and enjoy your stay."

"Goodbye, Mr. Chelovek. Thanks for making this experience so easy on the eyes, and thanks for the computer games too. I do enjoy them."

Once he was sure Chelovek was gone, the first thing Bubba did was pull up a search engine and entered a web address for a web site Kianna had made him commit to memory. Once it came up, he logged in as a guest using the special code Kianna gave him, which allowed him to access her cousin's cyber hacking tools on her dedicated pocket site. His Daddy had taught Bubba everything he knew about computers and all the tricks of the trade to navigate even the most complicated systems. Although he didn't have Ki's cousin's specialized skills, he was no slouch on the keyboard. He even knew how to create an undetectable encrypted access folder to hide his history.

Chelovek's web presence was not only complicated, it was also massive. As he entered the system, he felt like an ant wandering in Atlanta. He soon realized that he would be better off switching to a virtual reality (VR) venue, and when he did, Bubba reassessed his metaphor. It was more of a flea wandering around on a rat on a ship on an ocean. He really had his work cut out for him. The first thing he did was to activate what Ki's cousin called the 'cloak'. This particular code made his presence undetectable and allowed him to penetrate any firewalls Chelovek's techs had installed on the system. This was a whole lot more fun than playing computer games.

CHAPTER TWENTY-FOUR

"I believe there are more instances of the abridgment of the rights of the people by the gradual and silent encroachments of those in power than by violent and sudden usurpa-tions."

—James Madison

Kianna arranged to meet Chelovek on his own turf. He had offered to give her a personal tour. On the face of it, she knew it posed a greater danger, but she needed to know the layout and capabilities of his facility. And she did have one major advantage over him. She had developed a strategic plan for eliminating the threat he posed. After today's meeting, she would have a tactical plan in place in order to implement that strategy. He would then get the opportunity to present his case for folding her into his fantasy of working together to solve the problems of the world. Of course, she had an entirely different agenda. She planned on bringing down his entire international operation. Her team had their marching orders, and they were only waiting on the logistical data, which she should soon have in hand. After that, it was simply a matter of flawless execution with perfect timing. What could possibly go wrong?

As Kianna entered the seemingly derelict and abandoned warehouse, Chelovek was there to greet her. The holographic projections of serpents, as well as the nuance of virtual dust and cobwebs covering everything, was gone. In that moment, she realized the world Chelovek created full of subterfuge and obfuscation spoke volumes about who he was at his core. He was all about achieving his personal goals, no matter the cost, and whatever manipulation he could pull off was fair game. He was a puppet master, and he was highly adept at his craft. Additionally, her assessment of him was that he was a megalomaniac obsessed with gaining and maintaining control. On the plus side, her intuition told her he was honest with her. But the question was not whether what he told her was the truth; it was whether he was telling her the *whole* truth. You can know what you know, and you can learn what you know you don't know, but when you don't know what you don't know, that can really hurt you.

Ki entered the facility and coldly addressed Chelovek. "You do realize I am not very likely to be convinced of your ability to bring me around to your way of thinking."

Chelovek shrugged and offered a weak smile. "Yes. But, why don't we see where our conversation will take us? Follow me. In order to better understand what I am offering you, it is critical you have a better understanding of my operations, their scale and their scope. So, before we embark on our discussion, I believe the so-called 'nickel tour' I promised you would be in order. Please oblige me."

Kianna followed Chelovek to the elevator and kept her eyes open for anything useful or important she may have missed the previous time she had been there. The cloaking device for the elevator was also turned off and the corridor leading up to it was well-lit. "Well, Kianna, you must be wondering why everything is illuminated. Everyone on my surveillance staff, including myself, has a microchip installed subcutaneously. The system recognizes us as we move through the facility and turns off the deception devices. The same thing applies to the elevator. The code you so cleverly figured out was in place from an earlier security system. It was sheer good luck that you infiltrated our facility before that section was upgraded." Chelovek reached over and closed the elevator doors, and then pressed the number nine. "I think we will start on the top floor and work our way down. This will give you an opportunity to see that Bubba is being treated very well before we continue with the tour."

After disembarking from the elevator, Ki noticed that the holographic projectors had been fabricating more than dust. The rows of empty offices were all enclosed by bullet-proof plate glass. There did not appear to be any mechanism for accessing them. If she and Bubba had investigated a little further, she would have realized this their first time here. Chelovek walked up to a panel, and it slid open automatically. Ki followed him down a corridor with solid unmarked doors every twenty-five feet. He stopped at the third door, waved his left hand, and looked directly into what appeared to be a security peephole, but was more likely a retinal scanner. Sure enough. The door slid open silently. The entire space looked like an empty apartment with windows opening onto nothing but smooth grey surfaces. There was a low table near the entrance with several pairs of eyeglasses laid out in a neat row. Attached to them were small microphones. Following Chelovek's lead, she put on a set, and the smart plastic in the frames snugged to her skin and the convex lenses wrapped around her face to cover all of her direct vision as well as her indirect peripheral vision. Chelovek went to a wooden panel on the wall and again waved his left hand. The panel slid open silently, and there were twenty-five buttons with designations of A through Z beside each one. The oddity here was that there was no button beside the letter C. when he pressed the B button, she was astonished by what she saw.

"Impressive, isn't it," he said smugly. "We are currently in the Observation Room. Each of the other rooms on this floor are identical to this one, except for the fact that they are furnished with a refrigerator, sinks, toilets, furniture, and everything else that makes a house a functioning home. Through a projection on to their retinas, and with the help of hidden speakers, the occupant experiences a telepresence streaming from a remote location. I have twenty-six places around the world that are transmitting via live data in real time, reflecting what is happening at those places. The visual, auditory, and—something new I am very proud of—olfactory senses are all engaged. Every apartment has the identical furniture and utility placement, but what the occupant sees is based on the actual appearance from the projected telepresence."

Kianna was thunderstruck by what she saw. Truly amazed, she was hit with the strongest sense of cognitive dissonance. The room she was in looked just like a rustic cabin. As she moved around, she could see a lake outside the windows. She could smell balsam fir, and, in the distance, there was the sound of a loon. Then there was the biggest shock of all—Bubba, sitting at a computer playing a game of solitaire.

"Bubba, it is so good to see you. Are you okay? Has Chelovek been treating you okay?"

Bubba did not respond.

Chelovek smiled. "This telepresence really fools you, doesn't it? I call it TP for short. As for Bubba, he can't hear us unless I activate the microphone on our TP glasses. Would you like to speak to him?"

"Yes. Of course, I want to speak to him!"

Chelovek went to the wall panel and pressed a button. Kianna spoke.

"Bubba, are you okay?"

Bubba looked up with complete surprise on his face and spun around in his seat. "Miss Ki! Are you here? I just hear your voice."

"Yes, Bubba, I am here at Chelovek's complex. He is here with me now and is giving me a guided tour before we sit down and negotiate for your release. Has he mistreated you in any way?"

"No, Miss Ki. He's been a real gentleman. A little surprising, but he's been a really good host . . . except of course for me bein' locked up."

"Bubba, we are going to get that cleared up as soon as we can. You will not believe this, but you are actually on the top floor of his complex. I have to admit, it is very impressive. I need to leave now with Chelovek if I am going to get you out of here. Sit tight and I will be back as soon as I can."

Chelovek was taking off his glasses. "Satisfied that I kept to my end of the bargain?"

"Yes, but I still want him out of here as soon as possible, so let us move on. I noticed that there is no C button. Why is that?"

"I think you suspect the reason. That is my apartment, and of course there is no surveillance in my quarters."

Kianna huffed. "Of course not. What are the rooms used for? And what does the next floor down have going on?"

"I use these luxury apartments for special guests and clients. The next two floors down are for employees. I have approximately two hundred people working for me that are living on the premises. The rooms are considerably smaller, but there is the illusion of a much grander space, and they are attuned to the individual worker and their particular needs and fantasies. Needless to say, I have very satisfied and loyal employees."

"What about the ground floor of the warehouse space?"

As they left the observation room, Chelovek said, "Let's go check it out. Nothing fancy, really. It is the infrastructure for everything above it— plumbing, electrical, and other structural engineering elements that are critical for maintaining all of that living space. Are you sure you want to see it?"

"I have paid my nickel, so I expect the full tour. Lead on."

When they reached the ground floor of the warehouse, Chelovek opened an access door and Ki was duly impressed by the engineering design and layout of the maintenance floor. The panels were clearly labeled for electrical, plumbing, HVAC, fiber optics, and other electronics. Every section had redundancies and backups on top of backups, so there was no need to call a plumber or electrician in the middle of the night. She noted this was a smart preemptive security protocol.

Arriving at the elevator, Chelovek said, "The next floor down is really quite utilitarian. It is the parking garage for offsite guests, visitors, and in-facility transportation for workers who occasionally need access to the larger community. Do you want to see that as well?"

"As I said, show me everything."

They got off at floor five, and it was just as he described. It was essentially an underground parking garage. The odd thing about it was it appeared to be bathed in daylight.

"How do you get the daylight down here?"

"That is pretty old technology. It is the latest incarnation of Solatubes. On the surface of the roof there are light collecting stations and highly reflective tubes that snake down through the infrastructure and emerge in the ceiling of the garage."

Kianna let out a low whistle. "I must admit, albeit begrudgingly, I am impressed. I have already been to floors one and two, and based on what I saw, that included the third floor as well since those domes must have been nearly twenty feet high. That just leaves one more floor to explore. I am curious though, the elevator has stops at all floors, including a third floor. I presume that is maintenance catwalks connecting the viewing domes?"

Chelovek nodded. "Very astute, my dear. There is one catwalk that circumnavigates the entire space with perpendicular catwalks accessing the domes. I suppose you will not be needing to see that space or the lower floors since you have already been there. Is that correct?"

Kianna nodded. "Yes, please show me floor number four so we can get to our discussion. I am anxious to hear what you have to say, and I have a lot of unanswered questions."

Chelovek smiled. "I am glad we are saving my favorite floor for last. I have a certain level of pride for the whole operation, but I am particularly proud of the fourth floor."

When the elevator door opened on the fourth floor, Kianna gasped. A forest glade and open meadow sprawled before her. Beyond the meadow, lining the horizon, was a ragged mountain range. Birds were flying through the air. Squirrels were scampering in the trees. There was a red fox running along a nearby stream bed. She had never seen any place quite as exquisite as this space. Then she saw the dragon. It was meandering down a pathway away from them.

Chelovek was watching her and looked very pleased with himself.

"Do you like it?"

Kianna found herself nearly speechless, simply nodding her head.

"Wow. How?"

Chelovek spread his arms up in the air and said, "All of this is virtual reality without the need for headsets. The smells, the sights, and the sounds are all created by my computers. Fans create the breezes and occasional bursts of wind, but other than that, everything you sense is not happening. I have hundreds of programmers in China that toil day and night, configuring and modifying this environment. I have replicated this space at all of my properties around the world. It is the same program, so what you see happening here, is happening in all of those facilities simultaneously. But it is interactive, so each place responds to the people within it differently."

As they stepped away from the elevator, Ki turned around to see the closed elevator door hanging in the middle of the forest. The fact that the only real thing there, besides themselves, looked so illusory compounded the surreal nature of this place.

"You have certainly outdone yourself. I truly am at a loss for words."

Chelovek led them to what appeared to be logs with blankets covering them, and he motioned for Kianna to have a seat. "Shall we begin our discussion?"

"Absolutely. But before we go into the deeper topics, I have several questions that need to be answered. The power consumed by this operation is enormous, and the heat generated must be off the charts. How do you manage?"

Chelovek smiled. "Wonderful question. At each of my facilities, I have my own semi-fusion reactors occupying a separate sub-basement accessed through the first floor. I am producing more power than I consume, and I even feed the surplus back into the grid. I am also reducing my power consumption because I am using room temperature superconductors that were designed to operate at a peak efficiency of exactly 77 Kelvin, which is the same temperature as liquid nitrogen. There are nitrogen scrubbers and condensers on the roof processing the air and keeping the entire system in a balanced state. Next question?"

"Within each of my client's operations, you planted donors and even board members into virtual meetings. Were those employees of yours?"

"No. Those were all me. I would never trust any of my employees to do that sort of thing."

"But how? One of them was a woman."

"Simple, actually. The interactions were always virtual, and the computer modified my physical appearance and modulated my voice. The algorithm I used had adapted my movements and expressions to be conveyed in the form of the persona I was representing."

Kianna shook her head. "Incredible. One last question: when we were in the observation room on the top floor, we were like ghosts to Bubba. Is it possible to be virtually visible to him?"

"Yes, it is possible. In fact, if I am conducting a virtual meeting, I have a personal avatar that is an exact duplicate of me. You saw it once when you brilliantly figured out where this facility was located."

"Okay, let me hear what you have to say about Bubba and why you think I would choose to work with you."

"I have told you already about how my orphanage years and my experience with my mother helped to form my anarchist philosophy and the reactionary way I regard government of any ilk.. Societies that are dictated by the state are rife with examples of suffering. When you closely examine the solutions proffered by these nation states, you will find they create far more suffering than they alleviate. Nine times out of ten, they only exacerbate the problems they are trying to solve. If you try to combat structured governments from within, the idealists find themselves like Brer Rabbit and the Tar Baby. The harder they fight, the more they get consumed by that which they fight. It is only from an overthrow and dismantling of *all* nations and structured governments that any hope exists.

In order to abate suffering, we need to start from ground zero. The people in power will not give up their control easily, but they need to be made to understand the suffering the vast majority of people endure even as we speak. Yes, I know that what I am proposing is dramatic and, yes, it will cause a suffering. But that suffering will mostly be felt by the most sheltered, the most privileged. What I want to do is to facilitate a rebirth, or renaissance if you will, of society at large. A society where individual liberties can exist in a harmony that springs organically from a society where compassion replaces corruption. I want to establish a system that allows individuals to live freely without being yoked to a system that serves the privileged and elitist class. I envision a new system that will function free of restrictions and allow an autonomy of action throughout society. It has happened before, right here in North America. Native American tribes were not wealth and ownership-based power systems. Their society was based on equity and compassion for all people, not on power and wealth controlled by a minority of the population. We have the potential to create a world-wide society where it is not controlled by a handful of privileged individuals. A collaborative society where wealth is evenly distributed.

I am literally on the verge of initiating my plans, but I am looking for your support. If I trust only one other person to have the insight and intelligence to do the right thing, that person is you. I know you have concerns about an inevitable infiltration of corruption into my operations, so I am willing to let you spearhead a department whose sole purpose would be to circumvent any bribes, extortion or power grabs within the coming new world order.

"As to the issue of Bubba, no matter how much I regret circumstances necessitating I hold him hostage, I needed a certain amount of leverage in dealing with you. As an opponent, you have proven formidable. Here is what I am willing to do regarding Bubba. If you will verbally agree to drop any further defense of the Southern Commonwealth, Ebonée, and NAM, I am willing to release Bubba to you upon your departure from this facility."

Kianna sat silently regarding Chelovek for a good minute. Finally she said, "That is a whole lot to unpack. Your rationale for anarchism is intriguing, and I can tell you have given it a great deal of thought, however, I find there is a gaping hole in your logic. First, I believe you are not giving enough consideration to the very predictable nature of humankind. Most people are not leaders but more like sheep. Humans mostly avoid responsibility and seek the path of least resistance. This is one reason our societies are so addicted to the security we achieve by sacrificing our individual freedoms. We so easily relinquish control to other authority figures because we are essentially lazy and incompetent. Left without the infrastructure found in a governing body, people will seek a leader and, as you so astutely put it, people who desire power are going to seek it. And to be honest with you, the idea of being in charge of quelling corruption throughout the entire world is more than I can process right now. Corruption will certainly ensue. An anarchist framework as a strategy for a rebirth of a society is a topic I would like to explore further once I have had more time to digest what you are proposing. Give me a couple of days to process and explore further, and I would welcome meeting again to explore the idea of my working with you once you have responded to the questions that I am sure will arise.

"As for Bubba, here is my counter proposal. Release him to me as soon as we are finished with this discussion. I am willing to cease and desist in pursuing my clients' invasion of privacy issues, but on two conditions. You, in turn, will agree to disengage from your private surveillance of each of their operations, including their personal lives. Second, you will also stop any efforts to blackmail, extort, or manipulate them or any members of their groups. I cannot imagine, considering the scope of your vision, they are anything more than a minor inconvenience. Giving me your word will be sufficient for the time being. I have never sensed from you that you have ever been anything but honest with me, although my concern is not so much what you tell me, but rather that which you do not reveal to me that gives me the greatest pause. However, I am willing to put that to the test. If you do not comply, your life will quickly become very complicated. What do you say?"

Chelovek sat on the pseudo log with a smile on his face. "Let me go in reverse order. I accept your proposal regarding Bubba. He will join you on the main floor of this facility. I also grant you the time you need to think about what I've said. I can envision us having a lively debate. Of course, I will permanently suspend surveillance activities of the Southern Commonwealth, NAM and Ebonee. I will also grant your request for a couple of days. Touch base with me for the details of time and day."

Ki stood up. "I think we have made a very good beginning. I am glad we can put this cloak and dagger business behind us. I am sure my clients will certainly embrace this agreement. I will see you in two days. Now, let us get Bubba back into my care."

CHAPTER TWENTY-FIVE

"To a father growing old, nothing is dearer than a daughter."

—Euripides

The first thing Kianna did upon getting back to her office was call Marain Jagu and update him on her meeting with Chelovek and the fact that Bubba was back. She also told him she needed to schedule another total group meeting.

"I have discovered a great deal more about what is really going on with Chelovek, and I now have enough knowledge to add important tactical information to our plans. Please have your far superior Black Box ready for us."

Marain complied. "I will contact all the players. I am looking at tomorrow afternoon at 2:00 p.m. But before I talk to the Southern Commonwealth, I have a question about Colonel Tom. I can't tell you why, but I am sensing he is like a rat on a sinking ship. Can we trust him? And if not, what do we do about him?"

"That is a very good question. It is possible Colonel Tom may be trying to play a separate game with Chelovek to further the interests of the Southern Commonwealth. Colonel Tom is a wily person who is always looking for the best angle for his vested interests and likes to cover all his bases. I seriously doubt he knows who he is dealing with though. I am also not sure that what Chelovek tells Colonel Tom will be as honest as he is being with me. Even when he is telling the truth, he does not always convey the whole truth. My personal opinion, as it now stands, is we invite both Colonel Tom and Latitia to the meeting tomorrow. As a group we can confront him and gauge his responses, and then make our decisions from that point forward."

"Sounds reasonable. I will see you and Bubba tomorrow at two. I am glad you got your trusted assistant back safely."

****

At Ebonée, inside Marain Jagu's office, Kianna did a quick electronic scan of each person, including herself. To her surprise, everyone was clean, even Colonel Tom. Once they got into the Black Box, she immediately got down to business.

"Colonel Tom, I am very concerned about you and this whole affair. The last time we met, you were not able to be here and sent Latitia in your stead. On the face of it, that was wonderful. I know Latitia from my work with the senator from Louisiana. By sending her, you showed some growth in the acceptance of a black person in a position of trust and responsibility. I was impressed. Then, at the end of the meeting I noticed one of Chelovek's discrete listening devices secreted on her person. I suspect there was another one I did not find. I recognized it because he had placed three on me surreptitiously when we met in the cave. As far as Latitia could recall, the only person who had any close contact with her was you. What do you have to say for yourself?"

Colonel Tom fidgeted in his chair as all eyes fell upon him. "Well, you most certainly have me *in flagrante delicto*. However, I promise you, here and now, that I was not a willing traitor to our cause. I was approached

252

personally by Chelovek. He came to the Southern Commonwealth offices and gave me a personal invitation to his facility. He said he wanted to discuss the possibility of arranging an alliance of some sort between his organization and the Southern Commonwealth. I took him up on his offer to at least hear him out and get a chance to see behind the curtain, as it were. I couldn't resist. He gave me an address and met me outside. He then blindfolded me and led me to an elevator. We entered it and descended to his surveillance rooms. I believe it must have been the same place you found. It was just as you described. He showed me the ropes, and then we went to a private room for a discussion. I was amazed by what I saw. It is no wonder he can see what we are doing and know what we are saying. It confirmed everything you told us.

"He told me if I played along with him, he would stop all surveillance of the Southern Commonwealth and would personally feed vital secret information about Ebonée and NAM to the Commonwealth. He said he needed my assistance in breaking into your durn Black Boxes. He was very frustrated by your contraption, Miss Kianna. He gave me two tiny listening devices that he said were undetectable and could record our conversations. Although I was uncomfortable, I agreed to do that for him because I felt it was important for our efforts for me to gain his trust. I also said I needed some time to fully consider his offer and, to be honest with you, I was tempted. I was very tempted. In fact, it still is tempting, but I realized there is a price to be paid for everything. I have decided not to accept his offer, however, for two reasons. First, I realized it was likely I could not trust him any further than I could throw him. Second, regardless of how much I don't agree with Ebonée's and NAM's political perspectives, since I have gotten to know everyone, I'm not sure I could betray any of you. I also reflected on how I would feel if one of you were to do that to me. It just wouldn't be right."

Kianna frowned. "You know how to say the right things, Colonel Tom, but to be frank, I am still not sure I can fully trust you. I do believe Chelovek made that proposal to you, and I'm inclined to believe you did not accept. But, by going outside this alliance, you are endangering our entire operation. Here is something you do not know. I have already negotiated a deal that will eliminate his surveillance of the Southern Commonwealth's business operations. In fact, he has agreed to permanently stop any surveillance of each of you personally or your political organizations and the various boards associated with them."

Shock washed over every person in the room.

Obatala shouted, "That's great news. Finally, we can be done with all this subterfuge!"

Daniel frowned. "I don't think we are really done with him. I concur with Colonel Tom that he cannot be trusted. What reason does he have to stop doing his snooping? We may be small potatoes on the international stage where he plays, but he chose to be after us for some reason. The bigger issue for me is what is his master plan? Extortion and blackmail are lucrative, but they seem to be the proverbial tip of the iceberg."

Kianna nodded her head. "To answer your first question, the Black Boxes I designed have thwarted his efforts, and I did agree to not share their design with other businesses in return for leaving you all alone. I also agreed to stop investigating him. That part of it is likely the most attractive proposition. He is concerned about what I may uncover. I think your analogy regarding the tip of the iceberg is correct. There is a great deal he has yet to reveal to me, and that is what worries me the most. He is also still under the impression there is a chance I may join him as a partner.

"We have stumbled on a massive terrorist threat to the entire world community with our Mr. Chelovek. The extortion and the selling of information is merely a means to an end. I believe his primary objective is to somehow disrupt all the major governments of the world. If he pulls this off, we will suffer dire economic and social disorder throughout the world. Let me emphasize, this is not an idle threat. Now, I understand this is not what you signed on for, but it is in our best interest to put a stop to this narcissistic megalomaniac's plans. He has the ability to shut down the entire worldwide power grid as well as the free flow of data and commerce over the internet. He has been putting into place a complex web of control that essentially makes him the most powerful person in the world. We are in a unique position to stop him. I truly believe we have a great deal more to lose by ignoring his threat.

"Colonel Tom, I think I have a way that you can make up for your missteps. You are going to tell Chelovek you have decided to take him up on his offer, but that there are a couple of things he will need to do to justify your betrayal of our alliance. I am sure he will be more than willing to comply. And it is imperative that it be done by the end of the day tomorrow. You all will notice new packets in front of you. Each has detailed information and timing for what needs to happen the day after tomorrow. Follow those instructions to the letter. Colonel Tom. I need to speak to you separately."

*****

Mänsklig Chelovek sat in his private chamber in deep thought. He needed to be very strategic with his next move. If he revealed his hand too soon, it could easily jeopardize his plans for bringing Kianna into his world as an accomplice. He knew the emotional impact of what he had to say could possibly devastate her. However, depending on her reaction, it could very well work in his favor once she fully accepted the fact that she was his daughter. It could motivate her to join with him. At some point, he needed to tell her the whole story of what had happened.

As a young man, Mänsklig Chelovek had thought very little of other's needs. He was all about self-gratification. As an orphan, his will was constrained by the orphanage's rules and regulations. He was their marketable commodity and, as such, they had complete control over him. Breakfast was at 8:00 a.m., teeth brushed by 8:45 a.m., then classes from 9:00 a.m. to 11:30 a.m. They held recess until noon and so on. Each component of his day was ordered and predetermined, and that held true every single day of his life for close to eighteen years. Every step he took was dictated by the administrators of the orphanage. He longed to do what *he* wanted to do when *he* wanted to do it. So, on his eighteenth birthday, when he was finally liberated from that straight jacket of a facility, he fully embraced his newfound freedom. If he hurt some feelings along the way, that was just too bad. He was long overdue. It was *his* turn. Even as an employee, he rankled whenever he was told what to do. The mere thought of going into the militia made him physically sick to his stomach.

When he finally found his freedom, it was like adrenaline, and he exploded into the world. He could go wherever he wanted, whenever he wanted. He would go out at night and stay out until the wee hours of the morning, drinking until he was totally snookered. He answered to no one. He was finally his own person. The problem with being drunk, however, was he did not make the best decisions; any inhibitions that might control his behavior were gone. It wasn't until later in his life that he realized what he had sacrificed through his hedonistic compulsions.

It was during one of those bacchanalian releases that he came across Mary Smythe walking alone in a secluded park not far from his apartment. He was struck not only by her physical beauty but also by her poise. There was something about the way she moved that touched his heart. He felt he was in love with her, but she did not know he existed. He was drawn to her, even consumed by her. He told himself that somehow, he must possess her. He did not act on his original drunken impulse, but he followed her to see where she lived. He stalked her for several days while the obsession built up in him and he felt a compulsion to act on his need. Unfortunately, he got very drunk one night and the liquid courage of the bottle allowed him to finally approach her, but his inebriation led him to overpowering her and having his way with her. He immediately regretted his actions, realizing his wanton recklessness had ruined any chances he would ever have of wooing her. On the plus side, it was the last time in his life he was drunk, and he vowed to never again let alcohol take away his control.

He continued to stalk Mary Smythe, and when he realized that she was pregnant with his child, he felt such a loss that he fell into a deep despair. The unrequited love he felt for his child and her mother was like an empty space in his innermost being, and it was a space he felt he could never fill. He vowed to do all he could to have at least some part in his daughter's life, even if it was vicariously. He became a master of disguise and found ways to influence parts of her life and gain moments of access to her. He appeared as a substitute teacher, a grocery clerk, a homeless person, a school crossing guard, an old man feeding pigeons in the park. He was always in disguise, literally hiding in plain sight. He even found ways to subtly influence her through gifts of puzzles that he left in places he knew she visited. As she matured, his visits were less frequent but never really stopped.

He had her office bugged, and he hacked her computer simply as a matter of course because of the business he became involved in. It was a good way of keeping tabs on her. When she stumbled upon his surveillance of the Southern Commonwealth, Ebonée, and NAM, he was over the moon. He finally saw an opportunity to connect with her on a personal level. He was extremely proud of his daughter. She was his equal in intelligence, and she was clever with a keen eye and a sharp mind. He only hoped he hadn't driven her away with his heavy-handed abduction of Bubba.

Finally, he decided to reveal his paternity to her before their next meeting at his facility. If he presented his confession in person at the beginning of their discussion, the news could be too much and far too disturbing for her to having any cogent conversation with him. So, instead, he sent her an email.

*****

When Ki read the email, her universe unraveled. Normally, she was in complete control of her surroundings and her emotions. But, upon learning Chelovek was her father, her mind could not stop racing. She found herself hyperventilating and realized she was physically shaking. She had heard of panic attacks before, but she thought that only weak-minded people suffered from them. Never again would she judge those people negatively. Her emotions were a freight train running off the rails, and they jumped between rage, frustration, and (oddly) satisfaction. All these years she had wanted to know who had raped her mother, and now that she knew, a part of her was grateful, but a larger part of her longed for a blissful ignorance that would never be found again. The animal inside of her wanted to tear Chelovek to pieces.

The problem was, she had to meet with him, and soon. She wondered if Chelovek may have done this to throw her off her game. Not that she doubted the validity of his revelation, but his timing seemed to be calculated to upset her and make her vulnerable. Regardless of how she felt now, Ki needed to master her emotions and focus on how she was going to accomplish her goal of bringing him to his knees. Before, her motivation was to best a masterful, narcissistic terrorist, but now it was personal. She knew she would prevail, but the coming meeting was going to be a challenge.

CHAPTER TWENTY-SIX

"All war is a symptom of man's failure as a thinking animal."

—John Steinbeck

When Ki entered Chelovek's facility, he was waiting for her at the ground floor of the false front warehouse. Chelovek was all smiles and exuberance upon greeting Kianna. She, however, could not look him in his eyes. Her face was stern and unyielding. It was difficult for her to be there. She was consumed by so many emotions; she had a difficult time settling on any one of them. They rolled through her like a swelling and then ebbing tide. There was the anger she felt generally for what he was planning on doing to the world. The bile rose in her throat thinking about what he had done to her mother so many years ago. Her irritation grew the more she felt the pull toward him because, after all, he was her father and his game of intrigue fed her innate inquisitiveness and hunger for mental challenges. She could not fight her admiration for his massive intellect and the accomplishments he achieved through his perseverance and innovation in technology. But the emotion affecting her now, on the verge of his proposal of joining him, was the exasperation she felt for his inability to see that he was a toxic narcissist. His solipsistic paradigm combined with his far-reaching intellect meant he was likely the most dangerous man on earth. As if that mixed bag of emotions weren't confusing enough, she also felt guilty for being the one to bring him to his knees. She would have to play on his longing for a relationship to accomplish that, and the betrayal from his own daughter would cut deeper than anything.

"Good morning, my daughter! I am so glad you came to my facility to hear me out."

Hiding none of her disdain, she said, "You do not yet have the right to call me your daughter! Forcing your seed into my mother's womb makes you my progenitor, not my father. There is considerably more to fatherhood than simply engaging in a sexual union with someone. Considerably more! Besides, what choice do I really have? You are holding all the cards. You know literally everything about my clients and myself, and you abducted my personal assistant. You want to reconcile the situation, but I sense no remorse in your actions. You speak of the 'greater good', but I have yet to fully comprehend your position and how you justify your reprehensible behavior. I want to get this over with."

"Yes, I am looking forward to that debate. I can hardly wait to discuss your response to my offer now that you understand our true relationship."

Kianna frowned. "Mänsklig. I am willing to acknowledge the fact that we are biologically connected, but we do not have a *relationship*. As it stands, I am not sure you will respond positively to what I am about to say."

Chelovek went silent and his face became hard to read.

Kianna took a deep breath. "Let me start by saying something positive. I am impressed with the technology you have created. I had no idea there was anything like this type of advancement in surveillance and manipulated remote transmission. If you were the one that developed all of this, my hat is off to you."

"Thank you for the acknowledgement. That means a great deal to me. It has been a long time coming. Regarding the technology, however, I cannot take credit for its creation. I have enhanced it and fine-tuned it a great deal over the years. Surprisingly, it is quite old technology. You could say I inherited it. But that is a story for another time. Regardless, thank you for the compliment."

"Let me get to the point. Although I must admit, there is a part of me that wants to get to know you better, I am sure you can guess at the conflicting emotions I harbor. One that factors large is the rage I feel for what you did to my mother. I am not a violent person, but right now I want you to suffer." Suddenly, her face contorted with a righteous fury and she screamed at Chelovek. "I HATE YOU! I WANT YOU TO DIE!" Ki gained some small degree of composure, but her voice was shaking as she said, "Torture would be too good for you because it would not put you into the amount of pain you deserve." She took a beat and pulled herself together and then said in a calm that belied her true feelings. "I know I owe my very existence to you, but it is small recompense for your heinous behavior. I would gladly give up my life if it could take away what my *mother* had to go through because of your selfish actions! She has suffered needlessly and continues to do so. And as great as my ire is for you, as deep is the hatred I feel for you, it is not the main reason I would find the idea of joining you in *any* enterprise reprehensible. My biggest objection to joining you is what you are planning on doing to this world and its billions of people with your technology."

Chelovek shook his head vigorously. "You have no idea what I am planning on doing! I have revealed nothing about my intentions. I keep my plans very close to my vest. I am the only one who knows what I am going to do. I am solely in control of all my operations. Please don't dismiss this opportunity to establish some family bonds. I am even willing to see your mother and make my apologies if you will join me."

Kianna shouted. "Apologies? Do you think that will make up for what you have done? Regardless of what happens here tonight, I do want you to speak to my mother, but only to offer her some kind of closure. And, as to your intentions? You may not have explicitly told me your plans, but it is abundantly clear what you are going to do. I refuse to sit back and let you release your particular brand of horror upon the world.

"You say that your intentions are honorable and you talk about creating a utopia that will evolve out of the chaos you are hellbent on unleashing. It is abundantly clear to me you are only deluding yourself in order to justify your actions."

At that point, Kianna pulled a sheaf of papers out of her blouse and handed them to Chelovek.

He asked, "What is this?"

"After receiving your email, I knew it would be difficult to rein in my feelings and remain focused, so I drafted this projection of what your plans for all the governments of the world were, deduced from what you have told me. Read it and tell me I am wrong. Right now, however, I need to disengage or I will do something I will regret." She then turned and stepped away from him, closing her eyes to recenter and slow her breathing.

The note read:

Here is what I suspect are your plans for all the governments of the world and all the control they exert over you. This is worth noting because, ironically, I believe your motivation for all of this is rooted in the resentment you feel for having your personal rights and freedoms violated.

This is what I think will happen: The first thing you will do is broadcast by way of the internet and other streaming services, an announcement from the talking heads of each of the economically important countries of the world, stating there is an eminent threat, but with no details. Of course, none of these politicians will be the actual people. They will all be virtual duplicates created by your programmers. The words coming out of their mouths will be your words, and each of their voices will be your voice manipulated by your digital technology. On top of the supposedly credible fear that you will foment, you will saturate the internet with massive far-reaching conspiracy theories predicting the shutdown of the power grid and internet streaming services. They will appear to be far-fetched but will serve the function of exacerbating and spreading fear among the populace. Then, using your technology, you will sow doubt through various analog and digital media, which will include hijacked newspaper content, fake television, and fake radio programs, partially replacing and supplementing the authentic reports. You will then proceed to confirm all the rumors by actually shutting down the power grid, utilities, and the internet throughout Europe, Asia, the Americas, Australia and Africa. Finally, you will reward countries that fall in line with your image of an ideal form of government by returning limited control of their resources. How did I do?

Chelovek sat there in stunned silence. He was immobile for several minutes, his face blanched, until finally he spoke. "How did you come to those conclusions? Where did you get your information?"

Kianna opened her eyes. "From you. I have had my suspicions for some time now because of the dry runs you have recently been doing here in Atlanta. Power brownouts, news reports that were modified subtly, but to my ear and eye quite overt, and then there was a greater amount of internet content that seemed focused on large scale global dystopia. What you told me in the cave helped me zero in on specifics, but you also revealed a great deal to me in your highly informative tour of this facility. Up until that tour, I was not entirely sure of the mechanisms you would use to follow through on your ultimate plan."

A big grin slowly formed on Chelovek's face. "My first reaction to you knowing my plans in such detail made me think you had somehow gained the ability to read minds, but now I realize you aren't prescient, just a genius. And I am your father. It only makes sense. The proverbial apple does not fall from the tree. I am so proud of you, even if you do not agree with me. What is keeping you from joining me?"

Kianna sighed. "Mänsklig, there is so much I have a problem with. Thankfully, I was raised by an amazing and loving woman with strong principles, ethics, and ideals. You were not nearly so fortunate in your upbringing, so I understand the disconnect you have, and I do feel some sympathy, but not enough to overlook the reprehensible nature of your objectives and goals. There is a deep truth I abide in. Do unto others what you would have others do unto you. You do not want to be controlled, but you have no problem dispensing broad scale control over others. You have a compulsive need for privacy, but everything you do violates the privacy of nearly everyone in the world. You justify all of this by telling yourself you are going to be creating an Eden for these poor misguided miscreants. If you were to turn your massive intellect towards a realistic deconstruction of your plans, you would see the giant holes of logic residing in them."

Chelovek frowned. "Give me an example."

"Certainly. You put a great deal of faith in the ability of people to rise out of the ashes of your manifested social disaster and create a community of citizens capable of controlling their human nature. As you said yourself, and I agree, there are people who are predisposed to desire power, and the power that they wrench or wheedle within a governing body will be bent toward corruption. They yearn to have their own needs and wants met, even if that means sacrificing the rights of others in the process. While it is true there are truly good people in the world, there are also their opposites. It has been said, the most qualified candidates for public office choose not to seek any such office. The flowers that will come to fruit in your Eden will be rotten down to their roots. Corruption will reign supreme."

Chelovek interjected, "But you are wrong. As you pointed out, my plans will nip that nascent corruption in the bud because I will dole out benefits to those groups of leaders that follow through on my expectations. Not the corrupt ones. I will control the corruption even if you choose to turn down my offer to join me."

Kianna shook her head. "Or so you say. Since I am not going to be a party to your nonsense, you will have to relinquish control to some of your minions because, at this scale, you will be unable to effectively manage the complex dynamic that will unfold. You have said you do not trust any of the people working for you. Do you not think that corruption will weed its way into your own organization? You will have created the ultimate fascist state. Do not tell me that it will not attract power hungry individuals."

Kianna paused to collect herself, and then continued, "Enough of this debate. I am not going to delude myself into thinking you are going to suddenly see the light and truth of what I am saying. You have dedicated so much of your life, energy, and passion toward this singular goal that you are blinded. I am being forced by your actions to shut you down and put an end to this nonsense."

Chelovek snorted derisively. "And how do you plan on doing that?"

At that moment, the lights went out and Kianna smiled and thought, *Now that is what I call timing.*

Kianna had positioned herself to be standing beside Chelovek when the entire facility was plunged into darkness. She reached over and pressed two nerve points on his body simultaneously. Chelovek collapsed to the floor. As soon as he hit the ground, the power was restored and the lights came back on. The elevator door opened and Bubba stepped out. Her team had followed her instructions to the letter.

****

With Chelovek prostrate at her feet, she took in the splendor of the virtual world around her. The attention to detail was phenomenal. Even though she knew most of the woodland creatures she saw were a robotic simulacrum, the virtual texture and appearance made them feel authentic. Letting go of her awareness of the technological marvel allowed the virtual environment to become real for her, and the tranquility of this tableau swept her into a deep sense of peace.

The main elevator door opened and out walked Latitia, Tamba, Marain, and The Ghost. They had never seen the 4th floor VR illusion before and were taken aback as much as Ki had been. Marain said, "I have to get some of this technology. I am already redesigning my office in my head. I thought I had state of the art at my headquarters, but I can see now, I do not."

Kianna greeted them and asked, "Everything went as planned?"

Everyone nodded their heads. Marain looked around. "Where is Bubba? Is he okay?"

Kianna reassured them. "He is fine. He is just attending to some items on my assignment sheet. How did you and Daniel fare with accessing the lower floors?"

Daniel nodded. "We paid a visit to the nitrogen compressors on the roof per your request, and then accessed the parking area via the Solatubes. But it is a good thing Marain and I are lean of body. It was a bit of a squeeze. We did run into some security forces, but it wasn't anything we couldn't handle. Getting to the first floor above the reactor was a piece of cake thanks to your elevator code. By the way, those VR projections of the serpents near the circuit breakers were very convincing! I must admit they had us doing some high-stepping."

Kianna looked at them quizzically. "That does not make sense. Why would Chelovek put serpent projections around the circuit breakers?"

Chelovek had started coming back to consciousness and muttered. "That is because I didn't put serpent projections near the circuit breakers. Those are honest-to-goodness venomous vipers. I can see I didn't account for your good luck."

Marain and Daniel looked at each other with undisguised horror and then relief.

"It's not that I don't trust my employees, but I put them there as another safeguard against intrusion. It was just an additional precaution to keep the power on at all times. If you were trying to do this as a ploy to shut me down, you may have noticed it didn't work. I have a number of back-up generators in place, which kick in within a few minutes if there is any loss of power. While Kianna did catch me by surprise, and she took me down with a nerve compression, I won't be stopped that easily. I don't seem to be any the worse off for it. And it seems we are missing some members of your boarding party. You are short three people, I believe."

Just then, as if on cue, the elevator arrived and out stepped Obatala, followed closely on her heels by Colonel Tom.

"My goodness, I hope we are not too late for the party. Looks like the only one missin' is our Bubba."

This is when Colonel Tom looked around the space and began to take it all in. He slapped his leg and said, "If this ain't the damnedest thing. If I didn't know better, I'd think we were in the middle of the countryside. And lord have mercy, is that there a fire-breathing dragon?"

Obatala was equally impressed and glanced around, but soon she returned her attention to the gathering of nearly all the players in the drama that had been unfolding. Her attention shifted to the man who sat on the floor before them. She noted that Chelovek was sporting a sly smile on his face and Colonel Tom was acting very nervous all of a sudden. That's when she noticed the handle of a pistol mostly concealed in Colonel Tom's jacket. She slowly inched her way over to Kianna. Just then, the elevator door opened and Bubba made his entrance and joined the group.

Bubba had a big grin on his face and said, "Sorry if I kept everyone. I came as soon as I could. I haven't missed anything, have I?"

Chelovek stood up and brushed himself off. "Well, it is so good to see everyone all in one place. This whole thing about spying on each of you separately was becoming tedious, to say the least. I suspect Kianna told you that I have agreed to stop my surveillance of you, and in addition, I will cease my extortion and blackmail schemes. All I am asking you to do is return the favor. Stop your investigation of my operations. That being the case, I don't know why you are all here. I am no longer going to be in your lives. Why don't we all just peacefully go our own ways?"

Marain shook his head. "How can we ever believe anything coming out of your mouth?"

Kianna spoke up. "Marain, I beg to differ with you. I will grant you he is very deceptive and overflows with deceit, however, I have never known him to lie. He may be a despicable person, but he appears to be a man of his word. I believe he will honor that agreement. However, as I have explained, I do not want to live in a world under his control. That is why we are here. This may have started with privacy issues, but it has devolved into something far more sinister."

"My dear, Kianna. Thank you for standing up for my integrity. I am wondering how we are going to resolve this dilemma. You seem to have temporarily disabled my security forces, but that is of no real consequence. Knowing you as I do, I suspect they have fallen to no harm. All I need is one security person. Colonel Tom, I believe you have something to reveal."

Everyone turned to look at Colonel Tom. He was sidling up to Chelovek with his pistol drawn. He did not look comfortable as he spoke.

"Well, everyone I am really sorry about this, but I just could not turn down the opportunity that Mr. Chelovek offered me. I am ashamed of myself, but I know I will get over it." Turning to Chelovek, he said, "What do you want me to do with these folks?"

"I abhor violence, so eventually they'll be set free once I have returned to Beijing, or at least until I am safely out of the country. I'm thinking we should put them on ice for the time being. I have several unoccupied apartments currently. Let's put the ladies in B and the gentlemen in F. Bubba, since you are well acquainted with apartments, you'll be able to give the men a tour of their new accommodations and Kianna, you can do the same for the ladies. Colonel Tom, after we secure them, you can accompany me, and I will give you a deeper peek into the inner sanctum. Once we have done that, I need to check my operations in case something else has happened that I was not aware of. Colonel Tom, you and I can then discuss how to handle things between us going forward."

Chelovek walked the group down the wooded trail and reached down to touch a massive, moss-covered rock in front of a large oak tree. Immediately, the tree disappeared and what stood in its place was a clear glass elevator and shaft rising straight up into the air. Once they all were gathered inside, the elevator automatically ascended directly to the apartments. Everything was going as Chelovek had hoped. However, he was disappointed that his daughter failed to give him more of a challenge. One thing in particular that confused him was Kianna's total acquiescence. She could have used her Aikido skills but had not, and then there was her current lack of emotional response to him. Maybe she was simply accepting the inevitable.

One of the truths he neglected to tell Colonel Tom was that within the next three weeks he would be overthrowing the world. Much better to let him live in his comfortable balloon of security. Once he had unleashed his reign of controlled chaos, he would let his new guests go their merry ways. There was nothing they could do to stop him. He could only hope Kianna would come around once civilization had collapsed around the world. Maybe then she would realize that his vision would become a reality. Although she made a valid point about the power-hungry people out there, he felt confident he could suppress any moves for power those people might employ. NAM would fit nicely into his hopes for society's renaissance and Ebonée would also instill some catalyst for change as well. He did feel sorry for Colonel Tom though because his neat and tidy world was going to come crashing down around him.

When he got to his apartment, he immediately went to his master computer terminal. He needed to check his security and find out why they had failed to show up in his moment of need. He mumbled to himself as he attempted to turn on his system.

"Now that's odd."

The computer did not seem to recognize him. He had a retinal scan, a fingerprint ID, and a state-of-the-art DNA sequencer to affirm who he really was. But it was saying he was not an authorized user. A sick feeling settled over him as he heard the door open to his apartment. Standing in the doorway was everyone who should have been safely ensconced in their apartments. As the representatives of NAM, Ebonée, and The Southern Commonwealth made their way in, the Smythe Detective Agency rounded everyone up to confront Chelovek. Latitia, Obatala, and Tamba stepped forward and ceremoniously pulled out their remotes for the explosives on the roof. Pressing them simultaneously, they triggered the small explosions on the nitrogen condensers above their heads. As the realization of defeat settled on Chelovek, another unknown person entered the room and proceeded to place handcuffs on Chelovek.

The man with the cuffs said, "I hereby arrest you in the name of the United and Honorable Militia of the Southern Commonwealth for suspicion of high crimes and terrorism. You will be taken to a prison where you will await arraignment, trial, and sentencing."

CHAPTER TWENTY-SEVEN

"The best way of keeping a secret is to pretend there isn't one."

—Margaret Atwood

Kianna knew prison would be the most unbearable punishment her father could face. It was real, it was stark, it was confining. Nearly every moment was controlled—when he could eat, exercise, sleep, or go outside were all at the discretion of the warden, or worse yet, the system. After he left the orphanage, he built a life that granted him the maximum control over other people and the world around him. She knew he would resent her and what she had done, but she had a clear conscience. She was somewhat surprised that he agreed to her visitation, but there he was sitting at the hard metal table in the visiting room with a serene look on his face.

"Hello, father. You are in a better frame of mind than I expected."

"Hello, daughter. Wallowing in self-pity and resentment never achieved anything other than suffering. One of the most important lessons I learned in my Buddhist studies was suffering comes from how we entangle with the world. In letting go, we exercise the only control we can ever have. Don't get me wrong, I would change my situation in a heartbeat. I am glad you asked for this visitation. I was hoping you could enlighten me about how you did what I considered impossible."

Kianna smiled broadly. "I would be happy to share what we did. How would you like to proceed? With a timeline or a detailing of who did what?"

"Let's go with the timeline."

"Okay, we'll start with the journey to the cave. I placed Bubba there to do two things. One was to disable your communications jump station. I knew you would try something like setting up that device. And yes, I saw you place it on the rock. You could have a second career as an illusionist. Wonderful sleight of hand. The second thing is that I was actually hoping your people would abduct Bubba. You did not fail me there. If you had not done it then, I would have had to come up with another way to achieve my objectives. But you took the bait. I had hoped you would put him in your personal apartment. Unfortunately, I realized after my visit to your operations, you had numerous living quarters. Ultimately, it did not matter because you gave him access to your computer system, and Bubba is a sophisticated hacker. With his daddy being a computer nerd for a long time, Bubba learned a great deal about navigating cyberspace. That, combined with my cousin's security expertise, enabled him put an open backdoor into your network to be accessed later from inside the building.

"I used your miniature bugs to send you contrary messages via our clandestine meetings. I presented our team with handwritten notes warning them about your subterfuge. Knowing what to look for, I scanned the other members of our group and there was Latitia, leaking the same information I was. After the meeting I pulled her aside and, via written notes, I informed her of what she was inadvertently providing. The bugs had to have been coming from Colonel Tom, which immediately made him untrustworthy. I confronted him and he gave you up without a moment's hesitation. He had already decided he could not betray the people within our group. Although, he was sorely tempted. I told him to play along with you so he could be microchipped and gain your confidence, and I gave him the gun that he used. It was loaded with blanks.

"Our meeting and tour of your facility was extremely helpful. That aided in the development of a tactical plan of operations in closing you down. The teams were broken into twos, with the exception of Bubba who needed to work solo. Marain and Daniel started on the roof, planting small plastic explosive charges on the nitrogen compressors and accessed the facility via the Solatubes into the parking garage. They were met with a small security detail that had been alerted by sensors you had on the roof, but they were easily dealt with and subdued quickly. With the information I had given Daniel and Marain, they used the elevator to get to the lower maintenance floor, and then it was easy to find the ramp down to the reactor and circuit breakers. The real serpents were not expected. Thank goodness Yhprum's law occasionally comes into play and favors the unprepared. Before they flipped the circuit breakers, they locked entry and exit to all but one of the surveillance pods on the second floor. I had been orchestrating our conversation on the 4th floor to coincide with the power outage. I knew you were expecting the power outage because I had told Colonel Tom to share that bit of misleading 'insider' information. I made sure, just to be safe, that none of the teams knew what the others were doing, so Colonel Tom sincerely knew nothing other than what I told him.

"I needed the power outage to create the opportunity to disable you and to eliminate the virtual reality of the 4th floor. When the power came back on, I knew it would take several minutes to reboot. With it turned off, the infrastructure revealed itself and I saw the second elevator. I knew you would have made sure to have an immediate access to your personal apartment, and getting there was my primary objective. Once you were unconscious, Bubba entered from where he had been hiding and helped me carry you to the personal elevator. Because of the master control microchip embedded in your body, I knew it would allow us access to any place I wanted to go. Once we were in your residence, I had full access to the central control processor and communication system for all of your far-flung international operations through the backdoor we created. Once your retinal scan, fingerprint, and DNA were provided, Bubba was able to change your personal settings so they would now recognize him as an alternate administrator, and he had full control. Using your avatar, he contacted all operations managers and basically told them all activities were going on a temporary hiatus and all employees were on a paid leave of absence. He then went to each country's intelligence services and made a full confession of crimes and provided detailed directions and access information for each of your centers of operation. He also dismantled all security functions at those facilities.

"While all of this was going on, Tamba and Latitia accessed the one surveillance pod that was accessible and searched the archives to find any recordings of conversations between you and Colonel Tom. I needed to be sure I had not misplaced my trust in him. Meanwhile, Colonel Tom and Obatala were immobilizing your security forces and other employees from the ground floor maintenance level of the apartment complex. There is a switch there which locks entire blocks of doors. They waited until the momentary power outage. That way, the employees thought it might be because of a glitch caused by the blackout.

"Once you came to and Colonel Tom appeared to take sides with you, we needed to allow you to retreat to the one place you felt the most secure: your apartment. Once you thought we were safely locked away, we then let in the head of the Southern Commonwealth Militia's intelligence operations. Our final coup was taking out the nitrogen compressors and destroying any backup systems that might be in place. You were arrested and that was that."

Chelovek sat there smiling and shaking his head. "Once again, I feel that sense of pride in being your father. Fascinating! By the way, I don't think I have ever heard of Yhprum's Law. Would you care to enlighten me?"

"It is the inverse of Murphy's Law. If anything can go right, it will, and at the best possible moment. The universe tends to be balanced in its unfolding."

Chelovek chuckled heartily.

Kianna pulled back from the camaraderie they had begun to enjoy and said somberly, "Now is the time for the real reason for my visit. I have brought someone with me today who wanted to have some alone time with you."

At that moment, the door opened and in walked a beautiful, tall black woman. It was readily apparent she was Kianna's mother because Kianna shared many of her features. There was some white in her hair, and she wore a simple black dress. Mary held herself erect and proud and walked with confidence. Her manner was serene, but it was just barely masking a darker and more serious tension that was palpable in the small room.

As Mary entered, Kianna left. Mary stared intently at Chelovek with a variety of emotions showing on her face—grief, relief, anger, sadness, and finally acceptance. She sat down in front of him.

He could not bring himself to make eye contact. He looked past her and meekly uttered, "Hello, Mary."

Mary's face was drawn as she said, "I have been looking forward to and dreading this moment for a very long time. When Kianna told me she had found my rapist, I frankly did not know how to respond. I have wanted this resolution for so long, it almost seems a part of my DNA. Now that I am here, what can you possibly do or say that will repair the psychic and emotional damage you have done to me?"

Chelovek hung his head. "I never wanted this meeting to occur. I am so filled with remorse, regrets, and embarrassment, I find myself unable to verbalize anything that is in my heart. It feels as though that breaking heart cannot begin to contain, let alone carry, the burden of my guilt. I was a weak and insecure man who fortified my courage with alcohol in order to possess and control you. I soon realized I had gone down a path from which I could never return. I would apologize, but I know that any apology that I would make would be like being gored by a bull and putting a small bandage over the wound. Yet, I feel I owe you at least some recognition of my regret and shame. I never had the courage to do that while Kianna was growing up with a mother who struggled alone to put food on the table. Now, that strong, noble daughter of ours has forced my hand, and I offer that apology to you now."

Mary sat silently. When she finally spoke, she sounded exhausted. "Your words are hollow to me regardless of your sincerity. I take some small recompense in the pain that it is causing you, but on the whole, you cannot begin to comprehend the violation I felt at your hands. And although I would love to visit retribution on you for your actions, it would not alleviate my pain. In fact, it may only make it greater. If you are looking for me to forgive you, I can only say that it will be a cold day in hell before that will ever happen. The one bright spot in all of this evil is the amazing woman who is my daughter. But, be clear on this: you are not her father. You do not deserve the title of father. Now, I think we are done here. If we ever see each other again outside of this environment, do not expect me to acknowledge you."

With one final glance, she stood and left the room, leaving Mänsklig Chelovek, aka Frank Brown, collapsing in a spasm of sobbing regret.

CHAPTER TWENTY-EIGHT

"When you compare the sorrows of real life to the pleasures of the imaginary one, you will never want to live again, only to dream forever."

—Alexandre Dumas

Mänsklig Chelovek found himself becoming more and more despondent. Although he knew he shouldn't dwell on the circumstances of his imprisonment, that was where he found himself. At first, he had talked himself into embracing an attitude of acceptance. Although he talked a good game to his daughter, there was a huge difference between complacency and truly accepting the life unfolding around him. The crux of his problem was the resentment that kept rising to the surface and dominating his thoughts. As much as he would like to think he was a master of his own mind, he fell far short in the practice of meditation. Unless he changed his focus, he would continue to dwell on what he had lost. He felt certain, over time, he would lose his mind.

Repeatedly contributing to his downward spiral of depression was his memory of the fourth-floor fantasy world he had installed in all of his facilities. He relished the feeling he had with the falling away of reality that was replaced by a world in which he was in control.

Suddenly, it struck him! His fourth-floor fantasy served not only his escape from reality, it may just be his escape *to* reality. He needed to understand its value to the rest of the world and position himself in a way that he could market it or have someone else market it. If he played his cards right, he might find the opportunity to leave this prison compound.

His daughter had taught him many important lessons about what he had done wrong and how he had been defeated. If he were to get out of this hell hole, he would not make the same mistakes. That was a big *if*, but he was now feeling like there was a chance to put himself back in the game. It reenergized him. The first thing he did was reach out to Colonel Tom. He knew how to read the man and had a fairly good idea of what Colonel Tom was looking for.

Colonel Tom was hesitant to reply to the formal invitation from Chelovek. Tom did not trust him, and perhaps not even himself for good reason. He let the invitation lie on his desk for nearly a week before he opened it. All it had said was Chelovek wanted to talk to him about a project that could be beneficial to the Southern Commonwealth. The Southern Commonwealth was, to a large degree, what defined Colonel Tom's existence. But he had concerns regarding Chelovek and what his larger plan might be. Still, he could not know for sure until he knew more about it. His mind went round and round like this for nearly three weeks. Finally, he accepted Chelovek's invitation and decided to go to the prison with his personal assistant, Latitia. He felt far more confident with her along because she would be a good counterbalance to any temptation coming from Chelovek.

When they arrived, Chelovek was sitting at the hard metal table in the visitation area. Everything about the space spoke of bland and neutral. The gray walls, the dark gray tables and chairs, the light gray floor, and the drab demeanor of Chelovek's garb. Colonel Tom was, of course, dressed in his usual outfit of brilliant white with black accents. His neutral theme contrasted well with the dull décor, and it would normally have made him the center of attention in this monotonous abode, if not for Latitia. She wore a fluorescent yellow dress and lipstick-red shoes that, when contrasted with her mahogany skin, commanded the full attention of any onlookers. Chelovek glanced up when he heard the door open, and as soon as he saw Latitia, he stood up and made a deep and respectful bow in her direction.

"My dear Latitia, you have literally brightened my day! I would go so far as to say you may be detained for causing a disturbance in this otherwise dull and dreary dungeon of a domicile. Your attire is a welcome conflagration for these tired eyes. Colonel Tom, thank you for bringing along this spot of color and visual excitement to my drab world."

"You are more than welcome, Mr. Chelovek. Latitia, however, is serving a more important role than mere eye candy. I don't trust you, sir, and I know I have been tempted before by your silver tongue. She is my insurance policy. I have learned my lesson."

Latitia smiled as she spoke to Chelovek. "Thank you for the compliment. I was very intentional in selecting my attire. But, rest assured, I will be listening carefully to whatever you are proposing. As the good Colonel conveyed, you are not to be trusted."

Chelovek nodded his head. "True. My reputation does precede me. However, what I am about to propose is something that can create a win-win-win solution for all the parties involved: the Southern Commonwealth, Colonel Tom, and yours truly. What I will receive from this proposal is an occasional brief respite from the cruel and excessive monotony of prison life. I fear that if I continue to be subjected to this lifestyle, I will slowly go insane."

Colonel Tom leaned forward. "What do I gain from this?"

"You will be the one who gets credit for this whole idea and become one of the most popular men on the planet."

Colonel Tom smiled. "You have my attention. What about the Southern Commonwealth? How will we benefit from your proposal?"

Chelovek leaned back in his chair. "One word: wealth."

Colonel Tom leaned over and whispered in Latitia's ear. "What do you think, my dear?"

Latitia said, "I think we need to hear him out."

Colonel Tom directly addressed Chelovek. "So, what is this brilliant idea of yours?"

Chelovek put his hands behind his head and grinned. Leaning back, he said, "The fourth floor."

Colonel Tom had a puzzled look on his face. "What on earth do you mean? Latitia, are you following him?"

"I am, and I will say, it is a brilliant idea and could very well work. For everyone concerned."

EPILOGUE

"They say when you meet somebody that looks just like you, you die."

—P. Wish, *The Doppelgänger*

Bubba leaned back on the couch in the foyer of the Smythe Detective Agency and cupped his hands behind his head.

"I don't know 'bout you Miss Ki, but I think we deserve a good rest from that last case. I was wound up tighter than a fat man's girdle. It feels strange to not have a pressin' need to fix the world."

"I know what you mean, Bubba. When you are going a hundred miles an hour and solving problems, your life is filled to the brim with meaning and energy. When it is over, you feel empty inside, like you should be doing something. Accomplishing something. I agree a respite is called for, but I hope not for too long. I have never been a fan of ennui."

Bubba sat up. "I have a feeling this break ain't gonna last long. When word gets out of what we did, we'll be able to pick and choose the cases we want to work on."

"I suspect you are right. That is, *if* the word gets out. I think the only ones who will ever find out we were on the brink of a worldwide economic collapse will be the law enforcement community. I predict that the next knock on the door will be from a police officer with an unsolvable problem."

Just then, their door opened and in walked a late middle-aged Latino man with some Arabic features who looked more than just a little worse for wear. The badge attached to his belt announced who he was.

"Miss Ki, you gotta stop doin' that."

Ki laughed out loud. "I do not know what you are talking about. THAT was just a lucky guess, but I will take credit for it. How may we help you detective?"

"Detective Omar Sanchez. I am with the Atlanta Crime Authority. You are Miss Kianna Smythe and Bubba Smith?"

He appeared to be someone who was used to hard work and wasn't overly concerned about appearances. He also looked tired, as though he desperately wanted to join Bubba on the couch. His button-up shirt was rumpled and his hair was unruly, but his disheveled appearance likely belied his innate intelligence and awareness. When he glanced at Ki and Bubba, they noticed there was a brightness in his eyes that showed him to be tuned in to his surroundings. His gaze was penetrating and when he spoke, it was with complete authority.

Bubba stood up and reached out his hand and said, "Right on both accounts. As Miss Ki said, how can we help you?"

Omar shook Bubba's hand and took off his hat and held it in front of him. "I guess you could say I have an unsolvable problem."

Bubba looked over at Ki and saw her smiling back at him. Bubba just shook his head and turned his attention back to Detective Sanchez. "What makes you say it is unsolvable?"

Omar said, "I consider myself to be pretty good at my job. I have solved a number of difficult and perplexing cases, but what I have now has me stumped. The word got around through the precinct what you did with that Chelovek fellow, and I naturally wanted to see if you all might rise to the challenge and join me in an investigation."

Kianna reached over and also shook his hand. "A pleasure to make your acquaintance, Omar. I must admit, you have whetted my appetite. Tell us more."

"Certainly. May I sit down?"

Ki said, "Maybe we should do this in my private office."

Officer Sanchez followed them into the office area and scanned the surroundings with an attention that caught the notice of Ki. Once they were seated, he looked around the office, taking it in as though it was a crime scene. Kianna knew that look.

"Excuse me detective, I could not help but notice you were scanning this room much like I would. May I ask what you can tell me about what you saw?"

"Sorry. Force of habit. I have been doing this job for over thirty years and have a procedure that has rarely failed me. I picked up a lot, but I think I'm going to file that information away in case I might need it later."

"I totally understand. It appears we are kindred spirits. I am sorry if I interrupted you. Please continue with your story."

"I was working on some cold cases and there was one file on a murder case that referenced an evidence box. I pulled the box and examined the sealed baggies. I found an eyelash with a DNA report that made no sense. It matched a long-time prisoner who has been incarcerated for over thirty years. Obviously, some sort of mistake was made. I ran it through our new DNA sequencer and came up with the same match in our database but discovered an additional match. I was excited, because I could reopen the case. The problem was the other match in the database didn't make any sense either. It was of a fellow police officer."

Kianna smiled. "That does not seem too odd. It could be that the investigating officer shed an eyelash that fell into the evidence bag."

"That's what I thought, but the officer was not on the police force at the time."

"Is it possible he was the perp?"

"No. I have briefly interviewed him and run a background check. He has a rock-solid alibi. He was a student at the police academy here in Atlanta at the time of the crime."

"Could someone be trying to frame him and planted the eyelash in the evidence?"

"I thought of that, but it is highly unlikely. The baggie had been sealed for over five years. If someone were trying to frame him, there would very likely be more corroborating evidence."

Kianna leaned in, becoming increasingly interested in this problem. "Did he have an identical twin brother?"

"The DNA match for an identical twin is 99.99 percent, and this one was a 100 percent match."

"You really have my attention now. Is there anything else?

"Yes. There was one very perplexing aberration. The telomeres on the chromosomes found on the eyelash indicated that the perp was ten years older than my police officer and about thirty years younger than the prisoner."

Kianna nodded her head. "We will take the case. When can we get started?"

Omar stood up smiling. "Wonderful. I can't wait to see how you are going to solve this."

Kianna smiled. "Oh, that is easy. I already have that part figured out. The hard part is coming to understand the consequences of the questions surrounding the answer."

AUTHOR'S NOTE

I came up with the idea for the Soushari Saga in 1997 when I had moved from Maine to South Carolina. Although I am proud of my New England heritage and roots, I became totally enamored by the history, mystery, and traditions of the Southern culture. Although, the overt good manners and gentility of these wonderful people were a comforting psychic balm, I noticed a certain passive aggressive nature to it all. Being a Yankee, people were polite enough to me but there was a certain line I could never cross. I would never be fully accepted into that esteemed culture, and I understood this all too well because it was the same way in the State of Maine. In Maine, if you weren't born and raised there, you were "from away," and you could never be fully embraced by the community. I believe this attitude is changing, both in the North and in the South, but it is a slow change.

In time, I came to realize the complexity of the Southern culture and the deep-seated resentment that came with what remains of "the unpleasantness" of that "War of Northern Aggression" (aka the Civil War). The memory is a long and deep wound, and for many Southerners it will never be healed. There is a pride in their heritage, and that heritage has become a part of their personal identity. I eventually came to understand and respect that. In fact, in my teen years, I was a fan of the "Stars and Bars" flag. To me that symbol represented *rebellion* or more simply *rebel*. That idea resonated with me. I was an advocate for questioning authority because power, in any form, needs to be questioned and challenged.

But I was raised by a wonderful mother who taught me the importance of respect. Once I understood that Black people during the antebellum South were not considered to be fully human, my mind shifted. Here was a symbol that meant one thing to me but meant something highly offensive to another group of people. If I put myself in their position, how would I feel? When people can be bought and sold at the whim of those in power, there is a problem. I can only imagine how I would feel if I were treated that way. I had early on embraced the Golden Rule as a guiding principle in my life, so if I were to do unto others as I would have them do unto me, I needed to reassess my relationship with that symbol. If I wanted to show respect, I needed to change.

I have been, and still am, a strong advocate for individual rights and freedoms, but I cannot conscientiously tread upon the rights and freedoms of others while I am in pursuit of my own because to do so is inviting the same behavior toward me. In the Lord's Prayer there is something about ". . . *and forgive us our trespasses,* **as we forgive them** *who trespass against us.*"

The idea for the setting and timing of the book became obvious when I looked at attitudes and considered possible futures over time in the South. If I were to stage the story in a future where the South had finally seceded from the rest of the United States, it would allow me to develop the storyline against what that South might look like. I focused on what I could see as the obvious unfolding of strong state's rights and fractured ideas of segregation and integration. I staged a great deal of the action in Georgia, and particularly in Atlanta. By having Atlanta represented as a Special Economic Zone, I was able to create what would likely become an independent "cultural island" within the surrounding dominant cultural milieu. In this cultural island it would only be natural for independent political entities to surface. Thus, Ebonée and NAM.

I also introduced a number of Japanese elements throughout the story because, in my opinion, the Japanese culture and the Southern culture are parallel in many respects. They both find manners, respect, and honor to be extremely important in their self-definition. They are both also adept at incorporating other cultural traditions and seamlessly making them uniquely their own.

A major theme of this book is about understanding *who* a person is versus *what* they consider themselves to be. Too often, we define ourselves by the boxes we put ourselves in. Am I my race, my gender, my nationality, my religion, my political party? It is my belief that who we are is more about our personal stories and histories and not the boxes that we put ourselves and others in. These boxes are a part of our identity, but it is not necessarily *who* we are. My favorite color is green, and your favorite color may be orange, but it should not define us or divide us. Until we understand the stories of other people, we can only define those people from the boxes and the fears and the lies we tell ourselves. Our shared personal stories, however, can help to create empathy and compassion in our own lives and the lives of those people we come to know. I am striving here to understand who we are as unique individuals vs. how we see ourselves within our group identities and how those identities influence and interact with each other. These group identities offer us succor and security, but we can find ourselves compromising our "true self" in order to find acceptance within the complex mélange of group identities. It is not a simple journey.

The technology that Chelovek has at his command is totally imagined, but it is based on capabilities that exist today. This story will unfold over three books and in the last book I will explain where and when and why that technology came into being.

THE SOUSHARI SAGA

BOOK TWO

DOPPELGÄNGERS

COMING SOON

ACKNOWLEDGEMENTS

I first of all want to acknowledge the incredible talents and insights of my editor, Cara Highsmith. Her ability to understand the sculptural aspect of the book's unfolding was instrumental to the flow and delivery of my writing. In addition, her help in navigating the complex world of self-publishing has been indispensable. Thank you Cara. I also want to thank Brian McLaren of the Living School for recommending Cara to me. My fellow writers in my writing community have also been instrumental in helping me better express my thoughts in a more lucid and readable manner. I thank Eric Kruger, Pamela Canler, Karen Claypool, Eleanor McCallie Cooper, and Brad Lepo for their sage advice. Finally, I have the deepest gratitude for my heart and head partner Barbara Ray who helps me write from my heart and takes the time to give me feedback that helps me grow as a writer and a person.

ACKNOWLEDGMENTS

ABOUT THE AUTHOR

R.L. Dube' is currently a writer, traveler, photographer, and arm-chair philosopher residing in Tennessee. He has been a landscape designer specializing in Japanese Gardens. His writing included articles for *Fine Gardening* magazine, *The American Horticulturist*, *The National Arborist Association* and other landscape inclined periodicals. This is his first venture into the world of fiction, but he has previously been published in the non-fiction realm. He co-authored two books, *Natural Stonescapes* and *Landscaping Makes Cents*, and wrote a design philosophy book, *Natural Pattern Forms: A Practical Sourcebook for Landscape Design*, which was translated into Chinese in the year 2000. A true bibliophile, he consumes dozens of books each year, sampling from nearly every genre.

An avid hiker and naturalist, he loves to explore the woods, caves, waterfalls, and lakes throughout the South. He had a career as a professional interpretive naturalist working for the State of Ohio and has employed his hermeneutic skills as a middle-school science teacher and adjunct professor at the Southern Adventist University in Collegedale, Tennessee. He was the director of the Chattanooga Audubon Society and was also the director of the NewsChannel 9 Science Theatre.

He made a two-year commitment recently to the Living School, associated with the Center for Action and Contemplation based in Albuquerque, New Mexico, where he embarked on a journey of self-discovery and learned how to live and act in a contemplative and mindful manner. He has been an advocate for and student of Zen for nearly 40 years.

www.ingramcontent.com/pod-product-compliance
Lightning Source LLC
Chambersburg PA
CBHW072346020726
47506CB00004B/1023